The Lore Adventure

The Lore Adventure

Lore: The Discovery

James D. Fletcher

Writer's Showcase
presented by *Writer's Digest*
San Jose New York Lincoln Shanghai

The Lore Adventure
Lore: The Discovery

Writer's Showcase
presented by *Writer's Digest*
an imprint of iUniverse.com, Inc.

For information address:
iUniverse.com, Inc.
620 North 48th Street, Suite 201
Lincoln, NE 68504-3467
www.iuniverse.com

Cover art by James D. Fletcher and Paul Johnson
Interior photographs by James D. Fletcher

This is a work of fiction. All characters and events portrayed
in this book are fictitious. Any resemblance to real people
or events is purely coincidental.

ISBN: 0-595-09996-3

Printed in the United States of America

For my family

"Everything was created from nothing. Look and wonder at everything around you. Then, think of all the nothing that's left and wonder what you can create with it."

Singer, the Singer of Songs
—from "The Wonder Of It All" Loral.

Contents

Acknowledgements

Of those I mention, they are but a few of all that deserve recognition. First I honor my students, past and present, who have taught me well. Paul Albright, one such student, for always stoking the creative fires in me and being a great friend. Heidi Neff Christianson, for wandering the forest with me and helping me find the location of the Lost City. John Doppler, thanks for the genuine vivacity and the editorial comments at the outset. Cary Haugrud, Scott and Lisa King, thanks for the enthusiastic reliance and the colorful persuasion in keeping me on track; and Cary, also, for scanning all those images. Paul Johnson, one of those terrific, former students who helped me with my cover design. Keith Klein, for always being supportive. Thanks Marcia Kyser, for all the little snapshots and giggles along the way. I will always appreciate two fine agents, Jonathan and Wendy Lazear, who saw life in Loretasia a long time ago. I must credit the Minnesota Department of Natural Resources and Maplewood State Park for allowing me to reveal Lore in those beautiful wilderness areas. James O'Rourke, director of Rourke Art Gallery and Rourke Art Museum for believing in the visual elements of Lore. Thank you Jaime Penuel, photographer and friend, for the early photographs and for all the rides in the van. Ryan Thompson, thanks for all the help with the computer. Scott Wonderlich, who will again raise a toast, draw a laugh and jest by the campfire, I appreciate all you've done. Jeff Zachmann, thank you for the friendship and the generous help in the beginning of it all. Most of all, to my most caring and understanding family—thank you.

PART ONE

Josh Clemens

One
Josh Clemens
Early Summer

Josh Clemens simply vanished. His car was found in a Minnesota wilderness area but there was no trace of Josh. Police reported no evidence of foul play; however, that wasn't completely ruled out. Most bizarre was Josh's trail that led to a small, secluded clearing in the middle of the forest. Police dogs led searchers into that remote area and that's where Josh's trail abruptly ended. It was as though Josh Clemens had left his car, went for a stroll in the woods and was suddenly snatched off the face of the earth.

The end of Josh's trail left the police dogs and searchers baffled. The dogs scurried in circles, barking, sniffing and bumping into each other, while the searchers stood quietly dumbfounded as they gawked at six unusual rock formations rising from the ground. The rock formations rose to different heights, from a few feet high to at least ten feet. Each formation consisted of various sized rocks and boulders that had been meticulously stacked and balanced one on top of the other. All were covered with lichens, moss and cobwebs and appeared ancient. One of the searchers later made the comment, "When I stepped into that clearing, it felt like I had left this world and entered another. All the while we were there I sensed we were being watched. It was spooky; I just wanted to get out of there." Others had felt that way, also, though they did not let on to that right away.

The clearing was natural and nearly perfectly round; fifty-feet in diameter and surrounded by a thick, hardwood forest and a perimeter of prickly underbrush. No paths led to the place, and the only evidence Josh was there was from the scent he had left behind for the dogs to follow. The tree crowns were widely spread and blocked out most of the sky, which kept the clearing dimly lit and dank. The pictographs and carvings on the rocks weren't discovered right away because of the low light and moss cover. Steve Adams, a close friend of Josh's, made the discovery while combing the grass beside one of the structures.

"Check this out," he blurted, surprised by the find.

"What do you have?" Officer Donald Ramsey asked. He was standing beside another officer who was taking pictures of the site with a Polaroid camera.

"There's some stuff on these rocks."

"Stuff? What kind of stuff?" Ramsey removed his sunglasses and revealed stern gray eyes. He was a twenty-five year veteran of the Sheriff's department and tagged as a diligent investigator. His peers considered him the best in the country, actually. Donald Ramsey was highly respected in Red Tail county and known to be a fair cop, but also tough when necessary. He was civic minded, and very active with youth groups; he particularly enjoyed teaching Boy Scouts wilderness survival skills. Ramsey was a well rounded, seasoned veteran. He had his share of unique experiences while both on and off the job, but this missing person search today, he had openly admitted, was probably the most unusual.

Adams peeled away some of the moss. "It looks like pictures."

"Pictures?" Ramsey said, approaching. He moved like a drill-sergeant. "What kind of pictures?"

"Look here," Adams said, peeling away more moss. "A lot of pictures of animals. There are some letters here, too. O L Y Q U A. Olyqua."

"What the hell's Olyqua?" Ramsey said, kneeling.

Adams didn't reply. He continued to clean off the rock as other searchers approached. He could hear the Polaroid camera clicking and humming behind him.

"What did you find?" Another voice from the search party asked.

"Look," Adams said, pointing to an area he had just uncovered, "pictographs. They're all over the place! Here's a bird of some sort, maybe a hawk or an eagle. And there's a bear."

"That one looks like a hand holding some kind of ball," Ramsey said. "What does all this stuff mean?"

"Beats me," Adams replied. He let his eyes float to the top of the rock formation. Every rock was covered with pictures, all barely distinguishable under the dim light and blanket of age.

"Wasn't Clemens writing about a couple of artists working in this forest?" Ramsey asked.

"He was," Adams said. "He never mentioned anything about this, though."

"Who are the artists?" Ramsey asked.

Adams stood slowly, following his eyes upward along the rock formation. "I can't remember their names, off hand," he said. "I've never met them. You can check the newspapers, though; he's written several stories about them."

"I'll do that," Ramsey said, also rising. "Do you know anything at all about the artists? Where they live?"

"All I know is they're local people, so they shouldn't be hard to find."

"How much has Clemens written about them?"

"Quite a bit, actually," Adams replied. "He was excited about their works and wrote several newspaper and magazine articles about them. Josh all of a sudden changed, though; he got a little funny."

"What do you mean, he got a little funny?"

"I'm not sure I know what I mean, exactly. After writing the stories about the artists, he just all of a sudden became tight-lipped about what they were doing. He said the artists were onto something really big; said it was the most important story he'd ever worked on. He became deeply immersed, or obsessed would probably be a better way of putting it. He said the story he was working on was beyond big."

"Beyond big, huh?" Ramsey said. "I think we'd better extend our search to include those two artists. If we find them, we might just find our missing Josh Clemens."

"Quite possible," Adams replied. "But I don't think those two artists had anything to do with these rock pillars."

"What makes you think that?"

"Look at their age; they certainly weren't built anytime recently."

"Maybe not," Ramsey said. "But we don't really know that. I have to get some help in here to figure out what all this means."

"The only thing it means to the dogs," a deputy said, petting his German Shepherd, "is that this Clemens fellow walked into this clearing and then vanished. His trail stops right here."

"The dogs could be wrong," Adams said.

"Not hardly," said another officer holding his own dog by a leash. "You can safely bet this is where Clemens' trail ends."

"Well, we've trampled this place down enough," Ramsey said. "Let's clear out of here before we create more damage. We'll get the right people in here to look things over; find out what all this stuff means." He turned to the officer who was taking pictures. "Don't spare any film; get as much of this as you can. And try to get every one of those, what did you call 'em? Pictographs."

*   *   *   *   *

Two

Steve Adams rifled through his bachelor's chest looking for the last correspondence he had received from Josh Clemens. The letter got shuffled into some other papers before he had a chance to read it and it disappeared. He never threw stuff like that away, so it had to be around somewhere. He grabbed a stack of papers from the chest and sat on the edge of his bed to go through them.

Clemens was a good friend. He was an excellent writer who wrote mostly human interest stories and sold them to various newspapers and magazines. This latest "beyond big" story involved two artists creating works in wilderness areas throughout the country. Josh's articles had attracted considerable attention because of the novelty of the artworks. The artists fashioned miniature clay buildings out of tiny blocks and hid them deeply in forests. They snuggled the buildings around tree roots, between rocks, and beneath waves of ferns. The buildings truly appeared to have grown into their surroundings, as though they were a natural part of the environment. They were difficult to find.

Simultaneously, the artists were developing legends about a mystical wilderness civilization that had lived secretly within the forests for thousands of years. These wilderness denizens weren't human. Supposedly, they were mythical beings patterned after the likeness of the American Woodland Indians. The unusual and amusing thing about these inhabitants was their implausible size: They were only two inches tall!

Adams couldn't help but smile as he thumbed through the papers. Clemens loved mysteries, and the more abstruse, the better. He was completely enthralled by the works of these artists. It was fun stuff. The articles he wrote attracted droves of people into the forests looking for them. It was an exciting time for Clemens, Steve recalled; his stories spread like grass fires.

Then, Josh all of a sudden got serious. He dropped everything else he was doing and devoted all of his time and energy to this legend. He called it, "The Lore Adventure."

For a while it was comical because Josh acted as though he believed in all the stuff he was writing about. But then he changed; he became quiet and more eccentric. People, including Adams, saw less and less of Josh Clemens. He had secluded himself. Eventually, Josh quit selling his stories and withdrew himself from the freelance market.

One night, at a popular pub, and on one of the rare occasions Josh was seen in public, he said to Adams over a bottle of beer, "It's amazing what these artists have found. It's a spectacular discovery. If I told you about it, you'd call in the white shirts and have me carted off." Then he chuckled to himself, downed the last swallows of his beer and ordered another round. He never mentioned it again.

Precilla Adams entered the bedroom. "Is this what you're looking for?" she asked, handing Steve a piece of paper.

He smiled at his wife, skimmed the paper quickly. "Where'd you find it?"

"Under your mess by the computer."

"I looked there," he said.

"Right," she replied.

"I'm going back to that rock site this afternoon," he said.

"I thought that place was off limits until the proper authorities were done investigating."

"I'm not going to disturb anything. I just have a feeling I missed something important."

"Do you think Josh is in some sort of trouble?"

"No. I think he's secluded himself to write. He's really caught up in what those artists are doing."

"How could he just disappear like that?" Precilla asked.

"Maybe he was abducted by the little people," Steve joked.

"Well, he's missing, and that's not amusing," Precilla retorted. "If he did just decide to venture off somewhere and seclude himself to write, then it was pretty inconsiderate of him not to tell anyone."

"Yeah, well, you know Josh."

"What's the note say?" Precilla asked.

Steve shot her a look.

"I didn't read it," she said.

He set the rest of the papers he was holding aside and read the note aloud. "It says, 'A quick note to let you know I've made a major breakthrough on this story I've been working on. It's an incredible adventure. I have to also let you know that *you* are deeply involved. If you don't hear from me for a while, don't be concerned, I'm okay. I'll be in touch. Josh.'"

Steve read it again to himself.

"So he has ventured off," Precilla said.

"Must be," Steve replied. "But it doesn't explain his disappearing act. The police are convinced his trail stops at that rock site."

"Do they suspect foul play?"

"There's absolutely no evidence to suggest that. He simply walked into that area and vanished."

"What does it mean in that note where it says, 'you are deeply involved?'" Precilla asked.

Steve shook his head, read the note one more time to himself. "I haven't a clue," he finally answered. "It makes no sense at all."

"Josh Clemens makes no sense at all," Precilla said, turning and leaving the room.

The phone rang. Steve picked up the receiver and watched his wife exit. "Hello," he said, reading the note again.

"Steve?"

"Yeah."

"Donald Ramsey here."

"Yes, sir, what's up?"

"I have the names of those two artists Josh Clemens was writing about. Cole Madden and Dakota Chase. It seems they've headed up North into the Superior National Forest and plan to spend most of the summer there. I've spoken with the Forest Service and asked them to let me know if either of them register at any of the national campgrounds. The department is also contacting the motels along the North Shore and, while at it, checking to see if they've applied for permits into the Boundary Waters Canoeing Area. If for any reason they want to be slippery up there, we'll have a hard time finding them; it's a million acres of wilderness."

"I just found an interesting note Josh wrote to me a couple of weeks ago," Steve said.

"What did it say?" Ramsey asked.

Steve read the note.

"Interesting, I suppose, but it doesn't really say anything about his whereabouts," Ramsey said. "What did he mean when he said, '*you* are deeply involved?'"

"I don't know."

"Well, his brother reported him missing, so we have to stay on it. But be sure to let us know immediately if Clemens makes contact with you. There's no evidence of any crime here and the man has a right to disappear if he wants to. He's not married, has no children or anybody to answer to. We just want to get this resolved as quickly as possible."

"Right," Adams replied.

"And Steve," Ramsey continued, "if you slip out to that rock site before authorities investigate, don't you dare mess with anything."

Steve smiled. "I won't."

"That's the most baffling thing of all," Ramsey said, "his trail just disappearing like that. The officers with the dogs are really perplexed."

"Well, there must be some simple explanation for that," Steve said.

"No, there's not," Ramsey said emphatically. "You don't know police dogs; particularly these dogs. You can be assured that's where Clemens' trail ended."

"I'll keep in touch," Steve said.

*   *   *   *   *

Three

Precilla Adams ran out the door after Steve and caught him as he was backing the car out of the driveway. She handed him a portable phone through the window and told him Josh Clemens' brother, Oren, was on the line. Steve took the call, visited for a couple of minutes, then informed his wife he'd be driving over to see Oren before going back to the rock site. He told her Oren had just found something that Josh had left for Steve, but didn't elaborate. Oren was insistent Steve come by right away. Adams told his wife that he'd stay in touch with her by way of his cell-phone he kept under the passenger's seat.

Oren Clemens lived on an immaculate little hobby farm in the country, a quaint forty acres of fertile ground with plenty of water. A river ran through the middle of the property and fed a small, ten acre lake filled with plenty of pan fish. It was a perfect little homestead, Oren had figured when he bought the place, that would help his children learn about work ethics and responsibility as they grew up. The farm was home to several head of beef cattle, a couple of horses, and chickens. His wife, Claudia, and their three children, Duane, August and Demi, pretty much ran the place, as Oren owned and operated the only hardware store in Red Tail.

"I wish Josh and I had this opportunity when we were growing up," Oren would often say, referring to the farm, "then maybe Josh would have grown up and settled down some, instead of gallivanting all over kingdom come, living out of his car and writing nonsense."

Oren was Josh's senior by five years, a hard working, matter of fact kind of guy, who didn't believe in wasting any time dilly-dallying around smelling the roses. His hardware business was very successful and his beautifully manicured homestead kept the whole family busy seven days a week. "Hard work builds character," he said regularly. "You can't get ahead being aimless and undisciplined; you gotta get callused and dirty if you want to make something of yourself. Drifting ain't no sort of life."

Steve sat in Oren's living room, gazing quietly at a high school senior picture of Josh resting on top of the piano. "Senior picture," Steve thought, smiling to himself, "That was taken over ten years ago."

Josh hadn't changed a bit: Close black hair, meaty face as round as a full moon, thick black eyebrows and a pinched nose that held dark rimmed glasses close to frolicking brown eyes. He was as wholesome as one of the beef steers feeding in Oren's pasture and he moved just as leisurely. As casual as he was, though, his mind and thoughts ran ballistic. Josh Clemens had a definite talent for writing and could captivate practically anyone with his stories. Anyone except Oren, that is. Oren had no time for such "nonsense."

"Claudia found this stuff in our guest room this morning," Oren said, following his voice down the hallway.

Adams stood without speaking. Oren appeared carrying a large, cardboard box bound tightly with duct tape. It looked rather heavy.

"It's got your name on it," Oren said, setting it on the floor by Steve's feet. "I don't know what it is."

Oren rose and looked Steve in the eyes. They stood the same height, about six-feet, though Clemens was much heavier set. A quick glance at Oren Clemens told you he was a hard worker.

Oren had many of the same features as his brother, Josh, but his face and eyes were much more serious. He didn't wear glasses, but he had Josh's short, black hair, thick eyebrows and dark brown eyes. Oren's eyes pierced and stung, however, whereas Josh's eyes always bounced merrily about.

"I didn't open it," Oren said.

Steve pulled his eyes away from Oren and let them fall to the box. "It looks heavy," he said.

"It is heavy," Oren replied. "It will take you an hour to get through all that tape."

"Shall I open it here?" Steve asked.

"No, take it with you. You can let me know what's inside."

"Do you have any idea what it is?"

"It feels like a ton of paper."

"Paper," Steve repeated softly. Was it the "Lore Adventure" project? he wondered.

"I don't care much about what's in the box," Oren said, "but I am curious to know what's in this." He knelt and peeled an envelope off the side of the box and handed it to Steve. He stood again and remained quiet while Steve read the envelope.

TO STEVE ADAMS: PLEASE TAKE CARE OF THIS DURING MY ABSENCE.

Steve examined both sides of the envelope, then carefully tore the end open and removed a piece of paper. He unfolded it and scanned the handwriting addressed to him. Oren remained silent.

Adams read the note aloud, "Greetings, Steve: By now you are aware that I am gone. I can't explain in this note my whereabouts, but in the box you will find many answers to, I'm sure, a lot of questions. There's an enormous amount of material here, but please read it very carefully.

"I know you're all worried about me, so please tell Oren, who I'm sure is with you this very moment, that I am fine, with full faculties, and I will see him in the not too distant future.

"My car, as I'm certain you have by now found, is in Maple Forest. Please drive it back to my apartment; you will find a set of keys in the box.

"Before long, something very unusual is going to happen that will baffle many people. Don't get caught up in other people's doubts and suspicions; accept it as a real phenomenon that can be explained.

"Carefully read the contents of the box. You will know what to do with it. In the meantime, I wish you all well. I will see you sometime soon.

"Your friend,

"Josh Clemens."

"Damn fool," Oren Clemens grumbled.

Steve raised his eyes to meet the disgruntled voice.

"He's living in a fantasy world! He has no responsibility whatsoever!"

Steve wanted to read the note again but avoided the temptation and replaced it into the envelope. "Well, at least he says he's okay," he said.

"He's far from okay!" Oren retorted brusquely. "He's out of touch with reality."

Steve lowered the envelope and laid it on top of the box. He was careful not to defend Josh or try to pacify Oren. The last thing he wanted to do was set this guy off. He felt uncomfortable because he had nothing to say that would do any good, and his awkward silence was precisely that: Awkward. Young Duane Clemens' sudden, tumultuous entrance through the front door was an enormous relief.

"Steve!" he bellowed, barging through the door like a spooked calf. He looked like a miniature Oren, with the same husk, but his eyes danced happily like Josh's. "A phone is ringing from someplace inside your car!"

"The cell-phone," Steve said, almost to himself. "I'd better get that."

He spun quickly, hurried past the oldest of the three children and hastened his steps through the open door. August, the second boy, and Demi, the daughter and the youngest, were leaning against the car and poking their heads through the open windows.

"Answer that, August!" Steve hollered from the top of the steps.

"Where's it coming from?" August yelled back, pulling himself out of the window.

"Under the front seat on your side," Steve answered, striding two steps at a time.

August pulled the door open and fumbled under the seat, removed a soft black leather case that had a thin wire running to the cigarette lighter. He peeled the Velcro fastener and exposed the telephone. The phone was in the middle of a ring when he grasped hold of the receiver.

"Hello," the boy said excitedly.

Adams approached quickly.

"He's right here," August said, handing the phone toward Steve.

"Thank you, August," Steve said, patting the boy on the head and taking the phone from him.

"Adams here," he said.

"Hi, Steve, this is Donald Ramsey. Your wife said I might be able to get you on your cell-phone, that you were headed out to Oren Clemens' place."

"I'm here now."

"Any news about Josh Clemens?"

"I got a letter from Josh. He said he was going to be gone for a while. He didn't say where he was going, but wrote not to worry about him, that he was okay."

"Anything else?"

Adams held back about the box. "Not really."

"Have you been back to the rock site?" Ramsey asked.

"Not yet. I'm going out there this afternoon to have another look around...that is, if it's okay."

"I think you should come out here now."

"You're out there?" Steve said, surprised.

"I have some people with me. God, you're not going to believe this!"

"Believe this? Believe what?"

Steve turned to see Oren approaching with the box.

"Just come on out here as soon as you can. Okay?" Ramsey said.

"What's wrong? What happened?" Adams asked.

"Can you get out here?" Ramsey asked, ignoring Steve's question.

"I'll leave right now. Is everything okay?"

"I'll see you when you get here," Ramsey said. "Be ready for a surprise!"

"I'm on the way," Steve said, then hung up the phone. He turned to Oren who was now standing by the car.

"Where do you want this box?" Oren asked.

"Here," Steve said, moving to the back of the car, "let's put it in the trunk." He inserted the key and popped the trunk to the Grand-Am.

Oren leaned into the bumper and set the box inside. The car bobbed a bit as he released it from his grip.

"That was Donald Ramsey on the phone," Steve said to Oren.

Oren shut the trunk. "What'd he want?"

"He's out at that rock site where Josh disappeared and asked that I go out there right away."

"Is there something wrong?"

There! That was the very first expression of real worry Steve had ever seen on Oren's face.

"No, he didn't mention there was anything wrong. He said he had people with him; probably those specialists he was contacting to investigate the rocks."

"It's all a spoof," Clemens said. "I've got no time for that."

"Ramsey said I'd be surprised by something when I got there," Steve said. "He was urgent that I come right away." He paused for a moment, then asked, "Do you want to ride along?"

"No thanks," Oren replied. "We've got a shipment coming into the store in an hour and I have to be there. Josh said in his letter he's okay, so I'm not worried about him anymore. Tell Officer Ramsey I'm sorry for all this inconvenience, that Josh is okay and is off somewhere gallivanting around. He can call off his search now."

"I'll tell him," Steve said.

"Tell him I'll contact him Monday morning and formerly withdraw the missing persons report. This is embarrassing as hell!"

"I'll take care of Josh's car," Steve said.

"You might as well bring it out here where it will be safe. There's no sense having it in town where someone might bust into it; not that they would find anything of value, anyway."

"Precilla and I will drop it off," Steve said.

Oren turned to the kids who were goggling at Steve's cellphone. "Back to the barn, kids," he commanded. "It's time to finish up your chores."

"I'll see you later, Oren," Steve said, moving toward the driver's door.

"He's lucky he's got a friend like you, Adams; someone who'll put up with all his immature shenanigans."

"He is a friend," Steve replied politely. There was a bit of softness there in Oren's face...another first.

*   *   *   *   *

Four

Josh Clemens' car was still parked where hikers had discovered it, tucked behind brush, off to one side of the barely passable two track road leading through the forest. A ways beyond Clemens' car, four police vehicles blocked further entrance into the woods.

Several uniformed deputies were grouped together in conversation, two of which were holding leashes for their dogs sitting by their feet. On the other side of the two track, Ramsey visited with two people Adams didn't recognize. Both were dressed in khaki clothing and wore floppy fisherman caps. They looked like typical college professors, wearing scraggly beards and thick, unkempt hair that rolled out from under their hats. One was leaning against a tree, puffing on a pipe and sending blue pillows of smoke into the established cloud floating above their heads. Ramsey just looked and nodded at Adams as he climbed out of the Grand-Am.

"Steve," Ramsey said as Adams approached, "This is Dr. Milton and Dr. Schepp. They're archeologists from the University."

"Pleased to meet you," Adams said, offering his hand. They exchanged greetings and small talk while Ramsey excused himself for a moment to visit with the officers nearby.

Milton and Schepp were specialists in Native American Indian cultures, specifically the early woodland civilizations that had occupied the forest regions in the upper mid-west. They were quite familiar with this particular region. Both had done numerous excavations of burial sites and discovered many locations the Indians had used as temporary villages along the lakes nestled within the dense woods. They were often called to investigate construction sites when heavy equipment inadvertently exposed remnants of the past. By law, of course, all construction ceases until proper authorities complete investigations. Adams quickly bored them when he told them he was a video production freelancer.

Ramsey returned, stood quietly for a moment as he watched the other officers separate and move into the woods. When they were out of sight, he quickly said, "Let's go," and wheeled in the direction of the rock site. It would be a thirty minute walk up and down hills, around bogs and through several dense patches of low brush and prickly ash. Milton and Schepp followed loosely behind, while Adams puffed to stay abreast with Ramsey.

"What's the big surprise?" Steve asked, pushing every muscle to keep up.

"I don't want to spoil it," Ramsey replied.

They remained quiet as they trudged through the wilderness. Ramsey seemed upset about something and his silence was a little haunting. Steve felt relieved as they made their way up the last large hill before the descent into the rock site. At the top of the hill they rested and waited for the archeologists.

"You're convinced Josh Clemens is all right?" Ramsey finally spoke.

"Everything indicates that," Adams replied. "With the note he left me, he included the keys to his car and asked that I drive it back to his apartment." He still didn't mention the box.

"What the hell's he up to, Adams?" Ramsey asked, watching Milton and Schepp struggle upward.

"He's on to a hot story, I guess."

"Hot story," Ramsey grunted. "We checked on those two artists, Chase and Madden. They're highly respected people in their communities and among the art community. They work mostly outdoors. One is a wildlife artist who sculptures in wood, and the other does anything from painting to installing works in wilderness areas around the country. They're harmless, decent people."

"Have you seen any of the newspaper articles Clemens wrote?" Steve asked.

"I read a couple of them last night. They're interesting, but I don't know anything about art, so it's all a little strange to me. It has attracted a lot of attention, though."

Dr. Schepp grappled with a small sapling and pulled himself toward Ramsey and Adams. "How much further?" he gasped. Milton was nosing his heels.

"All downhill from here," Ramsey said, half smiling. "The clearing is in the ravine below us."

They rested a while longer as the university fellows caught their breath. Milton clutched the pipe sticking out of his shirt pocket while he panted but he didn't remove it. The heavy canopy of leaves above them provided a soothing shade that protected them from the hot afternoon sun.

"Ready?" Ramsey finally asked. Everyone seemed to be breathing more normally now. The archeologists nodded and took their positions behind Ramsey and Adams as they continued down the hill.

It was a steep decent and the foursome had to carefully watch their footing as they proceeded along. The trees thickened as the ground leveled off and just ahead rose a dense grove of prickly ash they would have to ford through. A couple of hundred feet beyond, the large maples and thorny stand would yield to the mysterious clearing.

"After you," Ramsey suggested to Adams at the bottom of the hill.

"Thanks," Adams said with a hint of sarcasm. He hated wading through this brush, as it snagged clothing and tore the flesh. His arms were already battered up from the previous day's hike into the area.

The trek was slow and conversation free as they negotiated the spiny brush. An occasional, "Damn it!" did, however, erupt behind Ramsey and Adams. Mosquitoes hummed in the tree crowns and blended with the scratching barbs raking across their clothing. Adams had to stop several times to pry thorns loose from his shirt and pants. Fresh, fine pink lines appeared on both his forearms and a slight stinging sensation nipped at his cheek. He silently cursed his friend, Josh Clemens.

The cursing abruptly ended in humor, however, as he turned around to see Milton and Schepp wound up tightly in the scrub. Milton's hat dangled from a branch above his head and exposed a large, shiny bald spot in the middle of all those oily curls. Schepp's hat was pressed against his face as he battled to untangle. Both looked like bony puppets entwined in concertina wire. Adams nodded for Ramsey to take a look, then continued on. "Gads," he heard Ramsey grumble to himself, "I ask for experts and they send me Mutt and Jeff.".

The brush thinned as the clearing lay just ahead. Adams was intrigued. What was the big surprise going to be? Should he wait for Ramsey and the puppets, or should he bore his way on in? Bore on in, he decided with little hesitance.

At the clearing he locked dead to his tracks and stopped breathing. His eyes danced uncontrollably. He finally managed to gulp his breath.

The Rock structures were gone!

"Can you believe this?" he heard Ramsey's voice.

Adams couldn't speak.

"I discovered it this morning after I spoke with you on the phone," Ramsey said. "There's not one damn sign to suggest those rock towers were ever here!"

"What the hell is this?" Adams finally breathed.

"I asked the exact same thing when I got here this morning," Ramsey said.

"Where did they go?"

Ramsey joined Adams. "Look at the ground, Adams," he said pointing. "It's not in the least bit trampled. You can't even tell where the towers stood."

"That's impossible!"

"Apparently not impossible," Ramsey retorted. "They're all gone and there's not one sign they ever existed."

Milton and Schepp approached. "Is this the site?" Milton asked.

Ramsey appeared uncomfortable. "This is where they were, yes," he replied. His tone was sickly.

"Do you mind if we enter and have a look?" Schepp asked, moving around them.

"Be my guest," Ramsey said, gesturing with his hand.

The puppets eased into the clearing, walking lightly, as though barefoot on glass.

Adams leaned back and scanned the small opening between the treetops.

"That was my first thought," Ramsey said, following Adam's eyes and guessing what he was thinking. "I thought pranksters might have extracted them with a helicopter, but realized right away, that would have been impossible. Look at the ground. The grass is virtually undefiled. A ground crew would have chewed this place into a crater. And there's no way a helicopter could have raised the larger boulders."

Milton turned back to look at them. "How large were the rocks?" he asked, looking puzzled.

"A couple of them half the size of a car," Steve Adams replied. "Especially the base of the largest structure. That tower stood at least ten-feet high."

The puppets looked at each other blankly. "Where?" Schepp asked.

"Right where you're standing," Ramsey replied. "There were six of them, all different sizes, right about where you're standing."

"Not in here," Milton said.

"I beg your pardon," Ramsey said.

"There wasn't anything like you're describing in here, anytime recent, I can assure you of that, Mr. Ramsey."

Steve saw fire in Ramsey's eyes and there was a sudden, deathly stillness.

"This is the site," Steve quickly assured them, before Ramsey could blow. "At least ten witnesses could testify to that."

"Look at the grass here," Schepp said, his voice sounding a bit frustrated, "There's no matting or discoloring where the structures were suppose to have stood. There should be holes, indentations, bare spots. There's nothing here! This is virgin ground!"

"I showed you the pictures!" Ramsey barked.

"The pictures could have been doctored," Milton retorted.

"OOPS!" Adams thought, stepping away from Ramsey. The puppets were about to dance.

Ramsey puffed up like a threatened peacock. "I am a police officer!" he bellowed. "I am investigating a missing person's report!" He marched directly toward the archeologists.

Both took a couple of steps back, looking quite white.

"I did not drag you two up here to be participants in a hoax!" He squared up nose to nose with both of them. "Those damn rocks were right here, and by the blazes, we are going to find them and get to the bottom of this!"

"I-I'm sorry, Mr. Ramsey," Milton stuttered, "I didn't mean to discredit your integrity."

Ramsey didn't reply, but Adams figured he was whip lashing both of them with grating eyes. Donald Ramsey had that 'Don't mess with me' reputation and, at present, it was in full color.

"May we please see the pictures again, Officer?" Schepp said carefully.

Ramsey unbuttoned his shirt pocket, removed a stack of pictures and handed them to Schepp. Before he released them, he said, "Don't let these disappear."

"No, sir," Schepp replied.

Ramsey returned to Adams and they both looked toward a slight commotion in the brush behind them. The two officers with their dogs appeared; both dogs leading them to the same spot in the clearing they'd arrived at yesterday. The dogs circled the spot and whined.

"This is it," one of them said. "It's the same as before. This is where Clemens' trail ends."

The archeologists left the pictures for a moment and studied the dogs.

"Fridley and Johnston are combing all around this clearing," the other officer told Ramsey.

"You fellows do the same," Ramsey said. "Circle around and keep widening your search. If you see anything at all suspicious, mark the spot and let me know right away."

"Yes sir," they replied, pulling the dogs away.

"Any ideas?" Adams asked.

Ramsey chuckled. "Pretty elaborate hoax," he replied, looking back at the archeologists, who were again thumbing through the pictures.

Dr. Schepp held a photo at arm's length and stepped back a few paces. He glanced at the picture then the surroundings. "Quite astonishing," he said aloud. "These pictures are legitimate."

"What do you make of it?" Milton asked.

"I don't know what to make of it. Let's use these picture to first mark the exact location of each rock formation." He paused, looked up into the tree crowns, then back at the picture. "Whoever took these pictures did a good job. If we get them enlarged, they might better reveal the pictographs; those might tell us something."

"I'll get them enlarged for you," Ramsey said. "What else do you need?"

"We have rope, stakes, and the necessary items in our vehicle to get this place mapped out, but we could use a couple of your deputies to help us."

"No problem," Ramsey said. "I'll have them in here A.S.A.P."

"Would you mind having them bring our stuff with them when they come?" Milton asked. "Schepp and I can get things started while we're waiting."

"Of course," Ramsey said. He used a small radio pinned to the front of his shirt to summon for help. It took only a moment to relay orders and set things in motion for Milton and Schepp.

"What about you?" Ramsey asked Adams, "Are you going to stick around?"

"There's no reason to," Adams said. "I'll get my wife and we'll pick up Josh's car. I'll go through it to see if he left anything inside."

"It's clean," Ramsey said. "Clemens left everything unlocked and we've already searched it."

"Then I'll be heading back now," Adams said, scanning the empty site one last time.

"I'll walk with you. I want to have a chat with the D.N.R. and the forest managers. Maybe they can lead me to some of the things those artists left in the woods."

*   *   *   *   *

Five

Precilla Adams was wearing jeans, a sweatshirt, and a Mickey Mouse baseball cap, with her ponytail hanging through the adjustment strap in the back. She was sitting cross-legged on the living room floor, rifling through a stack of papers. Beside her was Josh Clemens' box. Steve Adams was a few feet away, kicked back in the recliner, also skimming papers.

"It looks like Josh is writing some kind of fairy tale," Precilla said, looking up. "He must be writing a book."

"It's a mighty hefty book," Adams replied, waving his stack of papers at her. "We haven't even put a dent in the contents of that box."

"A lot of these papers are notes and drawings," she said. "He's laid out maps, directions, all kinds of stuff. He can write well, but he can't draw worth a hoot."

"Have you found anything about rock structures?" Steve asked.

"Some. He calls them Amity Pillars."

"Amity Pillars?"

"Yeah, you know, amity, as in peace, harmony...."

"I know what amity means, but why are they called Amity Pillars?"

"It doesn't say yet. What do you have there?"

"Some of the characters he's developing for his book, I imagine. Here's one: Singer, he calls him; the singer of songs. He's a storyteller. I think he's one of the little people."

"Why do you think that?"

"Because the character is sitting on an oak leaf and talking about the stars."

Precilla raised her eyebrows and half smiled, then went back to her papers. She was quite engrossed.

"Ah, here we go," Adams said with a chuckle, "Here's a bad boy. Noctumba, possessed with greed and power—must be stopped."

"Noctumba?" Precilla repeated. "I saw that name somewhere…" She began backtracking through her pages.

Steve said, "This word, Olyqua, keeps popping up in his notes. I don't have a clue as to what that means, but I saw the word on one of the rocks at the site. It was actually the first image I discovered."

"It's an Island!" Precilla said excitedly. She quickly crawled to the recliner with a piece of paper in her hand. "Look here," she continued, waving the paper in front of Steve's face. "It's an island he calls Olyqua. It's surrounded by water and six smaller islands. Josh has made each island a different color."

"He's become a painter now, eh?" Steve laughed.

Precilla leaned back, sat on her heels and rested the paper on her lap. "Do you think Josh is really okay?" she asked.

Adams studied his wife's concerned, blue eyes. "I think so," he replied. "There's no way to really be certain, but in my gut I feel he's all right. He has done some pretty weird things in the past; but, I have to admit, nothing like this. I just don't feel he's in any kind of trouble."

"And his brother, Oren, feels the same?"

"I'm certain of it. After reading the letter that came with that box, Oren seemed relieved. Satisfied."

"It would have been nice if Oren was home when we dropped off Josh's car," Precilla said. "I'd have liked to have talked to him."

"Oren doesn't talk much. He certainly doesn't approve of or say much about Josh's lifestyle. It's probably best to just leave him be."

Precilla looked at the pile of papers on the floor, then at the nearly full box of them. "How are you going to handle all of this? Are you going to read through every paper?"

"I've got an idea," Steve said smiling and winking at her.

"Oh no," Precilla retorted, shaking her head and scooting away from the box. "I'm not reading all that; there's at least five reams of paper in there!"

"You don't have to read all of it."

"No!"

"Come on, Precilla, it's interesting. We're a team, remember? For better or worse?"

"Forget it!" Precilla puffed. She slapped the paper she was holding in her hand on top of the stack she had been going through. She stood and walked to the window.

Steve heard a car pull into the driveway. "Is someone here?" he asked.

"It's your new buddy, Ramsey," she replied.

"Ramsey? What's he doing here?"

"Maybe he's located Josh."

"What should we do with all this stuff?" Steve asked, rising out of the chair. "I never mentioned anything to Ramsey about the box." He gathered all the papers he and Precilla were examining and neatly replaced them.

"You go to the door," Precilla said. "I'll drag the box into the bedroom."

"Okay. While you're in the bedroom, maybe you can keep going through the box. See if you can find some clarity to all this...."

"Go get the door Steve," Precilla interrupted.

"Right, the door."

When Steve arrived at the front door, Ramsey was standing on the porch holding something rather large in his hands.

"Do you have a place I can set this down?" Ramsey asked, obviously struggling with the weight of it.

"What is it?"

"It's one of those artist's creations. I took it from the forest, and it's heavier than hell."

"Yeah, sure, come on in. Set it on the dining room table."

Ramsey followed Steve into the dining room. "One of the rangers led me to it," he said. "There's a whole bunch of them out there."

"It looks like a small castle," Steve said as the deputy set it down.

"Yeah," Ramsey replied with a soft chortle. "Look at it closely. You won't believe the detail on this thing. It's made out of some kind of clay, stoneware, I think the ranger said. There must be a couple hundred of them in the woods, all arranged to make up a village."

Steve lowered himself to inspect the structure. It appeared to be made of tiny blocks, complete with windows, balconies and stairs. "I've seen a lot of pictures Josh took," he said, "but I didn't realize how intricate they were."

"Intricate," Ramsey again chuckled. "I'll say they're intricate. Look through the windows; the inside of that thing is as detailed as the outside."

"Pretty incredible," Steve said, peering into one of the windows.

"Incredible, indeed," Ramsey said. "What Mutt and Jeff found in the woods is even more incredible."

Steve rose. "Mutt and Jeff?" he asked.

"Milton and Schepp, the archeologists."

"What did they find?" Steve asked.

"Something similar to that building. The building they discovered, though...."

"Yes?" Steve wheedled.

"The archeologists believe the building they found is thousands of years old."

Steve Adams tilted back.

"Seriously, Adams! They dug it out of the ground at the rock tower site! They discovered it underground where one of the rock pillars had stood. They're talking about excavating that whole site!"

"Thousands of years old?" Steve said in disbelief.

"That's what they claim. They're going to do some kind of testing to make certain. Schepp said there's some kind of dead bacteria or something on the bottom of the building and that he can get a pretty accurate age reading from that."

"Do they know where it came from if it's that old?"

"No," Ramsey replied. "And I don't think I want to tell you what else they said."

"What?"

Ramsey laughed.

"What?" Steve demanded.

"They said it appeared as though the structure they had found was actually inhabited at one time."

"Inhabited? Inhabited by what?"

Ramsey simply grinned.

"Inhabited? You've got to be joking!" Steve said. "You can't be serious."

"I'm not joking. They're like two little kids out there, Adams, claiming the most remarkable find the world has yet unveiled. I knew they were a little odd from the start, but I didn't think they were that wacky. Both those guys have great reputations, respected world wide. They're considered to be the best at what they do. When they told me the building they found seemed to have actually been occupied at one time, well...."

"Precilla!" Steve hollered for his wife.

"I heard everything," Precilla Adams said, entering the dining room.

"We're not to say anything about this," Ramsey said, then snickered. "Like I would tell anyone about this, anyway. Those archeologist boys don't want a word of this breathed to anyone. They don't want that site disturbed at all. They don't want anyone other than us to know about it. Absolutely no one."

"Do they know what happened to the rock pillars?" Steve asked.

"No," Ramsey replied. "A couple of deputies found a few smaller rock towers that are similar, but nothing like the ones we discovered."

"Where did they find them?" Steve asked.

"Back in the woods. They were quite a ways away from the original site, close to where these little buildings are located. The rock towers are next to a swamp."

"What are you going to do with this thing?" Adams asked, referring to the building on the table.

"Leave it with you to examine. I have another one in the car. If you look closely at all the details inside, you'll see there are a lot of symbols on the walls that are similar to those you discovered on the rock pillars. Maybe you can make heads or tails out of them."

"What about Josh?" Steve asked. "Are you going to continue to look for him?"

"No; not for the time being, at least. Since there is no evidence of criminal activity, and Oren Clemens is withdrawing the missing persons report, the investigation is terminated. I am, however, in charge of securing the site in the forest for the archeologists. As long as I'll be spending so much time out there, I'll continue my own *off the record* investigation. I have to say, though, that this is all beginning to look more and more like one huge, elaborate hoax. An incredibly huge, elaborate hoax.

"And just out of curiosity," Ramsey continued, "I have to ask you something."

"What's that?" Adams asked.

"When the dogs led us into that site, and while we were examining the rocks, did you happen to feel anything peculiar?"

"Peculiar?" Adams said. "How do you mean?"

"Several in the search party said they had this haunting feeling they were being watched."

"Watched by whom?"

"They really didn't elaborate that much, but several made the same comment. They said that while inside the site, they got this eerie feeling that they were being watched by someone or something. I was just wondering if you experienced anything like that."

"Not that I recall," Steve said. "It was all pretty amazing. Exciting. I think returning and discovering the disappearance of the rocks was more alarming. As far as having had a feeling of being watched, I don't recall anything like that."

"I just thought I'd ask," Ramsey said. "It's all so bizarre. While Mutt and Jeff were shooting compass directions inside the site, they claim their compass needle all of a sudden started spinning out of control. They, too, admitted to having had the sensation they were being watched."

"What do you mean their compass needle started spinning out of control?"

"I'm not sure. They just said the needle all of a sudden started spinning. Schepp said while that was happening it felt like someone or something was watching them. Both of them claimed to have had that sensation."

"I can't say as I had that impression while I was out there," Adams said.

"Neither did I. I'm just very curious about all this. I don't know where this is leading or what the hell's going on, but I would like you to keep me informed of anything you find out; let me know if Josh Clemens makes contact with you."

"I'll do that," Adams said.

"The way you informed me about the box Oren Clemens gave you?"

Steve Adams stammered with a rush of guilt. "Oh, that," he said with a forced, apologetic tone, "Yeah, well, I was going to tell you about it after Precilla and I looked through it."

"Do you mind telling me what's inside?"

"It's filled with Josh's notes. We think he's writing some kind of book. We really haven't had a chance to go through the whole box yet because there's a ton of papers."

"I'd appreciate it, Adams, if you stay up front with me and tell me about anything you find. I don't appreciate information being withheld."

"I'll keep you informed. And I'm sorry I didn't tell you about the box right away."

"Let's just work together."

"Agreed," Adams said.

"Good. I have to scoot now, as I've got to assign some deputies to guard that site. Someone has to be there twenty-four hours a day."

"Thanks for bringing the artwork by," Steve said, walking Ramsey to the door. "Precilla and I were going through the box when you arrived. There's so much stuff in it, it will take a long time to sort through it."

"Better you than me," Ramsey said. "Just keep me posted."

"I'll do that. And, again, I'm sorry I didn't tell you about the box right away."

*   *   *   *   *

Six

"Josh Clemens, where are you?" Steve Adams thought. "What are you up to?" He was standing in the middle of the artist's miniature village secluded in the woods. He had just finished videotaping the site. Donald Ramsey had drawn a map to all the tiny buildings for Adams; otherwise, he'd have probably never found them.

"Most of these little buildings have signatures on them," Precilla said, kneeling beside one of them. "Many of them were made by art students. Josh's newspaper article said one of the artists, Dakota Chase, spent some time as an artist in residence at a nearby school, and this village is part of a class project. It's called the Lost City."

"Yes, and Josh's notes refer to it as a decoy city," Steve said.

"What does that mean? A decoy city?" Precilla asked.

"I'm not real sure. Josh's notes are random, with no particular order whatsoever. I read somewhere, though, that while this site was being established openly to the public, the artists were creating another site in secret. For some reason the artists wanted this site known to the public, but the other Lost City kept secret."

Precilla Adams stood and joined her husband. "Another newspaper article said the purpose of this site was to lure people into the wilderness. Its intent was to reacquaint people with nature. It said, while exploring the forest in search of this site, people would rediscover some of the wonders of nature."

"That's the underlying purpose of The Lore Adventure," Steve Adams said, "according to Clemens. The Lore Adventure is supposed to lure people back to nature, back to themselves. At least that's the explanation Josh has in his notes."

"Lets go find those rock pillars the deputies discovered," Precilla said. "Josh calls them Amity Pillars. His notes say each rock in a pillar represents a different life form, and the stacking and balancing of them represents the delicate balance among all living things."

"It said that in one of the newspaper articles too," Steve said. "The article went on to say that in the future, Amity Pillars will be seen all over the world. People will just start building them everywhere. The world's human population will return to nature and become more aware of life's delicate balance."

"This place is amazing," Precilla said, kneeling again to a small building beside them. "Every one of these buildings is made of tiny, individual blocks of clay."

"We have to organize all Josh's notes," Steve said. "If this is really a decoy Lost City, then I'd like to find its counter part, the secret city, if it actually does exist."

"There's supposed to be a city like this underwater, too," Precilla said, rising, "somewhere at the bottom of one of the lakes around here. Do you actually think those artists built a city like this underwater?"

"I don't doubt anything right now. This is all so eccentric."

"Eccentric?" Precilla said. "It's a little beyond eccentric. Eccentric doesn't explain the disappearance of those rock towers at the site where Josh supposedly disappeared."

"There's absolutely no explanation for the disappearance of those rock towers. It seems impossible that they could be there one day and gone the next without a trace. It's unimaginable."

"This is unimaginable, too," Precilla said, scanning all the little buildings. "It's all so elaborate."

"It's an elaborate hoax, as Ramsey calls it," Steve said. "I think Josh is in cahoots with those artists for the purpose of creating a myth. That's all it can be; it's the only explanation for any of this."

"Well, whatever is going on, we're getting pretty tangled up in it," Precilla said. She scanned the surrounding trees. "Where are those Amity Pillars Ramsey said the deputies discovered?"

"Just over this closest hill," Steve said, pointing. "They're supposed to be standing next to a swamp. Ramsey said the ground around them is a little soft, but there's supposed to be a couple of them. They're not anything like the ones we discovered with the dogs, though. Those were really impressive. Ancient looking."

Steve and Precilla left the Lost City and started their way through the trees and up the hill toward the Amity Pillars. Both scoured the surroundings as they hiked, keeping lookout for anything unusual.

"Do you think the building the archeologists discovered—the building Ramsey said they found underground—could be part of the secret Lost City Josh wrote about? The counterpart to this one?" Precilla asked.

"Not if the building they found is as old as they claim it to be. Those archeologists are a little odd, that's for sure, but as Ramsey said, they have reputations for being the best at what they do. If they say the building is thousands of years old, then it must be. I'd really like to see it myself."

"They won't let us near that site, now, will they?" Precilla said. "They won't let anybody near it."

"No, not yet. I'll have a chat with Ramsey, though, to see if we can get permission to watch some of the excavating. He'll get us in there."

"What are you going to do with the videotape you're making?"

"I'm just documenting everything. The tape will be interesting to look at in the editing suite. It might help, too, in organizing all that stuff in Josh's box."

"In Josh's note that came with the box, he said you would know what to do with the box's contents. Do you know what you're going to do with all of it?"

"I don't have a clue," Steve answered.

"If Josh has gone a little wacky, then he's pulling us right along with him," Precilla said. "I'm really getting caught up in all this. I'm hooked."

"I know. I am too."

After ascending to the top of the hill, Steve and Precilla took a seat in the grass along the ridge. Steve rested quietly and scanned the steep grade they had just climbed.

"It's going to take forever to go through everything in that box," Precilla said. She was picking pebbles out of the ground and bouncing them off a nearby boulder.

"I know," Steve replied. He absentmindedly watched Precilla toss the pebbles and gathered a handful off the ground for himself. "I really appreciate all your help and your coming out here with me today. This is all so overwhelming; there's no way I could go through all those papers by myself. I only wish Josh had arranged that stuff in some kind of logical order. If there's, indeed, logic to any of this."

A small shadow drifted across the ground beside them. Steve looked up to see what had caused it and saw a large crow land on a tree branch above their heads. Precilla tilted back and followed his gaze.

"Did you come here to tell us something, big bird?" Steve said, tossing a pebble at the branch. The crow flew off and disappeared.

"We should get going," Precilla said. "I don't want to sit too long, or I'll never want to get up and start climbing again.

They rose to their feet, walked past the boulder and started down the hill. Steve searched the slope and saw sunlight reflecting off water at the bottom. Then he spotted the rock towers.

"I can see the Amity pillars from here," he said. "There are three of them, right along the edge of that swamp." He stopped and raised his video camera to his shoulder and began taping. He zoomed in on one of the pillars.

"They're not very big," Precilla said. Her tone sounded disappointed.

"They're not nearly as large as the ones we discovered at the first site, that's for sure," Steve replied. "Those were really awesome." He scrutinized the pillar through the camera's viewer and said, "These don't appear to have any pictographs on them. The pillars at the first site were completely covered with them."

"Steve," Precilla said quietly.

"What?"

"Look."

"What?" he said, lowering the camera.

"Look at the boulder we just walked by."

Steve glanced back over his shoulder and saw a large painting on the downhill side of the boulder.

"It's a crow, Steve. It's a painting of a crow!"

Steve Adams set his video camera on the ground and turned in disbelief. Precilla was already beside the painting examining it.

"This is really eerie, Steve. Has anyone mentioned painted rocks to you?"

Steve joined his wife. The painting was a large image of a crow and done in fine detail. The eyes of the crow were bright red and seemed to shimmer, even in the shade.

"You just spooked a crow away from here, Steve!"

"Ramsey never mentioned anything like this. His deputies must have missed it. Have you read anything in Josh's notes about this, or anything like it?"

"No," Precilla replied. She leaned close to the painting for a better look. "This is an old painting," she said. "There's fungus or something growing on top of the paint."

Steve ran his fingertips over the contour of the crow. "How long have those artists been working out here?" he wondered aloud. "How much stuff have they actually done?"

"This is really creepy," Precilla said. She stared at Steve. "Now I have the feeling we're being watched by someone."

Steve stood upright and searched the trees surrounding them. "So do I, actually. It's not a threatening feeling, but it does feel like someone or something is watching us."

"What's that up there?" Precilla asked, pointing toward a tree branch.

Steve followed her aim and spotted something dangling from the branch. It looked like a mask of some sort, with chimes hanging from the chin. The face of the mask appeared human, but the nose was fashioned in the shape of a bird's beak. He stared for a moment.

"What is it?" Precilla insisted.

"It looks like some kind of a mask."

"Why is a mask hanging in the middle of the woods?"

"Why is any of this in the middle of the woods?" Steve replied. He approached the mask and reached for it, but his fingers could only touch the chimes. They tingled slightly to his touch.

"That's a different sound," Precilla said, joining him. "They make a clinking noise."

"It's tied to the branch with a rawhide lace," Steve said. "Let's get it down and have a look at it."

"How?"

"I'll hoist you up on my shoulders. You should be able to reach it and untie it."

Precilla looked down the hill, then back at Steve. She had that, 'You've gotta' be kidding me' look in her eyes.

"What?" he said. "I won't drop you." He squatted, tapped his shoulders. "Come on, climb on. It'll be easy."

"God, this is crazy," Precilla said, mounting Steve's shoulders. She gripped his hair tightly.

"Geeeze!" he howled, rising, clasping her legs. "Go easy on the hair." He staggered a bit to get upright.

Precilla squealed as he hoisted her and wobbled to keep his balance. "Don't drop me!" she cried. "Don't let me go!"

"I'm not going to drop you!"

Steve braced himself beneath the tree branch and positioned Precilla beneath the chimes. "Get the mask," he said, holding her legs firmly.

Precilla released her grip from Steve's hair and reached for the mask. She fumbled with the rawhide lace but couldn't untie the knot holding it to the branch. "I can't untie it," she murmured.

"Break it!" Steve ordered, struggling with his balance. "It's only rawhide."

Precilla yanked swiftly on the mask and the rawhide lace snapped free. The chimes of the mask rang out loud and Steve staggered forward and back from the sudden jolt. Precilla screamed.

"Don't squirm!" Steve hollered. He quickly regained his footing. "I'm going to kneel down and let you off now."

"Don't drop me!"

Steve felt a heavy blow to the top of his head and the chimes of the mask dangled and clanged against his face. "Owe! Don't hit me with that damn thing! What's it made of anyway? Rock?"

"Clay!" Precilla yelped, as Steve knelt down and bent forward. She plopped to the ground and scrambled forward on her hands and knees.

"Are you okay?" he asked.

"I'm fine."

Precilla turned about and sat down. She brought the mask up before her eyes to inspect. The chimes dangled along her forearms.

Steve sat beside her. He rubbed a small welt rising on top of his head. "It's beautiful," he said.

"These chimes are made out of clay, too," Precilla said. She raised the mask upward and tickled them with her fingers. They made a soft clinking noise.

"The mask looks like it has been painted, not glazed," Steve said. "Nobody has mentioned anything about masks out here. Nobody has mentioned masks or anything at all about that rock painting over there. I wonder if anyone else knows about any of this?"

"Look here," Precilla said, turning the mask to look at the backside. "Here's a signature. Dakota Chase. One of those two artists made this."

"They must have painted that crow on the rock, too," Steve said.

"What are we going to do with this mask?"

"We'll take it with us. Ramsey will probably want to see it. The archeologists will want to see it, too, I'm sure."

"That's stealing, isn't it?."

"Borrowing," Steve said. "We'll bring it back later."

"Are you going to borrow that boulder with the crow painting too?"

"Real funny. I am going to take some video of it, though."

"Why don't you quickly take some video. We'll hurry down to look at the Amity Pillars and then head for home. I'm getting tired, and this place is really giving me the creeps."

"Do you still feel like you're being watched?" Steve asked.

"No."

"Neither do I."

Steve rose to his feet and went for his camera. "Don't drop that mask," he said.

Precilla stood, made a face at him and wiggled the mask so the chimes rang.

"Damn it!" Steve growled.

"I'm just ringing the chimes; they're meant to ring."

"No, not that," Steve said, "I left the camera on record when I set it down on the ground and now the battery is dead."

Precilla chuckled. "Well, you're the professional."

"Come on," Steve said, "let's check out the rocks." He moved down the hill toward the Amity Pillars.

"They're really kind of neat," Precilla said, approaching the rocks. "How do they stay up like that?"

"They're balanced. It must take a lot of time to set them just right. These are pretty neat, but nothing like the first ones we discovered. There are no pictographs on these and they look as though they've been built recently. The others looked really old."

"It looks like one of the rocks fell off the top of that short pillar," Precilla said, easing toward the smallest of the three Amity Pillars. She walked lightly, as the ground was soft beneath her feet. She stooped to pick up a small rock that laid in the grass beside its base.

"Those artists have really been busy," Steve said, watching moisture ooze into her footprints.

"My God, Steve," Precilla muttered. "Look at this."

"What's the matter?"

Precilla held up the rock to show him.

"What about it?" he asked.

She shook the rock and it rattled.

"What's that?"

"It's hollow. It's got beads or something inside. And look," she said, turning the rock over to show him the other side.

A sculptured leaf protruded from the surface of the rock. The leaf was round and painted green. Precilla shook it again and listened to the rattle.

Steve approached his wife, took the rock and examined it. "It's lighter than it looks," he said. "Is it a real rock?"

"It looks like it, but it doesn't really feel like a rock. It seems too light, like you said."

"How could they hollow it out like that and put something inside?" Steve wondered aloud. He shook the rock and listened. It was a unique sound, somewhat soft, as though the beads inside were pliant.

"This is way too much for one day," Precilla said, gazing around the whole area. "I'm ready to leave this place."

"I'm ready to go through that whole box of Josh's and get to the bottom of all this," Steve said.

"Are you going to *borrow* that too?" Precilla asked, pointing to the rock. She raised the mask she was holding and wiggled the chimes.

"Let's go home," Steve said.

A crow cawed in the distance as they left the Amity Pillars. For a brief moment Steve again felt eyes on him; then the sensation disappeared.

* * * * *

Seven

Papers were scattered all over the floor around Steve Adam's video editing suite located in the basement of his home. For several days he and Precilla had sorted through materials and arranged them into similar categories. Josh Clemens' box was full of notes, maps, drawings and photographs. In the center of the chaos were two thick manuscripts handwritten by Josh. Steve had found them buried at the bottom of the box. The titles of the manuscripts were "LORE: THE LEGEND," and "KINTU: THE DISCOVERY OF ONE."

After quickly skimming through the manuscripts, Steve and Precilla were convinced Josh Clemens was in the process of writing at least two fantasy novels evolving around the works of the two artists. Nowhere in the papers they had looked through, however, could they find any clues as to why Josh suddenly disappeared, or where he might have disappeared to. They had shared all their information and findings with Officer Ramsey, and he had asked them to continue with their investigating. He was quite intrigued over the painted rock, mask, and the unusual hollow rock Precilla found by the Amity Pillar.

The mask, as Precilla had discovered in Josh's notes, was called a "Windtickler Spirit Mask." Presumably there were many such masks hanging in the trees throughout the forest. Josh also had photographs and made mention of several full figures with chimes. He called them Dream Dancers and they were similarly fashioned out of clay. The rock painting was still an enigma and Steve was as yet booting himself for allowing the camera battery to run down after the discovery. He wanted to document everything with video, so he was planning a return trip to that site.

Precilla sat in Steve's chair at the video editing suite and sipped from a glass of orange juice. She was thumbing through a stack of papers and photographs piled on her lap. "This word, Loreduchy, keeps popping up," she said.

"I've seen that," Steve replied. He was sitting on the floor in the middle of the paper puzzle. "Dukes of the Lore," he said. "It says Loreduchy are dukes of the Lore."

"What are dukes of the Lore?"

"Who knows? Look at this mess," Steve said in disgust, "How are we ever going to put all this stuff in a seemly order?"

"Here," Precilla said, setting down her glass. "It says here, 'anyone who participates in the adventures of Lore, becomes Loreduchy.'"

"What does participate mean?"

"Becomes involved with, I suppose, interacts," Precilla replied. "Which would mean you and I are Loreduchy." She giggled.

"I feel like a Lore Duck swimming in all this paper," Steve said. "What the hell are we doing, Precilla? This is nuts!"

"Hey, Josh is your friend. You're the one that got me involved with this mess, remember? I'm just trying to help you wade through it."

"Maybe we should just start with these manuscripts and read them thoroughly."

Precilla inserted Steve's videotape into the play deck. "You haven't reviewed your tape yet," she said.

Steve rose from the floor and carefully stepped through the paper maze to join his wife. He pulled up a chair beside her.

"You're falling behind in your work too, Steve," Precilla said. "You're supposed to have two flying logos done this month for those Minneapolis advertising firms. Are you going to meet your deadline?"

"The technical stuff is complete; I just have to consult with them on the colors they want to use."

"That's our bread and butter, you know."

Steve ignored her comment, reached for the video editing control pod and rewound the tape. "Look at that mess," he said, scanning all the papers on the floor.

"Here's that word, Olyqua, again," Precilla said, continuing through the papers on her lap. "Four shall meet at Olyqua and Olyqua shall become one. Olyqua will be victorious, and the Inner Kingdom will return to the peaceful Regions. He has Regions capitalized for some reason."

"Olyqua is an island, right?" Steve asked. "An island with six smaller islands surrounding it?"

"Six or eight, I can't remember off hand. I'll find the other information and add this to it. I especially remember the small islands because Josh had painted them all different colors."

"Josh Clemens, the artist," Steve chuckled. "Here are the little buildings in the woods," he said, nodding toward the monitors and slowing down the rewinding tape.

Precilla set her papers on the floor by her feet and turned to face the monitors. "Those are so neat," she said.

"Some of these buildings are far more detailed than others," Steve said. He started the tape forward at normal speed. "It's hard to tell if there's any particular design or layout to the overall village. They look organized but, at the same time, they seem randomly placed."

"Look how everything blends to the ground and the surroundings," Precilla said. "It's like they are part of the woods, supposed to be there. They look like they grew out of the ground."

"That was a big part of the assignment Dakota Chase gave his students," Steve said. "Josh wrote the buildings had to blend naturally with the environment, as though they were part of the environment."

"I'm surprised you weren't more involved with all this when Josh was introducing it to the public and getting so much notoriety," Precilla said.

"It would have been nice to have spent more time with him, but I had just bought all this equipment. I had to bury myself with work just to meet the payments."

"I know. You've done so well, Steve. Now you're turning away work."

"Look at the detail on this building," Steve said, slowing the tape to half-speed. "Look at the stairs and the balconies...it's incredible." He further reduced the speed to one frame at a time.

Precilla Adams smiled broadly and pointed to the monitor. "Look," she said. "There's a tiny Windtickler mask hanging in the window. It even has chimes."

Steve stopped the tape and froze the image.

"You did a very nice job of taping," Precilla said. "It looks like we're passing through a real village."

"It was a lot of fun to tape," Steve said. "It will make a nice documentary."

"Keep it going," Precilla said.

Steve resumed the tape to normal speed.

"When will we be able to go out to the dig site to see the building the archeologists uncovered?" Precilla asked.

"Ramsey's bringing us a pass. He told Milton and Schepp we were part of the investigating team and that we needed clearance."

"Why does he call them Mutt and Jeff?"

Steve smiled without reply, paused the tape as it faded to black.

"Is that all?" Precilla asked. "Didn't you tape the Amity Pillars, too?"

"Yeah, but my battery died, remember?"

"Let's see what you taped, anyway."

Steve resumed the tape. It faded from black to a shot of the Amity Pillars from above. The picture zoomed in on one of the pillars. A moment later Precilla's voice came over the audio: "Steve."

"What?"

"Look."

"What?"

The voices became obscured and the picture wobbled dramatically. It was at that moment Steve had lowered the camera to the ground to look at the painted rock.

Steve lowered the volume control dial on the audio mixer and watched the video.

"Very nice close up of the lower half of that Amity Pillar," Precilla chuckled.

"Professional work," Steve replied.

"Turn the volume back up," Precilla said, "I want to listen."

"Do you want to hear yourself scream while you're on my shoulders?"

"I wasn't that bad," Precilla said.

"Right."

Steve reached for the audio dial, but stopped suddenly. "Look!" he gasped.

Someone had stepped into the picture beside the Amity Pillar. Only the person's legs and feet were exposed to the camera. Steve bolted for the control pod and froze the tape. "My God!" he said, stunned. "Someone was there!"

Precilla remained quiet with her eyes fixed on the monitor.

"Who the hell is that?" Steve said, gawking at the frozen image.

"He's wearing moccasins," Precilla whispered.

"The pants look like they're made out of some kind of animal hide," Steve said.

"Continue the tape," Precilla said excitedly.

Steve resumed the tape at half speed.

The figure moved further into the picture and knelt. He was now fully exposed.

"It's an Indian," Steve said.

"Look at how old he is," Precilla muttered. "He's all wrinkled and his hair is silver."

The Indian held a rock in his weathered hands and rolled it around as though he were looking at it.

"That's the rock, Steve! That's the rock I found!"

Steve and Precilla watched perplexed as the Indian lowered the rock to the ground and gently laid it in the grass beside the pillar. He slowly turned his head to face the camera.

"My God Steve! He doesn't have any eyes!"

The Indian faced them. His eyes were pure white. His leather face and long silver hair made him look very old. His clothes of hide were quite worn and tattered. Steve and Precilla were silently glued to the image.

The Indian rose slowly and backed out of the picture. He disappeared as enigmatically as he had appeared. The video went suddenly black, then turned to snow.

Steve stared blankly at the flickering, snowy monitor. He didn't move. Precilla sat quietly beside him.

Finally Steve said, "I have to call Ramsey."

*   *   *   *   *

Eight

Officer Donald Ramsey stood quietly and watched the police dog sniff and circle the Amity Pillars along the edge of the swamp where Precilla Adams had found the peculiar hollow rock with the sculptured leaf. He was quite intrigued over Steve Adam's videotape, particularly the part with the Indian. It appeared obvious that the Indian in the video wanted the rock to be discovered. Why? That was the question that plagued Donald Ramsey. This *unofficial* investigation with the police dog was prompted by Ramsey's personal curiosities, and officer Tony Williams, the dog's owner, was there as a favor to Ramsey.

The hollow rock, as it turned out, was not actually a real rock. When it was shown to Milton and Schepp, they had quickly determined it was made out of clay. Schepp knew it the minute he held it. "This is a ceramic rattle," he'd said. He removed a pocket knife and made a tiny scraping to reveal the clay body beneath the painted surface. No one was really surprised. Ramsey, however, was still intrigued by the Indian and why he had left the rattle to be found. Tony Williams and his dog, he'd figured, might help lead to some answers.

Officer Williams was kneeling several feet away from the Amity Pillars, appearing to be inspecting something on the ground. He looked up at Ramsey. "We have footprints here, leading to the rocks and then away from them. They lead West along the edge of the swamp."

"Are there any features to the prints?" Ramsey asked.

"No markings. It appears the soles are smooth."

"The Indian was wearing moccasins."

"That would explain it," Williams said. "The ground is soft here and the signs are pretty distinct."

"Do you think your dog can pick up on a scent?"

"Probably. The tracks are a few days old, though, and moisture has seeped into the pockets. We can sure give it a try."

Ramsey turned to Steve and Precilla who were observing quietly. "Do you have time to do a little tracking?" he asked.

"We have plenty of time."

Ramsey returned his attention to Williams. "Let's find out where those footprints lead, Tony. We'll follow you off to the side so we don't trample over your trail."

Tony Williams stood, whistled for his German shepherd. "Come on, Saber!"

Saber was at his side in a flash. The police officer leaned over, grabbed the dog's leash and pointed to a footprint. The dog took to it immediately and, without hesitance, was on the move along the edge of the swamp.

"Wow," Steve said, "That didn't take long."

"That dog is good," Ramsey said with a hint of pride, "the best. Tony's considered the best trainer in the state."

The threesome followed Tony Williams and Saber, being careful to stay clear of the trail and the soft ground along the edge of the swamp. They visited quietly amongst themselves as they kept their eyes focused to the surroundings.

"What have Milton and Schepp found out about the building they uncovered?" Steve asked.

"It's as old as they had determined at the outset," Ramsey replied. "Some of their tests came back confirming it. They're really excited. Completely baffled."

"You said they believed the building was inhabited at one time. Anything more on that?"

"They said it appears as though the building had been inhabited at one time," Ramsey said, "they're careful not to suggest it actually was. They've corrected me a couple times as to how I've interpreted them. In fact, they down right blasted me for ever mentioning that."

"I haven't heard any scuttlebutt about the excavation site," Steve said, "you're keeping that tightly under wraps."

"There's no police investigation going on, so there's no public awareness. Mutt and Jeff aren't about to leak any information, and you can be sure the deputies guarding the site aren't going to divulge anything."

Precilla quieted Steve and Ramsey. "Listen," she said. "I think I hear chimes."

Steve came to a stop. Ramsey slowed and listened. "Hold up a second, Tony," he hollered.

Williams gave an automatic tug on the leash and the dog stopped dead in its tracks.

"Up there," Precilla said pointing into the trees. "Look at them. There must be at least ten masks hanging in the branches."

"More like thirty," Ramsey said softly. "It looks like at least one in every tree. Some trees have two or three. What the hell is their purpose?"

"They're called Windtickler Spirit masks," Steve said.

"I know," Ramsey said, "but what's their purpose?"

"We don't know yet," Precilla said. "We're still sorting through Josh's notes."

Ramsey turned toward Williams who was standing as still as his dog…"Do you see the masks, Tony?" He hollered.

"They're all over the place!" he returned. "Even in the dead trees rising out of the swamp. What are they?"

"We're not sure yet. We know what they're called, but we don't know anything else about them."

"Mighty strange!"

Ramsey chuckled. "Strange is a good word!"

Ramsey waved for Williams to continue. The dog owner gave another quick jerk on the leash and Saber automatically resumed the lead.

"Let's go," Ramsey said.

"What else have the archeologists found at that site?" Steve asked. He was mentally counting the masks as they continued on.

It seemed Ramsey's attention was also focused on the masks. His eyes remained on the trees as he answered. "They've found another small building similar to the first one, and a lot of pottery. Much of the pottery is in excellent condition."

"What kind of pottery?"

Ramsey chuckled, looked at Steve. "Why, the kind you would find in little buildings, what other kind would there be?."

"What?"

"All the pottery is made in proportion to the size of the buildings. A bowl would fit on the tip of your little finger. It's really pretty amazing."

"Is it decorated?"

"Intricately decorated. Every piece they've found has been finely detailed with paintings and designs. How anyone could paint designs that small is beyond me."

"Sixty-three," Precilla said, interrupting.

"What?" Ramsey replied.

"Sixty-three masks so far, and there's more in the trees ahead that I haven't counted yet. No two seem to be alike."

"Those artist fellows have way, way, way too much time on their hands," Ramsey said.

"Hey Don!" Tony Williams hollered.

The threesome stopped. "Yeah!" Ramsey barked in return.

"Check out that oak tree about fifty feet in front of you, downhill towards me. Look at the lowest branch pointing back at you."

Steve strained his eyes to find the tree Williams was talking about. "Do you see anything?" he asked.

"Wow," Precilla said. "A Dream Dancer!"

"A what?" Ramsey asked.

"Where?" Steve responded.

"Down there, hanging from that lowest branch. We have to go see it."

"What the hell's a Dream Dancer?" Ramsey asked.

"There it is," Steve said, pointing. "It's like a mask, but it's a full figure. The whole body is made out of clay, and really elaborately decorated. Josh has pictures of several of them in his box."

"Let's go have a look," Ramsey said, aiming toward the oak tree.

The Dream Dancer dangled quietly from the oak branch. All the joints of the body were connected with what appeared to be stovepipe wire or fencing wire, and all parts of the body, including the fingers and toes, could be moved independently. The figure was life size and finely decorated with colors. The face of the figure was fashioned very similarly to the masks, and polished stones and feathers were attached to different parts of the body. It hung from the branch by a heavy wire running through a hole in the top of the head.

"This is incredible," Precilla said.

"This is crazy," Ramsey replied.

"The shoreline of the swamp veers South," Williams informed them, "but the footprints deviate slightly and continue Southwest up the hill away from the swamp. The physical signs of footprints pretty much disappear on the firmer ground, but the scent is still there for Saber to follow."

"Lead on," Ramsey said. "We'll follow off to the side."

Tony Williams and Saber angled away from the swamp and started up the steep grade. The threesome followed quietly. Steve Adams scoured every tree along the way, but as they moved further from the swamp, the trees became free of masks.

"I wonder if that was Loreduchy Swamp?" Precilla said faintly.

"Loreduchy Swamp?" Steve asked.

"Remember Loreduchy?" She asked. "In Josh's notes he mentioned Loreduchy. He said something like, 'Anyone who becomes part of the adventures of Lore becomes Loreduchy.' I read somewhere else that there was a place called Loreduchy Swamp, a meeting or gathering place of some sort. I'll have to check that when we get home."

"How long is it going to take you to go through all Josh's stuff?" Ramsey asked.

"There's so much," Steve said, "but we have most of it assembled into categories. It's a matter of finding time to read through it all now."

"I should bring the Boy Scouts camping out here this summer and have them comb through this whole forest," Ramsey said. "That would be a cheap investigation."

"There's a thought," Steve said.

"A very passing one," Ramsey said, chuckling, "I'd end up with another thirty missing persons out here."

Tony Williams came to a stop and turned to face the trio. "Saber is headed toward that large boulder sticking out of the ground just ahead. It's a pretty impressive boulder."

Impressive indeed. A large granite boulder jutted out of the earth and overhung the hill a good twenty feet. The rectangular outcropping extruded outward at an angle perpendicular to the slope and was the only boulder of its kind in the area. It was an unusual sight, to say the least.

"The glaciers did some pretty remarkable things when they came through this region," Steve said.

"Do you notice anything strange?" Williams asked.

"Like what?" Ramsey replied.

"Look at the ground here, it's covered with a sandy material. It looks like ground up granite. There are fragments of rock mixed in with it. It looks like someone had a rock crusher in here."

"What do you make of it?" Ramsey asked.

"I don't know what to make of it, it's very odd. Look at the trees overhead, all of the branches that are hanging dead, and those lying on the ground. It looks like something very large came crashing through this part of the forest and tore everything up. There's even gravel in the trees."

Ramsey, Steve and Precilla studied the trees around them. Strangely enough, it did look as though something had created a path through the crowns and busted up the tree branches along the way. "A small twister, maybe?" Ramsey suggested.

"Possibly," Williams said. "Though the branches look more like they've been sheered or snapped by something, some kind of object making a path. I would think a twister would have tied things together more, twined them up, and actually leveled some of the trees. Who's to say?"

"Continue with your tracking," Ramsey said, "let's find out where your trail leads."

Ramsey, Steve and Precilla hung back as Tony Williams and Saber approached the boulder. The dog sniffed around the base, led Tony to the backside where they momentarily disappeared from sight, then reappeared on top of it. Saber sniffed his way to the pinnacle and then stopped. Williams stood quietly watching his dog.

"Well?" Ramsey said, breaking the silence.

"It ends here," Tony said, looking confused. "The trail ends right here on the tip of this boulder."

"How can it end there?" Ramsey asked.

"Probably the same way Clemens' trail ended at the first site," Williams replied. "These characters have definitely mastered the magic of disappearing."

"Check all around the boulder," Ramsey ordered, "see if your dog can pick up another scent." He scanned the area and grumbled, "He couldn't have just vanished into thin air."

"I'm going to have a look around," Steve said. "The hill dips down a little to the North, I'll check to see if there's anything unusual on the other side."

"I'll come with you," Precilla said. "This is all too weird."

"Yeah," Ramsey said, "just don't disappear."

A crow cawed from someplace in the direction Steve and Precilla were headed. Adams chuckled, said, "That must be our friend on the painted rock."

"All this gives me the shivers," Precilla said. "Painted rocks, little buildings, little people, people that disappear, boulders that disappear, the Indian with no eyes, masks, and that stupid crow..."

"Pretty outlandish isn't it?" Steve said. "I'm okay with everything except for the Amity Pillars that disappeared from the first site."

"What do you mean?"

"Well, people, I suppose, can somehow elude dogs and disappear if they want to, for whatever reasons. The little buildings and masks were made by those artists, Madden and Chase, as was the painted rock, I'm sure, and the little people are simply a fabrication. All that stuff I can deal with and understand. The Amity Pillars, on the other hand, were huge granite boulders, weighing tons, and there's absolutely no logic for their disappearance. That's what really gets to me. How could they have vanished without a trace? Without leaving behind any signs they were ever there?"

"Have you thought about the hollow rock the Indian left by the rock pillar?" Precilla asked.

"What about it?"

"Could the Amity Pillars you first discovered have been hollow too? Made out of clay like that rock?"

"What do you mean?"

"If they were made of clay and hollow, then they would have been much lighter than rock and a whole lot easier to move."

Steve Adams stopped. "No," he said, "there's no way those rocks and boulders were made of clay. No possible way."

"How do you know that? Did you move any of them?"

"No. But I know they were real. I touched them, peeled moss off them. They were solid granite."

"You're absolutely positive about that?"

"I am positive. They were real, and if anything gives me the shivers, it's those missing Amity Pillars. Of course, Josh's disappearance troubles me a little, too."

"I don't know why, but I feel there's something more to all this than meets the eye," Precilla said, "something more than a fabricated myth. I feel it. I can't put my finger on it, but I feel it."

Another crow's caw, this time closer, ruffled the air and sent Steve's skin crawling. He quickly searched the direction of the squawk.

Precilla Adams rubbed her arms. "That damn crow," she muttered.

"There he is," Steve said, pointing. "In that tree over there, just over the hill."

Steve walked toward the slope leading to the tree. The crow side stepped along the branch it had been perched on and quickly took wing and withdrew further into the forest.

"There are some small Amity Pillars at the base of the tree," Precilla said as they approached the crest of the hill. "I'm going to check them to see if all the rocks are real."

"Neat tree," Steve said. "Kind of ghostly looking. It should be standing next to Disney's Tower of Terror."

"It's so scraggly looking," Precilla said.

"For a maple tree it's very scraggly. I thought it was an oak at first. It's got a lot of character, I'll say that." They descended the slope toward the tree.

As they approached, Steve noticed a hole in the tree above the branch the crow had been perched on. At the base of the tree trunk, another hole faced the Amity Pillars. Something seemed peculiar about the latter. The rim of the hole looked as though it was lined with some kind of material. Nearing, he realized the lining was made of tiny bricks.

"Look at that hole in the base of the tree," he said softly to his wife. "The rim is lined with little bricks."

"I feel like we've been lured to this place," Precilla said. "The feeling I have is uncanny."

"Check the Amity Pillars," Steve said, "I'll check out the tree." He approached the tree trunk and knelt beside the hole at its base.

The grass in front of the hole was worn down to the soil, obviously due to heavy traffic by some kind of animal. He didn't see any distinguishable tracks.

"All the rocks appear to be real," Precilla said. Her tone seemed almost disappointed. "There doesn't seem to be anything unusual about them."

Steve lowered himself closer to the hole to peer inside. It was dark and he couldn't make anything out, only that it opened into a large, hollow cavity. He dug into his pocket for a small pen light attached to his key ring.

"Don't tell me those guys put a building inside the tree," Precilla said. She joined Steve and knelt beside him.

"I don't know what they did," Steve said. "It's too dark inside, I can't really see anything." He removed his keys and turned on the light.

Precilla started giggling.

"What?" Steve asked.

"Look at us," she said chuckling.

"What?"

Precilla tittered, shaking her head. "Nothing."

Steve ignored her and aimed the light into the hole, lowering himself for a better look. Precilla snorted uncontrollably.

"What?" Steve said rising to question her humor.

"Just look in the hole."

Steve returned the light to the opening and looked inside. At first he couldn't tell what he was looking at, as the cavity looked as though it had been lined with something dark and furry. After closer scrutiny he realized the entire cavity was lined with feathers. Crow feathers!

"I can't believe this," he said, rising.

"What?"

"The whole cavity is lined with crow feathers."

Precilla's eyes and wordless expression gave away her wonder.

"Take a look," Steve said, handing her the light.

Precilla took the light and looked inside. After a moment of quiet examination she finally asked, "Did you see the stairs?"

"What stairs?"

"A set of stairs rise along the inside of the trunk. They enter a hole in the topside of the cavity, then disappear out of sight. The whole ceiling is lined with feathers, too. This is really weird Steve. That stupid crow led us here, you know."

"That was coincidence," Steve said, reaching for the light. "Let me have another look."

"There was nothing coincidental about it," Precilla said, rising.

"A minute ago you were laughing and now all of a sudden you're unsettled."

"I am unsettled," Precilla said. "Here's this unearthly looking tree in the middle of this huge forest and we just happened upon it? I don't think so. Consider how we got here."

Steve's light found the curved staircase Precilla had discovered. His eyes followed the stairs to the top of the cavity where they disappeared through a small hole. The staircase appeared to be made of clay. "How the hell did they get those stairs in there?" he asked. "And all those feathers?"

"Where do you suppose the stairs lead to?" Precilla asked.

Steve rose to his feet and walked all the way around the tree trunk, inspecting it carefully. "I wonder if I could see anything through that hole above the branch?" he said looking up. The branch was a good six feet above his head.

Precilla chuckled, said, "Now that would be a sight watching you try to shimmy up that trunk."

Donald Ramsey appeared on the crest of the hill. "Steve!" he hollered down to them. "Tony found our missing Amity Pillars!"

Steve moved away from the tree. "The ones that disappeared from the first site?" he hollered back.

"They'd be the ones!"

"Where?"

"Not far from here. Come on up and have a look, I want to make certain they're really the same ones."

"Unbelievable," Steve said, turning to his wife. "You've got to see these pillars to believe them."

"What about this?" Precilla asked, pointing to the tree. "What are you going to do about this tree?"

"I'll tell Ramsey about it and we'll come back later. I really have to go see those Amity Pillars."

Precilla followed Steve up the hill to meet Ramsey.

"Pretty incredible," Ramsey said as they approached him. "It's like the pillars have never been moved. They're in a remote little area and standing just as they were at the first site. Tony's there now, waiting for Mutt and Jeff. I called to have them brought over from their dig site."

"They might be interested in what we found, too," Steve said.

"What?"

"That tree down there," Steve said, pointing, "by those pillars. Part of the trunk is hollow and the whole cavity is lined with crow's feathers and a tiny staircase made of clay."

"Crow's feathers?"

"Yeah, the whole interior is lined with crow's feathers."

Ramsey snorted. "Tony claims it was a crow that led him to the Amity Pillars. He said a crow was sitting on top of one of the pillars when he discovered them."

Precilla took Steve's hand into hers but didn't speak.

*   *   *   *   *

PART TWO

Dakota's Dream

Nine
Dakota's Dream

Enlarged photos of the pictographs confirmed the Amity Pillars Tony Williams discovered were the same ones that had disappeared from the first site. The archeologists were as perplexed as anyone as how they could have possibly been moved. The ground around the new site was virtually undefiled and showed absolutely no signs that anyone had walked there. The pillars themselves were arranged exactly as before.

Williams' recollection of his discovery was odd. He said if it wasn't for a crow he probably would have never found the pillars. He told Ramsey, Steve and Precilla that he was headed in another direction when a crow suddenly appeared out of nowhere and flew inches over his head. He said the crow turned a complete 360 in midair, flapped one wing as though it were injured, and tumbled seemingly out of control. The bird plummeted out of sight behind a small rise off to his right. Curious, Williams followed the path of the crow.

When he reached the crest of the rise he spotted the crow sitting on top of a rock formation. Upon eye contact, the crow flew off, leaving Williams stupefied and gawking at the six Amity Pillars. He knew immediately what they were. His call to Ramsey was automatic.

The tree Steve and Precilla had discovered was just as bewildering to everyone, especially the archeologists. They had spent much time investigating the tree, even to the point of fishing a surveillance camera into the cavity, up the stairs and through the small hole where they disappeared. What they discovered astounded them. The camera entered a small chamber and revealed a table, several thimble shaped stools, some ceramic vessels, tiny masks along the walls, and other items. The archeologists extracted what appeared to be a miniature ceramic bowl from the table. Their judgment was that the bowl was extremely old but had to be tested to be certain. They had no explanations as to how the items they found with the camera could have gotten inside the tree. They were confident that much of what was being discovered in this forest was created by another culture centuries ago. Even longer. Milton and Schepp disclosed their professional findings to Ramsey and the others, but were careful not to divulge any personal opinions or speculations. Steve and Precilla believed they were holding back plenty.

Steve, now, like Precilla, was beginning to feel there was something more here than a mere hoax or fabrication by the artists, Dakota Chase and Cole Madden. What it was exactly, neither had a clue, but they felt certain they could find some answers in Josh Clemens' notes and manuscripts. It was now their quest to get through them all and to get them organized into some kind of rational order. If that was possible.

Steve was sitting in the middle of the floor of the editing suite rounding up all the *unknowns* he could find among the twenty some stacks of paper arranged around and about the studio. The unknowns were words, symbols, names and such, that made absolutely no sense to either of them. Precilla was going through all the photographs and sketches, trying to match them with the rest of the papers. She had a knack for organizing things into a broad picture, where as Steve always got hung up and lost in all the little details. He was hung up on one such detail now.

"What the hell is a Ulambent?" he asked flipping through papers on his lap.

"A Ulambent?"

"Yeah, I keep finding stuff that refers to a Ulambent. It seems to be a key element in all this."

"Ulambent," Precilla repeated quietly to herself. "Lambent I think means clear or transparent, something like that, but I've never heard of Ulambent. Is it even a word?"

"I can't find it in the dictionary, but it appears in a lot of Josh's notes. Here's another word that's driving me crazy: Kimirente. What in the blazes is a Kimirente?"

Precilla looked up. "A what?"

"Kimirente. It surfaces often, and on a couple of drawings, too." Steve held up a sketch of a human stick figure and a bird. There was an "X" drawn between them. The word, "Kimirente," appeared below the drawing. "What's it mean?"

"I don't have a clue. Maybe you should keep those off to the side and start going through the other papers. When you come across them again, match them up, then maybe you can tie them together."

"I wonder if any of this would make sense to those archeologists?" Steve said. "I really think they know more than what they're telling us."

"They're certainly not generous with their assumptions and speculations. I think it would be worth a trip to the dig site just to have a chat with them. I'd really like to see all they've uncovered, too."

"We'll take a run out there this afternoon. I want to start going through one of Josh's handwritten manuscripts first to see if any of this mess comes together."

"Which one are you going to start with?"

"'Lore, The Legend,'" Steve said, reaching for the manuscript. "It looks like there's a lot of material written about the artists, Dakota Chase and Cole Madden. It seems a likely place to start."

"When I'm finished with all this," Precilla said, "I'll take a look at the other one, the Kintu manuscript."

Steve placed all the other papers in a pile beside him and scooted along the floor to the wall so he could rest his back while he read. He stared a moment at the title: "Lore: The Legend." He then flipped to page one.

Page one contained one line in the center of the paper: "Something's out there…something in the woods."

"Now there's an understatement," he thought to himself, turning to the next page. He began to read.

"Bright Feather"

Dakota's dream was a recurring one. He told his friend, Cole Madden, about it as they scaled the sharp rise leading toward a mysterious rock pillar he'd discovered while sketching in the woods. The dream, he'd explained, always began with a haunting chorus of voices singing a mantra. "One…," Dakota hummed, letting his voice trail softly.

"The sky is always turbulent," Dakota said, "with black clouds rolling like a sheet flapping in the wind. The air along the ground is mysteriously calm. A figure, who I don't see clearly because it's night, makes his way down a hill through dense trees, then stops along the edge of a lake. In the unruffled water before him is an island.

"An anomalous light begins to glow beneath the water and the figure wades slowly toward it. As the figure sinks deeper into the water, the mantra intensifies. Then, when the figure is completely submerged, the chanting stops; everything becomes still and deathly silent. Even the clouds hang motionless in dark suspension.

"The light begins to rise toward the surface of the water. The chanting commences again, at first very softly, then concentrates as the light nears the surface.

"The light emerges from the water, held by a hand. The light is a perfect sphere, blinding bright. Once again everything hushes. The figure follows his hand through the surface of the water and his exhaling breath echoes across the lake.

"The clouds begin to roll apart, opening a hole in the sky far above the light. The figure tilts back and looks up.

"No...!" the chorus howls.

"A lightning bolt rips through the hole in the sky and strikes the brilliant sphere. The sphere explodes with a blazing flash, and I bolt awake startled and in a cold sweat."

Steve Adams set the manuscript in his lap and looked at his wife. She was deeply absorbed in her sorting. "Have you come across any pictures or sketches of a hand holding a ball or some kind of round object?" he asked.

"Not yet," she said without looking up. She stopped what she was doing. "Why?"

"When I discovered all the pictographs on the Amity Pillars at that first sight, Ramsey pointed one out. It was a hand holding some kind of ball. This manuscript begins with a reference to it."

"How so?"

Steve told her about Dakota Chase's dream.

Precilla set her papers aside and joined her husband. "Read some more," she said, sitting beside him.

Steve raised the manuscript, flipped to the next page and read aloud.

"How often does your dream recur?" Cole asked.

"There's no pattern," Dakota replied.

"Is it affecting your life?"

"I don't know. I think it somehow ties in with what I'm about to show you."

"How much further?"

"There," Dakota said, pointing. "At the very top of this hill."

Cole Madden's silence revealed his astonishment. They approached the rock pillar quietly.

Cole circled the enormous pillar several times. "This is amazing," he finally said. "It looks very old."

"So, what is it?" Dakota asked.

"You've got me," Cole replied. "Is this why you've begun building rock pillars throughout the forest?"

"I haven't built anything of this magnitude but, yes, this is the reason."

"Have you found others like it?"

"No. I haven't really searched for others yet. I've been waiting for you."

"I wonder who else knows about this?"

"I haven't mentioned it to anyone besides you."

"Who would do this?" Cole asked, again walking around the pillar. "One person couldn't have done this alone, it has to be at least ten feet tall."

"It tossed me for a pretty good loop when I discovered it," Dakota said. "It's really seductive."

"What brought you out here, this deep into the forest, in the first place?" Cole asked.

"I don't know if I want to tell you about that," Dakota replied with a chuckle.

"Humor me."

"I followed an injured crow."

Cole's look was vacant.

"Seriously," Dakota continued. "I tried to chase down a crow with a broken wing. It scrambled along the ground and hobbled up the hill. I was going to try to help it, take it to a veterinarian if I could catch it. The next thing I realized, I was looking at this tower of rocks, and that rickety crow was perched on the very peak of it. Then the damn thing flew off as though there was nothing wrong with it."

Precilla Adams interrupted. "Coincidence, huh?" she said. "At the tree you said everything was a coincidence. What are your conclusions now, my dearest, still a coincidence?"

Steve set the manuscript on the floor. "I'm getting a cup of coffee," he said, "do you want anything?"

"Get me a glass of orange juice, please," Precilla replied, reaching for the manuscript.

Steve rose, carefully stepped through the stacks of paper on the floor and made his way up the stairs. In the dining room he stopped for a moment to look at the brick building Donald Ramsey had brought from the forest. He thought about his friend, Josh Clemens.

"Where are you Josh? What are you doing?" he thought to himself. He slipped into a chair in front of the building and lowered himself to study it.

Through the windows he looked at the designs, symbols and relief sculptures that decorated the interior walls. The images were plentiful. They consisted of representations of birds, cats, spiders, bears, dogs or wolves, and symbols or icons that didn't seem to depict anything recognizable. One image in the central room was obscured by darkness, but seemed to be a relief sculpture, dominating the others.

Steve reached into his pocket and removed his key chain with the penlight. He turned on the light and aimed it through the window toward the relief sculpture. The light struck something shiny and the room burst suddenly into a dazzling array of luminous colors! He straightened upright with surprise.

Light particles danced inside all the windows of the building, creating a kaleidoscopic exhibit of every color in the spectrum. It was a majestic display. Steve again peered through the window for a better look. The beam of his penlight was striking what appeared to be a small crystal ball being held by a sculptured hand. Above the crystal ball, carved into the wall, were letters. He strained his eyes to read them. ULAMBENT.

Steve sat upright and turned off the light. "Ulambent," he said to himself.

Precilla hollered something from downstairs.

"I'll be right there!" he answered. He got his coffee and his wife's orange juice and returned to the editing suite.

Precilla was so engulfed in Josh's manuscript she didn't realize he was standing beside her. "You have to see what I found in the building Ramsey brought over," Steve said.

Precilla winced. "What?"

He handed her the orange juice and sat down beside her. After a sip of coffee, he told her about the sculptured hand, crystal ball and light display. Then he mentioned the word, Ulambent, above the crystal ball. He was certain the word Ulambent referred to the crystal ball.

Precilla absorbed what he said then held up the manuscript. "Those two artists, Chase and Madden, were lured into all this just as we are being lured," she said. "They just encountered the blind Indian."

"How?"

Precilla explained. "After Dakota Chase showed Cole Madden the Amity Pillar, they went on to explore the forest in search for others. While walking, Madden kept making reference to Dakota's recent landscape paintings, how dramatic they had changed. He said they had gone from natural earth tones to extremely vibrant and luminous colors, completely out of character for the artist. He said every recent painting Dakota had done looked as though it had been dipped in a rainbow. Everything seemed to glow with its own light, very unnatural.

"While descending a hill," Precilla continued, "Chase spotted a cluster of rock pillars near some dense scrub in the hollow below. As they approached, they noticed a figure moving around them. The figure looked old, but it was difficult to see clearly from such a distance. The two artists crept closer for a better look.

"Madden was the first to realize it was an Indian. He was carrying what appeared to be a wooden staff and, with it, was probing a large black object on the ground between the Amity Pillars. As the two artists made their way closer, the Indian stopped what he was doing and looked in their direction. He had no eyes!

"While the artists gaped in their confusion, the Indian retreated into the thickets and disappeared. Chase and Madden stood fast in their bewilderment. Both were quite alarmed."

Precilla paused and sipped from her orange juice.

"Then what?" Steve asked. "What did they do?"

"After some time and serious deliberation, they decided to approach the Amity Pillars. What happened next is very curious."

"What happened?"

"When they reached the Amity Pillars, they realized the large black object the Indian was toying with was an immense slab of rock. It was described as black and highly polished, like onyx. On the rock, or rather carved into it, were pictographs and symbols.

"Now get this," Precilla said. "When Cole Madden stepped between the Amity Pillars to look at the strange rock, the hair on his head and arms stood on end, and he became enveloped in, what Josh described as, blue squiggles of static electricity. The same thing happened to Dakota Chase when he followed his friend between the pillars."

"Give me a break," Steve said.

Precilla ignored him. "It was late afternoon and the artists had to leave the forest before dark. Before leaving, Dakota Chase removed a large sheet of paper from his pack, unrolled it and laid it on the black rock. Using a graphite stick, he rubbed the paper to capture all the images on the rock. While making the transfer rubbing, he watched the image of a hand holding a ball appear. He was completely dumbfounded. His haunting dream came back to him."

Precilla removed the manuscript from her lap and set it on the floor between them. She sipped her juice.

"Then what?" Steve asked. "Where did they go from there?"

"That's as far as I got. I don't know what happens after that."

"I think Josh is embellishing things a little bit," Steve said. "I mean, really, the hair on the artists' heads and arms standing on end, blue squiggles of static electricity...."

"And the crow and the Indian?" Precilla interrupted. "That's embellishment too? I don't think so. I think we should take all of this," she said, gesturing with her hand, "everything scattered around this room, very seriously."

"I wonder if any of Josh's maps pinpoint the location of those Amity Pillars and that mysterious black rock?" Steve said.

"I'm wondering if it's the same site where the archeologists are doing their excavating," Precilla replied. "I can't tell my right hand from my left, so North and South are meaningless to me. You're going to have to be the one who goes through that stack of maps over there to see if they make any sense and figure out where they lead to."

Steve reached for the papers he was looking at before he started reading Josh's manuscript. "This word, Ulambent," he said, "I'm sure refers to the circle or ball being held in the hand in those pictographs. You have to see that building upstairs on the dining room table to believe it. When my light strikes that crystal ball, the whole interior of the building explodes with bright colors."

"I want to see that," Precilla said. "Why don't you go through that pile of maps first, see if there's any reference to the Amity Pillars and that black rock we just read about. I don't know why, but I just have a feeling it's the excavation site. Afterward, you can show me the crystal ball. Then," she added, "I think we should head out to that dig site and have a chat with the archeologists."

* * * *

Ten

Josh Clemens' maps were very crude but readable. Out of a stack of twenty some drawings, Steve Adams found a map that located the large black rock the two artists had discovered. The map led directly to the excavation site. Precilla's instincts were correct.

Along with the map, Steve found more references to the pictograph of the hand holding the ball. In all the references, the image of the hand with the ball was enclosed within an odd looking freeform shape. One such drawing included the words, 'Comet Lake.' Steve dug out a county map and compared the shape of Comet Lake with Josh's drawings. They were the same. Steve felt certain that whatever the hand with the ball referred to, it was located somewhere at the bottom of Comet Lake.

Precilla Adams was quite amazed with the colorful light show the building presented when Steve shined his light on the small crystal ball in the central room. As he moved the light around the ball, every color in the spectrum danced brilliantly along the interior walls. As he demonstrated this to his wife, Steve recalled part of Josh's manuscript his wife had read to him. While the artists were exploring the woods in search of Amity Pillars, Cole Madden made mentioned of Dakota's recent landscape paintings and how colorful they'd become, how out of character they were for the artist. He'd said every recent painting Dakota had done looked as though it had been dipped in a rainbow. "Were Dakota

Chase's recent paintings and this crystal ball somehow related," Steve wondered. It was a passing thought.

It was quite obvious the archeologists weren't real thrilled about Steve and Precilla Adams being at the excavation site. When they arrived, Milton and Schepp emphasized they were extremely busy and didn't have a lot of time to visit. They said they would talk while they worked.

All of the cuts into the earth looked very neat and precise. Three people Steve didn't recognize were in different parts of the dig area, carefully cleaning and brushing dust and debris from the surfaces of rocks and other things. They were graduate students from the University helping with the excavation, so Steve was informed. They paid no mind to the visitors.

In the center of the site, below ground level, a brown plastic tarp covered a relatively large rectangular form. All the way around the form a uniform trench had been dug. To the right of the tarp and also below ground level, a pedestal of earth supported an interesting looking building, similar in shape and size to the building on Steve's dining room table. On the opposite side of the tarp, several feet away, stood another building. Intricately cut furrows led away from the central trench surrounding the tarp, past the two buildings to other areas around the site.

Upon Precilla's request, Dr. Milton escorted her and Steve into the dig area to see the buildings they had uncovered. The archeologist was very emphatic about their not touching anything and to carefully walk and stay within the furrows. He was quite concerned about cave-ins or damage to yet uncovered areas. He was gruff and obviously despondent over this intrusion.

The larger of the two buildings was the most interesting and detailed. It looked very old and parts of it had crumbled or collapsed over time. It was a fascinating, miniature architectural ruins. Even though parts of the building had collapsed, the fine particulars of its design had prevailed. When Precilla asked how old the building actually was, Milton's reply was that it was over a thousand years old.

Steve's attraction to the tarp in the center of the site was compelling. It seemed to him as though Milton was deliberately avoiding that area. Steve asked him flatly, "What's under the tarp?"

"It's an area we're protecting. We haven't had a chance to examine that ground yet," he replied.

"It's been dug out," Steve said, "the tarp is below ground level."

"Yes," Milton replied, "we've removed the topsoil."

"It looks like it's been dug deeper than topsoil. The ground looks very rigid under the tarp."

"It's virgin ground," Milton replied, "there's a lot of firm clay in the soil."

"Are you sure it's not a large black rock?" Precilla blurted out.

Milton stared blankly, looking quite muddled. Schepp and the graduate students stopped what they were doing and ogled at the threesome. Milton cleared his throat. "Excuse me?" he said.

"She asked if it might be a large black rock under the tarp," Steve said. "A flat, shiny black rock with symbols and pictographs carved into its surface."

The graduate students remained frozen like cast statues. Schepp stood quietly nearby tapping a soft brush against his leg. Milton looked stony. He wrung his fists, glared intensely at Steve.

"Hello?" Steve said.

"Who told you there was a rock under there?" Milton finally spoke.

"No one."

Milton fired a glance at the deputy on duty guarding the site. The deputy shrugged his shoulders.

"Someone had to have told you!" Milton snapped.

"No one told us," Steve replied. "My friend Josh Clemens, the guy that disappeared from this very site, left me some things he'd been writing about. Among them, my wife and I found reference to that shiny black rock." Steve pointed toward the tarp.

Milton's eyes followed Steve's aim. "What else did your friend leave you?" he asked.

"On the black rock," Steve said, "is an image of a hand holding some kind of ball. Whatever the image refers to, it's at the bottom of Comet Lake."

"Damn," the archeologist mumbled. He moved to the edge of the furrow they were standing in and sat down. Particles of loose gravel fell from where he sat and trickled down by his feet.

"You're disturbing your bank there," Steve said.

"Do you know what the hand is?" Milton asked, ignoring Steve's warning.

"No. Whatever the ball is, I think it's called a Ulambent."

"A Ulambent," Milton repeated softly. "Do you know where this *Ulambent* is?"

"In the hand, I suppose," Steve replied.

Milton shook his head. "No," he said. "It's not in the hand."

"How do you know that?"

"We've seen the hand."

Steve stepped toward him. "Where?" he asked.

"At the bottom of the lake. There was no sphere in the hand."

"You saw the hand?"

Milton gave a casual wave to Schepp. "Get the photographs," he said.

Steve watched Schepp leave the trench, looked back at Milton and asked, "You have photographs of it?"

"The students helping us are specializing in underwater excavation and research and all three are licensed scuba diving instructors. We pinpointed the location of the hand at the bottom of the lake and they found it. There was no sphere in the hand."

"How did you pinpoint the location?"

"From pictographs on some of the artifacts we've uncovered."

"What kind of artifacts?"

"Pottery, stone fragments, these small buildings...they're all abundant with assorted images. The hand with the sphere appears often and seems to be a central element."

"A central element to what?" Steve asked.

"We don't know for sure."

"You must have some idea."

"We know for certain many of these things were created prior to this millennium, but we don't know for sure who created them...or why."

"But you speculate," Precilla said.

"Speculation is dangerous," Milton replied. "We have to base our conclusions on the physical evidence we find."

"Yeah, but, theory is a big part of investigating," Steve said. "You must have some thoughts as to the meaning of all this."

"None," Milton replied.

"Ramsey said you believed the small buildings were actually inhabited at one time," Precilla said.

"There! You see?" Milton snapped, stiffening. "A prime example of the dangers in speculating! I did not tell Officer Ramsey we believed the buildings were inhabited! I made the comment that it had appeared as though the buildings had been inhabited at one time; I never said they actually were. Officer Ramsey has a unique way of twisting everything around."

"He's a professional interrogator," Steve said, "that's his nature. How is it, then, that the buildings *appear* as though they'd been inhabited at one time?"

Milton was obviously quite agitated with this conversation. "All the furnishings in the buildings are worn in respect to actual usage. Stools, tables, pottery...everything, including the fire pits, are consistent with natural wear. There's no rational explanation for it."

"How about the tree we showed you?" Steve asked. "You took a small ceramic bowl to have it tested. Have you heard anything about that?"

"It's very old," Milton replied. "The pictures our camera took inside the tree show the furnishings are similarly worn with usage. How on earth those objects got inside that tree, or how they were used, is beyond any of us."

"And you don't speculate," Precilla said.

"Look," Milton said, leaning back to look at both Steve and Precilla, "the only reason I am having this conversation with you is because Officer Ramsey said you may have some information that might help us with our investigations. You confirmed that when you mentioned the black rock. We are being very careful to not let anything we find go public before we know what's going on ourselves. We don't need a lot of press or people coming around here interfering with questions and getting in the way of our job. Can you imagine the storm of people into this place and the destruction it would cause if any of this got out? I hope the two of you can respect our grave concerns."

"We understand and we do respect your concerns," Steve said.

"Maybe we can share some of our information," Milton said humbly.

"I think that would be in everybody's best interests," Precilla said.

Schepp returned to the edge of the bank carrying a large leather portfolio. "Do you want to look at these here?" he asked.

"No," Milton replied. He stood, said to Steve and Precilla, "We have a table set up outside this perimeter. Let's go there."

The two followed Milton and Schepp out of the trench and into the trees nearby. A large, collapsible table was set up beside a Jeep Wrangler and two cabin style tents. On the table were boxes, laptop computers, papers, small rocks, and objects that appeared to be pottery fragments. Milton moved the computers to one side to make room for the portfolio.

"I'll go help remove the tarp," Schepp said, handing Milton the portfolio.

Milton nodded, set the portfolio on the table and opened it. Plastic protective sheeting covered a myriad of photographs, notes and drawings. He started to flip through the first few pages when Steve stopped him.

"Wait," Steve said. "Go back to the first page, I saw something I'd like to look at more closely. Our friend, Josh, left a ton of drawings and one of the pictures looked familiar."

"Which one?" Milton asked, flipping the pages back.

"That one," Steve said, pointing. It was a pictograph of a human stick figure. Beside the stick figure was an image of a bird. Seemingly connecting the two images were two diagonal lines that formed an X.

"That's it," Steve remembered aloud. "There was a word with it, but it slips me."

"Kimirente," Precilla said. "It was something like Kimirente."

"That was it," Steve said.

"Interesting," Milton said. "There are other pictures similar to this one. All are stick figures with different kinds of animals."

"What are the diagonal lines between the images?" Steve asked.

"We're not certain, but there's a definite symbolic relationship between the stick figures and the animals. We think they symbolize some kind of chimera."

"No kidding?" Steve said, eyeing the archeologist..."What's a chimera?"

"It's like an apparition or an illusion. Many of the Native American cultures celebrated animals as well as other natural elements of the earth. Numerous created different societies around animals, such as, Buffalo Societies, Animal Dreaming Societies, and so on. Members would often take on the likeness of the animals during their celebrations, and some believed the Shaman could actually transform into the animal. These images could represent a similar type of celebration for the animals. The pictographs are too obscure to determine anything for certain."

"Chimera," Steve said softly. "And you have other pictures similar to this one?"

"Several."

"That's an interesting picture below it," Precilla said, moving closer, "the one with the fish designs."

Steve examined the photograph Precilla was pointing at. The picture consisted of a wavy, horizontal line, diagrams of fish below it, and below the fish, several images that looked like buildings.

"What's that all about?" Steve asked.

Milton removed a pipe from his shirt pocket and began loading it with tobacco. "We don't know yet, but that photograph and others similar are the reasons we contacted the underwater team. We think there's more at the bottom of the lake but we don't have any reference to a location. We were hoping you might have something in the materials your friend left you."

"I don't recall anything like that," Steve said, "but I'll keep it in mind as we continue to go through them."

The archeologist gripped the pipe in his teeth and drew a lighter to it. Long puffs caused the pipe to gurgle slightly while bluish clouds filled with the odor of chocolate floated from his mouth. "Maybe sometime Schepp and I can have a look at the materials you have?" he said. The smoke was fairly pleasing, actually.

"Of course," Steve replied.

Milton took a long pull from his pipe then set it on the table. "Here's the hand the boys found underwater," he said, flipping quickly through the portfolio to the right page. "It's not actually a real hand, of course."

It wasn't a hand at all. The object in the photograph looked like some kind of black, finger coral one might find in the ocean, and it was fashioned more in the form of a deer's antler than a hand. It appeared to grow out of the bottom of the lake and rose a good three feet.

"What is it?" Steve asked.

"A mystery," Milton replied. "It's like a fresh water coral, very hard, but we haven't taken a sample of it yet. Here's another view," he said, turning the page, "this one looks more like the pictographs we've found."

This photograph was taken from a view that made the material look more like the profile of a hand holding an object. Except there was no object. Five finger like extensions curved upward from the main mass and turned inward as though curling around a sphere. The tip of the smallest finger appeared as though a part of it had been broken off.

Precilla leaned over the photograph for a closer look. "It looks like a piece has been broken off," she said.

"Yes," Milton replied. "We didn't realize that until after the pictures were developed. The divers are going back to see if they can find a fragment by the base of the form. It's pretty murky down there and the slightest disturbance raises a cloud. We really don't want to touch the object until we know more about it."

"It really does look like a hand from this angle," Steve said. "And there was no ball or anything lying around it?"

"Not that they could find. But, again, it's very murky down there and the bottom is all silt. Things could settle quite deeply in the muck."

"Is there such a thing as fresh water coral?" Steve asked.

"I've never heard of it," Milton replied.

"Strange," Steve said, studying the photograph. "Do you mind if I skim through the other pages?"

"Go ahead," Milton said. "Schepp and the others are removing the tarp so you and your wife can see the rock. I'll go check on them and return for you when it's uncovered. If you find anything you can shed some light on, please let me know."

"I'll do that," Steve agreed.

Milton took his pipe off the table and lit it again. "How much stuff did your friend actually leave you?" he asked.

"A lot."

Milton nodded, turned in a cloud of smoke drifting around his head and departed. Precilla moved closer to Steve as he began thumbing through the pages. The book was quite thick, every page filled with meticulous research.

"You're not going to give them Josh's materials are you?" Precilla asked.

"No. They're welcome to come to the house and look at anything we have, but I'm certainly not going to turn anything over to them."

"What if they try a legal approach to acquire them?"

Steve's eyes followed Milton through the trees. "I don't think he would do that if we agreed to share information. I actually kind of trust the guy."

"Look," Precilla said, "there's another picture with images of fish in it."

Steve returned his attention to the portfolio. The picture was a diagram of an arch with a wavy, horizontal line cutting it in half. Half of the arch was above the wavy line, the bottom half below. In the middle, beneath the wavy line, was a circle with straight lines radiating from it. Around the sun-like circle were abstract images of fish. Below the fish, were representations of Amity Pillars and buildings.

"Could that arch be an island?" Precilla asked.

"Dakota's dream," Steve said softly. "Remember in Josh's manuscript, the dream the artist described? There was an island in it."

"Yes," Precilla remembered, "and a figure waded into the water toward a bright light between him and an island."

"There's a large island in the South arm of Comet lake and it's not too far from shore," Steve said enthusiastically. "In fact, if I remember right, there's a shallow sandbar connecting the island to the mainland."

"That's not too far from here," Precilla said.

Steve glanced at his watch. "It's 2:30," he said. "We may have enough time to go over there yet this afternoon. If you want to, that is."

"We can do that," Precilla replied. She turned the page to look at another picture.

"What's that one?" Steve asked.

"Oh, ish," Precilla said, wrinkling her nose. "It's a spider. I hate spiders!"

"What does it say below it?" Steve asked. "There's a word with it."

"MAKAI...Makai" Precilla replied. "It's not real clear."

"Makai," Steve repeated. "I think I've seen that somewhere before, probably in Josh's notes. I should videotape all the pictographs on the Amity Pillars, and ask Milton if I could tape the images on the Black rock, too."

"Did I hear someone mention my name?" Milton asked, emerging from the trees.

"As a matter of fact, you did," Steve said, leaning away from the table. "There are so many pictographs and images here, I was wondering if you would mind my videotaping the black rock sometime. It would be a great reference for all the materials my friend left me."

"I wouldn't mind having a copy of a tape myself," Milton said. "In fact, we should be documenting everything on video. We can talk about that later. Schepp and the others have the rock uncovered if you want to have a look at it now."

"Do you want your portfolio along?" Precilla asked.

"No, you can just fold it shut and leave it on the table."

Precilla closed the portfolio and she and Steve joined the archeologist. He was tapping his pipe to the palm of his hand and emptying ashes from its bowl. He no longer seemed so discontented at their being there.

"Did you find anything useful in the portfolio?" Milton asked.

"There's so much stuff," Steve replied. "Most of Josh's references are hand-drawn, except for the photographs he took of the artist's works. It would be nice to have actual photographs of everything so we could match them with his sketches. His drawing abilities lack in finesse, if you know what I mean."

Milton smiled. "Schepp and I would really like to have a look at the materials your friend left you," he said. "We have multiple copies of all our photographs and we would be willing to share them with you. Ramsey assured us you were very trustworthy and discreet."

"When would you like to come by to have a look at them?" Steve asked.

"Whenever it's convenient. We don't want to impose ourselves on you."

"Anytime is convenient," Precilla said. "Everything is in a bit of disarray right now, but we're slowly getting the materials organized."

The threesome returned to the dig site. Schepp and the others were busy in different areas, brushing off rocks and examining them in place. The large black rock in the center of the pit was just as it had been described in Josh's manuscript: It looked like a large slab of shiny black onyx with images carved into its surface. Steve came to a stop and turned to look up the hill the two artists must have been descending when they discovered the rock along with the Indian. Precilla followed his eyes.

"Something wrong?" Milton asked.

"No," Steve replied. "Josh left a manuscript and in it he described how Chase and Madden, the two artists, discovered this rock. They were descending that hill when they saw an Indian moving around the rock and the Amity Pillars that used to be here surrounding it."

"An Indian?" Milton said.

"Yes," Steve replied. He turned to Milton. "Did Ramsey tell you about the Indian we caught on videotape?"

"No. What Indian?"

"Wow," Steve said. "You definitely have to come by the house to see this for yourself."

"What?"

"I don't want to spoil it for you."

Schepp and associates were motionless with their necks cranked and heads turned in Steve's direction. He smiled at them. "How's it going?" he asked.

They returned to what they were doing. Milton pressed. "What Indian?" he asked again.

Steve moved into the trench and approached the rock. "In Josh's manuscript, when the artists discovered the rock, there was an Indian moving around it. When he became aware of their presence, he backed into some thickets...," Steve paused, looked beyond the dig area to a part of the grove of prickly ash and pointed, "...probably those thickets there. Then he disappeared."

"Is this manuscript fact or fiction?" Milton asked.

"We've seen the Indian Josh described. We have him on videotape."

"How do you know it's the same person that's in the manuscript?"

"Believe me, they're the same."

Steve approached the rock, was astounded by the highly polished surface and detailed carvings. The block appeared to be a perfect cube, a good four feet in every dimension. It was a work of art.

"If you notice on top, right in the middle," Milton said, "there's a square we think represents the rock itself. The square's position makes it look like a diamond. Surrounding it are images of the rock pillars that used to be here. If you notice that on the square, and on the rock, itself, there's a small triangle at each corner. The triangles line up with the four directions: North, South, East and West. The entire surface of the rock seems to be some sort of map."

"Amazing," Steve said softly. Precilla joined him. The rock was so covered with images it was difficult to focus on any one in particular. Milton moved around them and pointed to one.

"There's the hand with the sphere," he said. "That freeform around it represents Comet Lake. When we put our compass in the middle of the rock, right on the square, the image on the rock is in direct line with the form we found at the bottom of the lake."

Steve remained quiet and tried to absorb all he was seeing and hearing.

"Something else," Milton said, moving his finger to another area. "Do you recognize this?" He pointed to a representation of a tree. The shape of the tree was unmistakable. It was the hollow tree Steve and Precilla discovered.

"It's the same here with the compass," Milton continued. "When we set our compass on the square, the image of the tree on the rock is directly in line with the actual tree in the forest."

"And all these other images?" Steve asked.

"We don't know their meanings, nor have we had the time to search for any of them. There are no distance references on the rock, so any number of these images could actually be anywhere in the world."

"In direct line with the images on the rock," Steve said.

"Quite possible," Milton replied. "We don't think it's coincidence that the images we've checked so far line up perfectly."

"What is all this?" Precilla asked.

"Something pretty spectacular," Milton said. "Whatever it is, it goes far beyond your friend that disappeared and the works those two artists have been hiding in the woods."

"What are they up to?" Steve wondered aloud. "What are Josh, Dakota Chase and Cole Madden up to? What all do they know?"

Milton reached for his pipe and tobacco. "Whatever it is," he said, "they're way ahead of us."

Schepp stopped what he was doing and joined them. "Our work here is a very slow process," he said. "We have to be extremely meticulous and careful not to damage anything we're uncovering. We don't have the time nor the resources to investigate all these images on the rock. We could use some help."

"Our funding is somewhat limited," Milton said, "but we would be willing to negotiate some kind of stipend if you would be willing to assist us."

"A stipend?" Steve said.

"Within reason, of course," Schepp said.

Precilla took Steve's hand into hers. "What exactly would that mean?" she asked.

"What would it mean?" Milton repeated. "I guess it would mean you would be getting paid for what you're doing right now: Investigating."

"Employed by whom?" Steve asked.

"The University," Schepp replied.

"I don't know," Steve said. "We would have to have a little time to consider that."

"That's understandable," Milton said. "We've already discussed the possibility with our people and they are willing to negotiate a contract with you if you're interested."

"We'll think about it," Steve said.

"Good," Milton said, dropping the subject. He walked around to the North side of the rock, dragging his pipe stem over the shiny surface. He stopped and lightly tapped on an image below the triangle on the corner. "Have you seen this word before?" he asked.

Steve and Precilla moved closer for a better look.

"Olyqua," Precilla said. The word was enclosed within a circle. The enclosure was surrounded by six smaller circles.

"Yes, we've seen it before, several times," Steve said. "It was the first thing I saw among the pictographs on the Amity Pillars we discovered here."

"Do you have any idea as to what it means?" Schepp asked.

"It's an island," Precilla said. "The small circles surrounding the larger one represent smaller islands."

"If that rock is a map," Steve said, "then Olyqua is somewhere North of here."

"Do you know how far North?" Milton asked.

"No," Steve replied. "I haven't seen any references to a location. Is it of particular importance?"

"We don't know," Milton said. "The word has come up several times."

Steve pondered for a moment. While investigating Josh Clemens' disappearance, Ramsey said Dakota Chase and Cole Madden had gone up North into the Superior National Forest to spend most of the summer there. Olyqua could be there, or somewhere in the

Boundary Waters Canoeing Area. He tucked the thought into the back of his mind but didn't share it openly.

"Did something come to thought?" Milton asked.

"No," Steve said, looking back at the word. "I would really like to make a videotape of this rock and the buildings you've uncovered."

"I don't see a problem with that, and like I said earlier," Milton said, filling his pipe bowl, "we would like to have all this documented on video for ourselves. You should really consider our offer, too. You may as well be getting paid for all the time you're spending investigating."

"Yes, well, like I said, Precilla and I will consider that."

"There's an image that looks like one we saw in your portfolio," Precilla said pointing. "The one with the arch and wavy line."

"Yes," Schepp said. "We think the arch is an island. Our divers are curious over that one and want to find it. As you saw in the portfolio, there are fish, rock pillars and buildings below the wavy line."

"Have you lined the pictograph up with the compass?" Steve asked.

"Yes," Schepp replied. "The closest island in the vicinity, within a direct line with the image on the rock, is in the South arm of Comet Lake. We haven't had a chance to search that water yet."

"That would be an interesting search," Steve said.

"Do you have underwater housing for your video cameras?" Milton asked.

"No," Steve replied.

"If you should decide to work with us," Milton said, "I'm sure we could get that equipment for you." He lit his pipe and the odor of chocolate filled the air.

"That's another point to consider," Steve said. He looked at his watch and then to Precilla. "We should be moving along."

"When would be a good time for Schepp and me to stop by to have a look at the materials your friend, Clemens, left you?" Milton asked from his candy cloud.

"Tomorrow's fine," Steve said. "You should probably bring along your portfolio to cross reference some of Josh's sketches."

"Morning? Afternoon?" Schepp asked.

"How about noon," Precilla said. "I'll have some sandwiches and soup waiting for you."

"Now that sounds great," Milton said. "Anything home cooked, even if it's out of a can, would be wonderful."

Precilla smiled. "I'll make something special for you," she said.

*   *   *   *   *

Eleven

It was a tall and a relatively large, triangular shaped island. It rose out of the water about two hundred yards off the point below the hill where Steve and Precilla sat looking at it through the trees. The shallow sandbar connecting the point to the island could be seen easily below the water's surface. Large rocks and boulders lined the narrow sandbar and appeared to be barely underwater. The rocks would be ideal stepping stones to get to the island.

Steve sat quietly absorbing the picture and the background singing of birds filling the trees above their heads. The air was gentle and the cloudless sky allowed the late afternoon sun to paint the island's tree crowns brilliantly with rich, warm hues. It was too perfect for even a post card, he thought.

"What did you think about the offer Milton and Schepp made you?" Precilla asked, "about getting paid for working with them?"

"I'm leery," Steve said. "It would mean, I'm sure, that anything we find or, in fact already have, would become the property of the University. We could possibly even lose the rights to Josh's materials. I trust those guys, but I don't think I'd want to work with them."

"That's what I thought right away," Precilla said. "They pressed just enough to make the offer appealing."

"Look out there," Steve said, "do you think there are actually Amity Pillars and buildings underwater?"

"I wouldn't be surprised by it," Precilla said. "Why are we sitting on top of this hill, anyway? Why aren't we on our way to the island?"

"Because of Dakota Chase's dream," Steve said. "I wanted to visualize his dream and descend this hill as the character in his dream did. All of this is so surreal and hard to imagine. I'm hoping that by tracing the path of the character in the book, I can get closer to what actually happened."

"It's getting kind of late," Precilla said.

Steve rose and looked for the most suitable descent toward the island. He motioned for Precilla to join him and said, "Josh wrote that Dakota's dream always began with the singing of some kind of mysterious mantra; something like, 'One....'"

Precilla chortled softly as she stood. "You're not going to sing all the way down the hill, are you?"

"Come on," Steve said, ignoring her. He gazed out at the sky for a moment then began his descent. "He wrote the sky was always turbulent with rolling clouds, yet the air close to the ground was calm. Then a figure, who he doesn't see clearly because it's night, makes his way down this hill to the edge of the water. The water is calm, and before him is an island."

"Isn't there a light in the water?" Precilla asked.

They carefully made their way downward. "Yes," Steve replied. "When the figure reaches the shoreline, he sees a light underwater. I don't remember if the light was between the figure and the island or somewhere else in the lake. I don't think that was mentioned."

"The figure waded into deep water," Precilla said. "Remember? The strange song got louder as the figure waded deeper into the water."

"That's right," Steve remembered. "Then the singing stopped when he went completely underwater."

"And everything became dead silent and calm," Precilla said.

After reaching the base of the hill, Steve aimed for the point leading to the island. "If the figure waded into deep water, then he didn't follow the sandbar toward the island. He would have had to have gone to one side of the sandbar or the other."

At the point where the sandbar extended toward the island Steve and Precilla stopped. Off to the right of the point and sandbar, the water looked to remain shallow for a long ways. To the left of the point, the water appeared to get deeper very quickly.

"The figure went into the deeper water," Steve said, pointing to his left.

"Then the light rose from the water and the singing started again. The figure followed the light, holding it in his hand, high above his head." Precilla said.

Steve tilted back and looked into the clear sky. "The light is a perfect sphere, blinding bright. As the sphere, or the Ulambent as I believe it's called, rises out of the water, held by the hand of the figure, the singing stops and a hole opens in the clouds overhead."

"That's when the chorus of voices hollers, 'No...!'" Precilla said.

"Right, and a lightning bolt rips through the hole in the sky and strikes the Ulambent."

"And that's when Dakota Chase wakes up startled," Precilla said. "But all that was only a dream, Steve, why are you paying so much attention to it?"

"Because it's the way it all started in Josh's manuscript. It has to be significant in some way."

"But we're not even sure if this is the right island. We're guessing."

"This is the right island," Steve said. "I can feel it."

"Well let's feel how cold that water is before we start hopping stones over to it," Precilla said.

The stones and boulders made a perfect walkway. The water was mild. Neither took off their shoes as the rocks were too slippery and it would have been too hard on the bottoms of their bare feet. Negotiating the rocky path was easy and it wasn't long before they stood on the shoreline of the island.

"This is a big island," Precilla said. "Does someone own it? or is it part of the state forest?"

"I think it belongs to the state, but I'm not certain."

"The brush is pretty dense here," Precilla said, looking for a way to penetrate it.

"Let's walk the shoreline a ways," Steve said. "It didn't look quite as thick further down, and this area is loaded with poison ivy."

As they moved along, Steve noticed a hole in the brush, just large enough so the two of them could crawl through it. He stopped to look. "Let's go through here," he said. "Stay away from the shiny green plants with three leaves or you'll be scratching for weeks."

"That's all I need," Precilla said.

Steve entered first on his hands and knees and crawled through the entanglement. The brush thinned and opened to a forest covered hill dotted with rocks and boulders. He inched his way to a boulder in the open area and waited for Precilla.

"I feel like a little kid," she said, pawing her way toward him. "I can't believe I'm doing this."

"It's beautiful in here," he said, scanning the tree covered haven. "I thought it would be a mess of underbrush and a hassle to move through, but it's all open between the trees.

"Are you sure it's okay to be here?" Precilla asked, joining him. "This isn't private property, is it?"

"Like I said, I'm pretty sure it's state property. I didn't see any "No Trespassing" signs. I would think, if it was private property, there would be a sign posted along the edge of the island; especially at the end of the sandbar."

"Look at this place," Precilla said, rising. "It's so peaceful in here."

Steve rose to his feet. "It's unusually quiet, isn't it? I don't even hear birds chirping."

"That's odd," Precilla said. "I didn't even think of it until you just now mentioned it. There were a lot of birds on the mainland."

"We'll make our way to the top of the hill to start with, then go from there," Steve said. "I have no idea what we're looking for."

"Is that a path leading to the top?" Precilla asked, looking straight ahead.

Before them, some fifty feet away, was an abrupt rise with a path cut through the middle of it. Rocks and boulders were scattered about the base of the sharp incline.

"It looks like erosion," Steve said. "It's a natural run off for water. We'll follow that." He made his way toward the rise.

The ground was soft and quiet beneath them, lightly covered with the moist, putrefied leaves that were shed the previous Autumn. Steve began to notice occasional splashes of color where wild flowers poked their noses through the loam. He always enjoyed the forest flowers which were so typical of the region. He thought about the region as he approached the hill.

The area was quite unique in that it was the topical division that separated the Eastern woodlands from the Western prairies. The region was part of the Alexandria Moraine, where the glaciers had left innumerable forest covered hills and deep valleys filled with hundreds of lakes. It was a visual wonder, rich in agriculture and native wild. Steve treasured the mysteries of nature.

"Look there," Precilla said, pointing. "It's a small rock painting; just to the right of the path. It looks like a hand holding a sphere."

"It is a hand with a sphere," Steve said. He approached the rock and knelt beside it. "It looks like a very old painting. The color has nearly faded completely."

He tried to wiggle the triangular rock free from the ground but realized it was actually the tip of a huge boulder buried in the earth. "I guess this isn't going anywhere," he said.

"What's that up there, Steve?" Precilla asked quietly.

"Where?"

"Up near the top of the hill. What is that?"

Steve rose to look. "What do you see?" he asked.

"That shadow moving along the ground by the trees. What's causing that?"

"What shadow?"

"There," Precilla whispered, pointing. "Don't you see it?"

Steve strained his eyes in the direction she was pointing. A slow movement caught his attention. It looked like a dark shadow slipping noiselessly over the ground. "What the hell...?" he wondered aloud.

"That's not a shadow Steve!" Precilla whispered sharply.

"What are you talking about?"

"Look at it! It's not on the ground; it's in the air above the ground!"

Whatever it was, it was a formless thing. It undulated slightly as it drifted in the air before them, moving slowly like an amoeba through water. The more Steve watched, the less it seemed to be a silhouette or shadow. It was more like a black hole in mid air. He gawked in nervous wonder.

"It stopped," Precilla said, staring. "It's just...hanging there."

The shapeless hole pulsated in place, silently contracting and expanding like an uncanny lung. It began to move down the hill toward them, seemingly growing as it approached.

"It's coming this way!" Precilla shrieked.

"Shhh!" Steve hushed sharply. "Get down."

He took Precilla's hand and forced her to the ground as he crouched behind the rise. His heartbeat pounded the island's silence out of his ears. He squeezed his wife's hand tightly. She buried her face into his shoulder and curled up beside him.

"It'll be okay," Steve whispered.

"What is it?" he heard her ask.

"Probably our imaginations," he replied. "We'll wait a bit, then have another look."

"I don't want to see it again," she murmured.

Steve held his breath and tried to listen through his heartbeat. Off in the distance a crow cawed and other birds began chirping in the trees. It was a relieving sound that seemed to signal all was okay. He felt himself relax.

"Do you hear that?" he whispered.

"Birds?"

"Yes. Stay where you are, I'm going to have a look."

Precilla gripped his arm.

"It's okay," he said. "I'm just going to look."

Steve patted her hand and rose slowly to peer over the rise. The hill was empty of any movement. Whatever that thing was, it was gone now. He stood.

Precilla looked up at him with sullied eyes.

"It's gone," Steve said, reaching for her hand. "It's okay."

Precilla hesitated a moment then took his hand and rose beside him. She quietly gazed up the hill.

"That was the strangest thing I've ever seen," Steve said.

"What was it?" Precilla asked. "It wasn't human or animal."

"I don't know what it was. I don't even know if we saw the same thing. It looked like a black hole floating in the air."

"How could there be a hole in the air?"

"That's just what it looked like to me, I don't know what it actually was. It's easy for the eyes to play tricks in the woods."

"Let's go home," Precilla said.

"Listen, the whole island is lively with birds now. Whatever that thing was, it's gone. It's safe."

"I just want to go home."

Steve studied the hill before them. "I think we should hike to the top and have a quick look around," he said.

"Are you crazy?"

"No. Listen to this place. It has completely changed from a deathly silence to lively commotion. That's a sure sign that everything is okay."

Precilla sneered. "The birds are telling you this?"

"Come on, a quick look and then we're out of here."

"Steve, that thing came from the top of this hill!"

"But it's gone now, and it was probably actually nothing," he said. "Just a quick look around the top of the hill and then we'll leave." He tugged her hand gently in persuasion and started up the eroded path.

"You *are* crazy," Precilla said, resisting slightly before following.

Once past the initial sharp rise, the going was easy and but a moderate hike to the top. Precilla sniffed the air as they climbed and stopped suddenly to look around. "What's that smell?" she asked.

"I don't know. It's a sweet, pungent odor."

"There's nothing sweet about it. Is there a dead animal lying around?"

"It's not the smell of decay."

"Well it's not pleasant. It smells like that floating thing farted."

"Come on," Steve said, continuing on.

As they climbed, Steve searched the trees for anything unusual. He was hoping to spot Windtickler masks or Dream Dancers in the branches but saw none. At the crest of the hill he did see something peculiar and stopped to examine what it was. It was an arrangement of stones. The shape of a circle was laid out in the grass, between the trees, near a patch of brush. The circle was perfectly round, at least six feet in diameter and made of golf ball sized stones that were placed closely together.

"What's that?" Precilla asked, halting beside him.

"A circle of stones. Have you read anything about a circle of stones in Josh's stuff?"

"Not that I can recall. There are so many different things, I can't keep track of it all."

Steve stepped into the circle and walked around the inside edge. "There's nothing really unusual about the rocks," he said. He knelt to look at them more closely. "It must have some kind of purpose." Something seemed different inside the circle. The air or something seemed to have changed. Steve felt a little odd but couldn't pinpoint it.

Precilla joined him inside the circle. "Do you hear that?" She asked.

"Hear what?"

"It's quiet again. The birds have stopped chirping."

Steve rose and listened. Precilla took his hand. "Come on, Steve, there's something strange here," she whispered. "I feel something very strange. Let's go home."

Steve scanned the area outside the circle. Something attracted his eyes to the brush close by. It looked like someone or something was crouched on the other side. "Look at the brush," he whispered to Precilla. "Is something there? It looks like someone is hiding there."

"I see him," Precilla said. "I can see him!" She squeezed his hand tightly. "Let's go."

Steve tilted toward the brush and squinted his eyes. "Hello?" he said.

"Get off this island," a voice replied. "You weren't invited here."

It sounded like a young voice.

Steve straightened. "I'm sorry," he said, stepping back. "We were just looking around, we didn't mean to trespass."

"Leave now," the voice said. "You're not welcome here."

Precilla studied the brush. "It's just a boy," she said. "Look, through there, I see him. It's just a boy."

"Boy?" the voice said. "Just a boy?" The voice crackled and turned deep and gravely. The figure rose, pushed the brush aside and stepped into the clearing outside the ring of stones.

Steve and Precilla took a step back. Precilla gasped. Before them stood a giant of a man. He was a middle aged Native American with the fiercest eyes Steve had ever seen. His hair was pulled back tightly into a ponytail and he stood all muscle, wearing only pants made of hide.

"Who's a boy?" the man growled.

"She meant no offense," Steve apologized. The Indian's eyes shot holes through him.

"Get off the island now!" the Indian snapped. He started toward them but hesitated slightly and stopped just outside the circle of stones.

Steve noticed that. It was almost as though the circle was off limits for some reason. "We're leaving," he said. "We're sorry for the intrusion; we didn't see any signs marking the island off limits. We meant no harm and we certainly don't want to cause any trouble."

"Then go, or trouble you will have."

"Yes," Steve said, moving back and guiding Precilla by the hand. They were still inside the ring, and for some strange reason Steve felt safe there.

The Indian's eyes were now glued to Steve's and Precilla's feet as they neared the opposite edge of the ring. He moved a couple of steps along the outside border, seemingly avoiding stepping into the circle; evading the circle, as a cat would evade stepping into a pool of water.

"We didn't know this was private property," Steve said, turning with the Indian's movement. "We wouldn't have come here if we had known."

"Just go!" the Indian snarled.

"We want to leave peacefully," Steve said. "We don't want a hassle."

The Indian raised his piercing eyes toward Steve. He made a stern face and exhaled sharply through his nose. Precilla cringed at Steve's side.

A crow cawed from someplace unseen. The Indian turned his head and scanned the trees around them. He returned his eyes to Steve and Precilla. "Go now and you won't be harmed," he said.

"We're going," Steve replied. He and Precilla backed out of the ring and eased cautiously down the incline.

"Don't return!" The Indian warned. He remained where he stood.

"We won't," Steve said.

The Indian kept his eyes skewed to them as they backed slowly down the hill. He motioned sternly with his chin for them to keep moving.

"Let's turn around slowly and keep right on going," Steve said under his breath.

"You're going to turn your back on him?"

"If he wanted to do us harm he would have done it right away."

"Then let's go quickly," Precilla said.

Steve turned and guided Precilla by the hand. They moved briskly down the hill toward the sharp rise they had climbed. At the edge of the drop off, both crouched and scooted down the eroded path to level ground. Steve spun to look back up the hill.

"He's gone," he said.

Precilla turned to look. "Let's get out of here!" she said.

They hurried to the opening in the brush where they had entered and crawled toward the lake. Both lunged into the water and dashed along the edge of the island toward the sandbar.

"Go easy," Steve said, "we're safe now. Be careful on the rocks going back."

As they hastened along the sandbar, Steve continually cranked his head around to look back at the island. The memory of the Indian's fearsome eyes and outright mean look was haunting. The recollection of the strange, shapeless black hole floating in the air sent a stirring chill through his whole body. It was like a crazy dream; as though none of it was real. At the point on the mainland, both stopped to catch their breath and turned in unison to face the open water and the island.

"What was that all about?" Precilla breathed.

Steve leaned forward and rested his hands on his knees as he panted. "Who the hell was that?"

"That was the meanest looking person I have ever seen," Precilla said. "He was downright evil looking."

"Did you notice anything about him while we were inside that ring of stones?" Steve puffed.

"Like what?"

"He wouldn't come inside the ring. It was like it was off limits to him; sacred ground or something. He would only walk around it."

"All I noticed was he was evil looking. I've never seen anyone so fiercely evil looking and cold. He looked so cold." Precilla turned her back to the island. "Come on, let's get to the car. I just want to get away from here."

"He was keeping us away from something."

"Let's go Steve!"

Steve straightened. "There's something out there," he said.

"Yeah," Precilla snipped, "an evil maniac! Come on!"

Steve turned and they continued a fast pace through the woods to the car. He couldn't imagine what was out there, what the Indian was hiding or keeping them away from. All he could picture in his mind was the Indian's mean eyes—eyes so ferocious looking, they'd make Oren Clemens and Donald Ramsey look like baby puppies in comparison. The guy seemed almost supernatural.

At the car, once inside with the motor running, Steve pulled the cell phone out from under the passengers seat and put it in Precilla's lap. "Turn that thing on, hit recall and number eight," he said. "That's Ramsey's phone number."

The phone beeped when Precilla pushed the power button. "Do you want to use the speaker?" she asked.

"Yes," Steve said, driving away.

Precilla pushed the appropriate buttons and the ring blared through the speakers.

"Red Tail County Sheriff's Department," a female voice answered, "how may I help you?"

"Donald Ramsey, please," Steve said.

"I'm sorry, Officer Ramsey is out of town until day after tomorrow. May I give you his voice mail or transfer you to someone else?"

"Damn!" Steve said.

"Pardon?"

"I'm sorry," Steve said. "How about, Williams? Tony Williams?"

"One minute please."

Steve looked at Precilla. "He's the one with the dog, right?"

Precilla nodded.

"I'm sorry," the voice returned, "Officer Williams is on vacation and won't be back until next week."

"Could I get his home number?"

"I'm sorry, I can't give you that information. May I direct you to anyone else? the Officer in charge?"

"No. Thank you, no, that's okay. I'll call Donald Ramsey when he returns day after tomorrow."

"Very well."

"Wait. Could you just leave a note on his desk to call Steve Adams immediately when he returns?"

"Steve Adams. I'll put it on his desk right now, sir."

"Thank you."

Precilla ended the call. "Now what?" she asked.

"We wait for Ramsey, what else can we do?"

"Well, we're definitely not going back to that island," Precilla said. "I don't think we should go anywhere out here without having Ramsey along. This whole thing is getting too serious."

"Maybe there's not even a connection with what happened just now on the island to anything else," Steve said. "Maybe that guy out there was just contemptible; maybe he had a girl in the brush with him and just didn't want us around. Maybe he owned the island…"

"Maybe you're out of your mind," Precilla said.

Steve guided the Grand-Am along the gravel road and thought about Josh Clemens and the two artists. He thought back to the first letter he'd received from Josh, before he went to the Clemens' farm and got the mystery box. The letter said something like, "A quick note to let you know I've made a major breakthrough on this story I've been working on. It's an incredible adventure. I have to also let you know that *you* are deeply involved. If you don't hear from me for a while, don't be concerned, I'm okay. I'll be in touch. Josh." Steve chuckled with dismay.

"What's funny?" Precilla asked.

"*I* am deeply involved."

"What?"

"I was just thinking about that first letter I got from Josh, the one I lost and you found for me in all the papers by my computer. Do you remember that?"

"Yes. What about it?"

"In that letter Josh said, "you are deeply involved in all this." Steve paused, looked at his wife. "Remember that?"

"Yes. I thought it was a strange remark."

"So did I."

Steve drove in quiet reflection.

"Your point?" Precilla asked.

"Think about it," Steve replied. "Just think about it."

*   *   *   *   *

PART THREE

The Legend

Twelve
The Legend

Steve Adams had slept little during the night, or at least it seemed that way. Precilla was already up and busy in the kitchen at six when he made his way to the fresh pot of coffee waiting for him. He paused at the dining room table and noticed one of Josh Clemens' manuscripts resting beside the brick building Donald Ramsey had left with them.

"You're up early," he said.

"I couldn't sleep."

"What are you making? It smells great."

"Wild rice and pheasant soup for our noon guests," Precilla replied. She stopped what she was doing and poured a cup of coffee for Steve.

"What time did you get up?" he asked.

"Four o'clock," she said, handing him the cup. "Between your tossing and turning all night, and my not being able to keep my mind off that Indian and that floating *thing*, sleep just wasn't meant to be. I thought I'd get up and do some things."

"Have you been reading?" he asked. He sat at the dining room table, noticed a notepad and pencil lying beside the manuscript.

"I finished the first chapter of Josh's manuscript," Precilla said. "I found out the name of that Indian you caught on videotape. He calls himself Bright Feather." She joined him at the table with a glass of her usual morning orange juice.

"Bright Feather?"

"Yes. Do you want to hear about it?" she asked

"Oh, yeah. Is it pretty outlandish?"

"No more so than what happened yesterday, I don't suppose," she said, opening her notebook. "I've made some notes, figuring it would be easier to remember things this way, rather than backtracking through the manuscript. Do you remember how the artists, Chase and Madden, discovered the Indian?"

Steve recalled aloud, "They went off looking for more Amity Pillars after Dakota Chase showed his friend a large one he'd found in the middle of the woods. Chase said he found the pillar because a crow had led him to it. While searching the forest for more, they spotted the Indian moving around six Amity Pillars and the black rock at the dig site. The Indian disappeared after he became aware of the artists' presence. When Chase and Madden entered the site, they both became engulfed in some sort of static electricity and the hair on their heads and arms supposedly stood on end."

Precilla sipped her orange juice. "That's right," she said, "and after examining the black rock, Dakota Chase made a transfer rubbing of it."

"I remember," Steve said. "That's where you stopped reading, just before we went out to the dig site to visit with the archeologists."

"Well," Precilla said, glancing at her notes, "the following day the two artists returned to the site. When they entered the area, they discovered the black rock was gone. It had disappeared!"

"Disappeared?"

"The black rock was gone, but the pillars were still there."

"What's with all this disappearing?" Steve asked, almost to himself. "How can things just up and vanish like that?"

"I imagine those two felt just as you did when you returned to the dig site and discovered the Amity Pillars missing."

"Continue," Steve said.

"Dakota Chase was certain the black rock with all the images was some sort of map. He laid the transfer rubbing he'd made on the ground where the black rock had stood and began studying all the symbols. One in particular, besides the hand with the sphere, attracted him, and he and Madden plotted a route to find it."

"Which image was he attracted to?" Steve asked, sipping his coffee.

"One that showed two Amity Pillars separated by two lightning bolts crisscrossing each other."

"Lightning bolts?"

"Do you want me to find it in the manuscript?"

"No, keep going."

"Just before leaving the site to find the pillars with the lightning bolts, a rock on top of one of the Amity Pillars moved. Both Chase and Madden saw the rock move by itself. It rotated on top of the others, as though one end of the rock was following them."

"What?"

"That's not all. When Dakota checked his compass prior to leaving, the needle was spinning erratically."

"Wait a minute," Steve said. "Didn't Ramsey say something about that? Didn't the archeologists claim their compass went all haywire while they were inside the dig site?"

Precilla nodded. "It gets better," She said. "The artists' route led them to the shoreline of Eagle Lake where they found what they believed to be the two Amity Pillars that were shown on the map. They were somewhat disappointed, as there was nothing really unusual about any of the rocks. There were no markings; nothing unique or peculiar about them. Dakota Chase removed a rock from the top of one of the pillars to inspect, and this is where things got a little wild."

"Wild? How so?" Steve asked.

"As Chase was examining the rock, a loud snap crackled in the air and a bright flash, or spark, shot out from beneath the rock he was holding and scorched his fingers. The rock flew from his hand, sailed through the air and reset itself to the top of the rock tower."

Steve leaned back in his chair in disbelief.

"Pretty crazy, huh?" Precilla said.

"Impossible," Steve mumbled. He rose from his chair and went to the coffee pot to refill his cup.

Precilla turned and handed him her empty juice glass. "Pour me half a glass please," she said.

"The rock flew out of his hand by itself? That's what you're saying?" Steve asked.

"That's what it says in the manuscript. It was at that very moment Chase had the sensation he was hearing that strange One chant he had experienced in his dream. Cole Madden thought he heard it too."

Steve returned to the table, handed Precilla her glass and sat beside her. "What did they do?" he asked.

"They were both in a bit of shock, staring at Chase's scorched fingertips. Before they could really react to any of it, the Indian with no eyes appeared at the edge of the tree line."

Steve sat quietly gazing at Precilla's notes.

"For some reason," Precilla continued, "Neither of them felt threatened or frightened by the Indian's sudden emergence. In fact, when they noticed him, the moment became very calm. Even the tingling in Dakota's fingers seemed to go away."

"Out of pure wonderment, I'm sure," Steve said.

Precilla put her hands over her notes and looked at Steve. "You're accepting this as though it all actually happened," she said.

"I am," Steve said, surprised by his own, sudden awareness of it. "I am accepting it as real. If I had heard all this at the outset, what you're telling me now, I would have had a good laugh over it and passed it off as foolishness. But, when I consider everything we've experienced since Josh's disappearance, it all seems to support what you've just read. It's all so damn bizarre."

"I wonder if the archeologists have had any unusual experiences while they've been out there?" Precilla thought out loud. "Or the deputies guarding the site, for that matter?"

"Well, we know their compass went all screwy at the dig site, spun wildly, which must have been a novel experience for them. There's nothing ordinary about the buildings or the black rock they've uncovered, either. It was obvious, however, that neither Milton nor Schepp knew anything about the Indian. Milton was very blank when we asked him if Ramsey had mentioned anything about it. And speaking of that Indian, what happened after Dakota Chase and Cole Madden became aware of his presence at the edge of the tree line?"

"The Indian approached them and informed them that they had just encountered the energy of the rocks."

"The energy of the rocks? This is the Indian with no eyes, right? He approached them?"

"Yes. He said the rock towers, or Amity Pillars, represented the Regions of Influence, or forces of nature. The Indian told the artists they had just experienced nature's energy through the power of the stones."

"The power of the stones? Regions of Influence? This is so weird. I do remember something about Regions when we first started going through Josh's notes but it didn't make any sense to me. I can't recall exactly what it was, now."

"I remember," Precilla said. "We were going through Josh's notes just before watching the videotape you made; the video that captured the Indian placing the rattle by the base of the Amity Pillar. I found the word, Olyqua, and written with it was something like, "Four shall meet at Olyqua and Olyqua shall become One." There was also something about Olyqua being victorious and the Inner Kingdom would once again return to the peaceful Regions. I remember he had Regions capitalized for some reason, but couldn't figure out why. I wonder if Regions in that context referred to the Regions of Influence the Indian talks about in Josh's manuscript?"

"How the hell do you remember all that?"

Precilla smiled. "It's a woman thing, I guess." she said.

"So what exactly are the rock towers?" Steve asked.

"The Indian said they were symbolic of the Regions of Influence. The balanced rocks represent the delicate thread of energy that passes through all living things; that the balanced rocks are tokens of the delicate balance between all living things. He said we were all a part of this great Influence and its tender balance; that we are all part of a harmonious One."

"A harmonious One," Steve repeated softly, dragging out the word, One. "So who's building all these rock towers? Certainly this Indian isn't capable of doing all that."

"He said they belonged to Lore."

"Lore? What did he mean by that?"

"Josh's manuscript doesn't really elaborate, at least not yet, anyway," Precilla said. "But I looked the word up in the dictionary. The word Lore means knowledge and wisdom, teaching or learning. The way the dialogue went in the manuscript, though, made it seem as though the Indian was referring to *someone*, and not something. Just speculating, he could have meant the Amity Pillars belonged to someone wise, someone named Lore, meaning Wise One, or One of Knowledge."

"Hey, don't let Milton or Schepp catch you speculating, it's too dangerous."

"Think about it for a minute," Precilla said. "Maybe there is a secret society from the past, a society or culture living now and practicing ancient traditions that no one is aware of."

"What do you mean?"

"Maybe a few descendants from the early Native American Woodland populations have secretly held on to their ancestral traditions and beliefs. Possibly these modern descendants are celebrating those traditions and the Amity Pillars are a part of that heritage."

"Wow," Steve said. "Now there's something that could make some sense. But wait a minute; what about all the other extraordinary things that have happened? The rock flying out of Dakota's hand, if indeed it did happen; Josh's disappearance; the disappearance and movement of those huge Amity Pillars; the mysterious crow; the items we found inside the hollows of the tree? Some of the things that have happened are outrageous; they're just not humanly possible. And what about that eerie, floating black hole that we both saw on the island? Some of those events are way beyond natural."

"I can't explain any of those things," Precilla said, "I'm just thinking this through as we go along and trying to come up with something that makes sense."

"Well let's get back to what you've read," Steve said. "I'm to understand Chase and Madden, just after having this abnormal experience with the rock flying out of Dakota's hand, are simply standing there having a casual chit-chat with this Indian? Unmoved by his appearance?"

"Not unmoved," Precilla replied. "They were both dazed by it all, but in full faculties. Neither of them felt threatened by his presence, however."

"Then, who is he? Where's he from?"

"He called himself Bright Feather. He said he lived there, in the forest. He called the region, Loretasia. He said it was the Inner Kingdom."

"Loretasia? The Inner Kingdom?"

"That's what he told them."

"Didn't you just a minute ago mention something about an Inner Kingdom?"

"You need more Vitamin E for that short term memory, Steve. I said, in Josh's notes, he declared four would meet at Olyqua and Olyqua would become One. Olyqua would be victorious and the Inner Kingdom would again return to the peaceful Regions."

"I remember," Steve said. "Then what happened?"

"The Indian, Bright Feather I'll call him, told the artists they could identify Loretasia by its colors. He told Dakota Chase that he'd already captured part of Loretasia on canvas."

"His paintings!"

Precilla smiled. "Yes," she said, "his landscape paintings. His friend Madden said all his latest paintings appeared as though they'd been dipped in a rainbow."

Steve looked at the brick building beside the manuscript. "Those colors," he said softly. "The colors the ball inside that building give off when I shine a light on it."

"Exactly," Precilla said.

"We have to see some of Dakota Chase's paintings," Steve said excitedly. "Maybe we could recognize the area in the forest the Indian is talking about. This Loretasia, or Inner Kingdom place; whatever the Indian called it."

"Bright Feather," Precilla said.

"Yeah, Bright Feather, whatever."

"Isn't there something a little odd here?" Precilla said.

"Odd? It's all odd. What do you mean, exactly?"

"How did the Indian know about Dakota Chase's paintings?"

"What do you mean? If Chase painted them in the forest, then the Indian could have seen him, been watching...."

Precilla nodded as Steve stopped in the middle of his sentence. "Bright Feather is blind; or so he appears to be. But we've been watched and followed all the while we've been out there, Steve. Everyone that has been out there has been watched. The first mention of a feeling of being watched was where Josh Clemens disappeared, at the excavation site. Ramsey said many of the searchers on that day had the strange feeling they were being watched, remember? He even asked you if you had experienced that."

"And the archeologists," Steve said. "They, too, said they felt as though they were being watched."

"You and I felt the sensation, too, Steve. We sensed it when we discovered the painting of the crow on that boulder in the middle of the woods. We both felt it. Bright Feather was there all the time. He left the rattle by the Amity Pillar, specifically for us to find."

"But Bright Feather is blind," Steve said. "How could he be watching anything?"

"Is he blind?"

"Of course he's blind, you've seen him."

"Yes I have, and I've always been a bit haunted by him. Think about the way he appeared in the video, though."

"That was inadvertent."

"Was it? Think about how he aimed his vacant eyes right into the camera while he was kneeling there. He knew he was being taped. He wanted to be seen!"

"That's ridiculous."

"Is it? When you show Milton and Schepp that tape this afternoon, watch it very closely. Watch Bright Feather's eyes. He can see as clearly as you and I. If he couldn't see, how else could he get around in the forest like that?"

"All right," Steve said, "let's get back to that." He pointed toward the manuscript. "What happened after Bright Feather told Dakota Chase he had captured part of this Loretasia place in his painting?"

"Bright Feather told them if they wanted to know more, and if they really wanted to find the Inner Kingdom, they would have to do something. They would have to find a fragment of the hand holding the sphere. He called the sphere in the hand a Ulambent."

"I knew it! I knew it was called a Ulambent!"

"He said if they found a fragment of the finger from the hand, it would lead them to Loretasia. The Inner Kingdom."

"Wait a minute," Steve said excitedly. "The archeologist's photograph of the hand, or whatever that coral like thing is at the bottom of the lake, shows part of a finger missing. The artists must have found the missing piece!"

"So it would seem," Precilla said.

"Go on, continue," Steve said.

"Bright Feather departed from their company. Before he left, though, he gave them each a necklace."

"What kind of necklace?"

"Each was a tiny replica of an Amity Pillar. Both consisted of small pebbles, assembled into tiny rock towers and attached to rawhide laces. He told them to wear the necklaces while in the forest, as the necklaces would identify them."

"Identify them? Identify them to whom?"

Precilla shrugged her shoulders, sipped her juice.

"So? Then what?" Steve said.

"That's as far as I got."

"What?"

"That's as far as I got. That was the end of the first chapter. I had to stop reading and start making the soup."

"Are you going to read some more?"

"I don't have time now. I still have to make fried bread and get this place cleaned up and ready for our guests. Why don't you take the manuscript and read it before they get here?"

"I can't. I have to finish an advertising logo and get the disk to the Post Office before the mail goes out. It's an important job."

"Well, Milton and Schepp will be here for lunch," Precilla said. "I'm sure they're the type that will arrive early. You'd better get started soon if you have to get something mailed."

Steve rose from his chair. "If Ramsey doesn't call right away tomorrow morning," he said, "I'm going to try to get a hold of him. I want to find out who that was on the Island yesterday. I want to know why he threatened us and drove us off like that."

"He was dangerous," Precilla said. "His evil eyes penetrated my bones. I never want to see him again."

"There was an evil character in Josh's notes, I remember," Steve said, reaching for his coffee cup. "The very first day we started going through that box, the morning Ramsey brought that building over, I found something written about him. His name was Noctumba. He was referred to as an evil one that must be stopped; that he was filled with greed and lust for power."

"I vaguely remember that," Precilla said. "You found some other characters too, didn't you?"

"Yes, but the others were fictitious. There was one, Singer, I think his name was, a singer of songs, or something like that. He was sitting on a leaf and talking about the stars. Obviously he was one of the little people."

Precilla chuckled, rising. "Well, every culture has its fables, so why should a myth about little people be any more alien? The Norwegians have their gnomes and the Irish have their Leprechauns.

Shakespeare and other great writers wrote about pixies, elves and fairies. In fact, many people right here in this country believe in a 'Big Foot.' If there is a secret band of people practicing their ancient customs in the forest, then I can easily accept a legend about little people as being part of their inheritance."

"Yeah," Steve said, laughing, "that's exactly what I was thinking. How the hell do you make so much sense out of so much chaos?"

"Like I said before, it's a woman thing."

*   *   *   *   *

Thirteen

Both Milton and Schepp were disappointed Steve Adams hadn't accepted their job offer. During lunch Steve informed them he just couldn't make that sort of commitment but he would be willing to share information with them. Though it didn't appear their hopes were completely dashed, the archeologists didn't press the issue. They simply assured the offer would remain open to Adams.

The small building on the dining room table was, besides the wonderful meal, the center of conversation while eating. Milton and Schepp said they had visited Chase's and Madden's miniature hamlet in the forest, but they weren't aware it was a supposed decoy village and that a similar installation was hidden in secret elsewhere. The question as to why the artists would hide a second village came up several times. Adams told them he had no reference to its location.

The archeologists were quite taken with the light show the building presented when Steve passed his penlight over the small crystal ball in the central room. Steve confirmed for them that the mysterious ball was called a Ulambent in Josh's notes. He went on to mention that the notes suggested the colors emitted by the ball were somehow key to the whole mystery. He talked briefly about Loretasia and the Inner Kingdom and how one could recognize those regions in the forest by their colors; the same colors as those emitted by the crystal ball. He found it difficult, though, explaining everything without making it sound like a fairy tale. Precilla chimed in to rescue him.

Precilla detailed for the archeologists the first chapter in Josh's manuscript. They listened attentively. Both leaned toward her voice as she mentioned the artists' description of the mysterious movement of the rock on top of one of the Amity Pillars. They remained still as she talked about the erratic spinning of the compass needle the artists had witnessed before striking out to look for more rock towers. It was obvious by their craned necks and stretched ears that they, too, had experienced something similar. They took her narration very seriously. Precilla had that knack for tying loose ends together and creating order out of chaos.

After several helpings of soup, salad and fried bread, everyone retired to the fresh air and sat on the outside deck just off the dining room. A tray of bars and a fresh pot of coffee was waiting for them. It was there Precilla offered her theory about the possibility of a secret society practicing ancestral traditions in the forest. Her conjecture captivated the archeologists. At the conclusion of her rationale, Milton and Schepp finally admitted that they, too, had a similar theory, and that the small buildings they uncovered could possibly be traditional articles from the past; articles used for some sort of celebration. They said there was yet much to be learned about the early woodland civilizations that had inhabited these regions before the Eastern tribes drove them into the plains.

Most archeological findings, Schepp informed, revealed remnants of the latter Ojibwe people, but very little was known about the first inhabitants. He mentioned one human remains, a young girl, was unearthed in the early Sixties during road construction. Her bones were determined to be some twenty thousand years old. He added that after the body had been discovered, little else was found to substantiate a proper, fixed date.

Milton poured himself a cup of coffee, lit his pipe and explained through his chocolate cloud, that the location where Steve and Precilla now lived was once completely underwater. As a result of the glaciers from the last ice age, one huge lake, named Lake Agassiz, completely covered the region. He said it was believed that the girl, whose bones had been discovered while building the highway, had drowned in Lake Agassiz. He added, again, that nothing else has been found to suggest others had roamed or lived in the area during that time. He explained that after Lake Agassiz receded, it left behind thousands of scattered lakes that the state of Minnesota is now well known for. The new lakes, rivers and forests resulting from the receding glacial lake, became a welcome invitation for the early Woodland populations.

All the while Milton spoke, Schepp squirmed on the deck bench, obviously waiting eagerly to add his tidbits of knowledge, theories and information. It turned out, refreshingly surprising to both Steve and Precilla, Schepp was really quite radical in his thinking and suppositions. He said it was commonly believed that migration onto this continent occurred during the ice age by way of the Bearing Straight. He said that theory was based upon artifacts that have been found along the assumed corridors of travel between Europe and Mexico. He said that this popular belief was biased. He, himself, believed the migrations were just the opposite. He preached, and quite persuasively, that the migrations had stemmed outward from the once tropical paradises of this continent! It was comical how Milton had to pull the reins on his associate to keep him from giving a complete dissertation on his beliefs about early migrations.

When Steve asked if either of them had any thoughts about the peculiar, coral like hand at the bottom of the lake, Milton said the divers had gone back this morning to inspect it more thoroughly. They were also going to look for the fragment missing from the finger. He said he didn't want to disturb the object until a geologist was able to investigate it and identify it properly. That's when Schepp went off again on anther one of his tangents.

It was quite possible, he explained enthusiastically, being as the earth was once a great sea, that the mysterious coral hand could indeed be petrified coral the glaciers had heaved up during their journeys. Milton again yanked on his friend's reins before he had a chance to spin too far and suggested they stick with the facts and tangibles they had and knew for certain. That's when Steve suggested they visit his editing suite and have a look at the materials Josh had left them.

In the editing suite, the first thing Steve showed them was the videotape he'd made in the forest. When the tape reached the point where the Indian laid the rattle in the grass beside the Amity Pillar, the archeologists gawked in quiet astonishment and had Steve freeze the tape and replay it several times. While watching the reruns, Steve again informed them that the Indian's name was Bright Feather. After Milton and Schepp had seen enough, Steve led them through the paper maze scattered along the floor. They paused at the two manuscripts and the archeologists thumbed through the pages, obviously not reading, but rather looking at the volumes of each. They had a look of dismay as they held the manuscripts and scanned the remaining piles of papers scattered about.

There was just too much to look at in one visit. It was too difficult to focus on anything in particular. Upon realizing that, Milton asked Steve and Precilla if they would consider copying everything for them, that the university would, of course, supply the copy machine. Steve grimaced at the thought of that as his eyes absorbed the accumulation of materials. He said copying everything would take a great deal of time, that he would have to think about it. Schepp left the studio for a moment and Milton again offered to pay Steve and Precilla for their services. Steve felt a snare creeping slowly toward his feet.

A few moments later Schepp returned with a portfolio of photographs, gave them to Steve and said they were leaving them with him and Precilla. The pictures were duplicates of those they had browsed through while visiting the dig site. After handing the portfolio to Steve, he asked if it would be okay if he and Milton looked through the stacks of papers on the floor, that they would be careful not to mix them up. Steve passed the portfolio on to Precilla, then ushered the archeologists around the room and explained what was in each pile and that the materials weren't yet completely organized. Precilla took a chair by the editing suite while Milton and Schepp plopped to the floor to riffle through the piles. Steve remained close to the archeologists to answer any questions they might have. They rummaged for two hours, overwhelmed, then concluded there was just way too much stuff to sift through in one sitting. They again mentioned they'd be more than willing to supply a copy machine and pay them for the time it took to copy everything. Steve made no commitment.

Precilla sat by the video equipment completely absorbed in the portfolio. Something stirred her and she signaled Steve; then she asked Milton and Schepp if they had any idea what the symbol she was looking at represented. All three crowded around her and glanced over her shoulders at the image that was troubling her. Milton said it was one of the "Chimera" type figures, but wasn't really certain as to what they were supposed to mean or represent. The image sent a tingle along Steve's neck.

Precilla held her finger to a human stick figure facing a squiggled circle. Separating the stick figure and wavy circle were two diagonal lines forming an x. Steve at once thought about the peculiar floating thing he and Precilla saw on the island. "Kimirente," Steve thought, remembering the word and similar images in Josh's drawings. This image Precilla was pointing to, Steve felt certain, was that eerie, floating hole they both witnessed. The tingling intensified along his neck and shoulders. He noticed goose bumps rising along Precilla's forearms.

"Have you seen that before?" Schepp asked.

"No," Precilla responded quickly, turning the page. "Just curious. All the other images, like this one," she pointed to a stick figure with a spider, "have representational shapes I can recognize. The last one was just a wavy circle and made no sense at all." Neither Steve nor Precilla mentioned anything about the sinister Indian on the island or their experience with the floating mystery.

The afternoon passed quickly into evening. It was still light outside, but it was time for the archeologists to leave and return to the dig site. They were very appreciative for the opportunity to look through Josh's materials and, before leaving, offered again to pay Steve and Precilla for having everything copied. Still no commitments.

Precilla put the leftovers from lunch into plastic containers and sent them along with Milton and Schepp. They were very grateful. Sincere handshakes preceded their departure.

*   *   *   *   *

Fourteen

Officer Donald Ramsey called at 7 AM. He said he'd sensed urgency in Steve's message and returned the call immediately upon arrival at his office. Steve detailed for Ramsey his and Precilla's experience on the island, but he left out the part about the unexplained floating mystery. Ramsey was concerned about the alleged threats made by the Indian. He said he was coming by in an hour to pick up Steve, that they would go out to the island and have a look around. Precilla wanted no part in this investigation and was worried about Steve returning to the island with Ramsey. She said it was a police matter to investigate, not a private citizen's. Steve felt it was his obligation to accompany Ramsey.

The air was still, the lake was a flawless mirror, and the island shimmered brilliantly in its own reflection. The narrow, rocky sandbar that stretched between the point and the island looked as though it was lying beneath a sheet of glass. Ramsey wore hip waders to get across and Steve wore cut-offs and old tennies. Steve repeated his story as they made their way to the island, but still didn't mention anything about the floating phenomenon. How could he? How could he describe something like that without sounding like a lunatic? Steve retraced his and Precilla's path, led Ramsey along the island's shoreline to the opening in the brush, then guided him through the small passage to the eroded trail that led up the steep embankment. They paused at the base of the drop off and examined the rock painting of the hand holding the sphere. After a moment, they continued their climb.

At the top of the hill, Steve pointed out the circle of small stones laid out in the grass, then showed Ramsey the cluster of brush the Indian was hiding behind. He moved to where the Indian had emerged from and had made his threatening gestures. He explained as best he could how it seemed the Indian had deliberately avoided stepping into the circle of stones, as though the circle was for some reason off limits to him. Ramsey listened but made no comment. He walked around the brush and inspected the ground where the Indian was supposed to have been hiding. The grass was trampled and matted, looking a lot like a deer bed.

"It's too bad Tony Williams wasn't along with his dog," Steve said.

Ramsey knelt and dragged his fingers through the matted grass. "Yes, well, a trail leading from here would probably just vanish into thin air like the others. I wouldn't wage high stakes on finding anything here today. You can bet whoever was here is long gone by now."

Steve explained how he and Precilla backed away from the circle without taking their eyes off the Indian. He hesitated slightly, then added that when a crow cawed, the Indian told them if they left at that moment no harm would come to them. That's when they turned around and descended the hill quickly and left the island.

Ramsey stood. "The crow again," he said half under his breath. "About all we can do is walk the island and have a look around. There's nothing really here that'll help us solve anything."

"We first thought the person hiding in the brush was a young boy. Precilla saw him, said something like, it's just a boy, and the Indian got real upset. He came through the brush transformed into one huge, mean looking man. He was the most evil looking person I've ever seen."

"Could there have been two people here?" Ramsey asked.

"I never thought of that."

"Let's have a look around."

For the most part it was easy walking around the island, as the density of the tall trees kept the low brush to a minimum. It was only along the island's perimeter, near the water, where the brush thickened and became nonnegotiable. They descended the hill to the edge of the scrub and began their walk, studying the trees and scrutinizing every rock and boulder they came across.

Steve mentioned as they walked, that according to one of Josh's maps, there was supposed to be an assemblage of small buildings somewhere at the bottom of the lake near the island. He told Ramsey that a similar reference was found on the black rock the archeologists uncovered. He explained that the black rock, itself, was some sort of an elaborate map. Ramsey listened attentively as Steve explained that the direction to the hollow tree they had discovered was also etched into the rock. There was no reference to a distance between the black rock and the tree, however, only a direct line between the two. Steve said there was no distance references for any of the images on the rock, only lines of direction. He believed the island of Olyqua was a large piece in the puzzle and that the black rock showed Olyqua to be somewhere North. How far North he wasn't certain.

"Somewhere in the Superior National Forest or in the Boundary Waters Canoeing Area," Ramsey said. "Probably the latter. That's where the artists, Dakota Chase and Cole Madden are spending the summer."

"Have you gotten any word on them?" Steve asked.

"No. We continue to check the national campground registrations and permits into the boundary waters, but their names haven't appeared. I'm sure they won't register anywhere. I don't think they want their whereabouts known to anyone."

"They have to park their vehicle somewhere," Steve said.

"We've had all the parking along the trails checked, but there hasn't been any sign of their vehicle. You can hide a vehicle pretty easily in a million acres of wilderness."

The conversation quieted for a few minutes as they walked, then Ramsey asked, "What do you think is really going on, Steve?"

"I don't know. All we have are theories. Milton and Schepp have finally opened up a bit and suggested a similar theory to one Precilla came up with."

"What theory is that?"

Steve explained Precilla's theory about a possible secret society celebrating ancestral traditions in the forest, and that the Amity Pillars, small buildings and all the mysteries were parts of the customs. He said he personally believed that Dakota Chase and Cole Madden had inadvertently come across the society's members and somehow became involved with them. Josh Clemens had been following the artists' works for some time and eventually he, too, became personally involved. Josh's manuscripts, he was certain, were the developments of elaborate myths evolving from this society's conventions.

"I can buy that," Ramsey said, "but what I can't get past are those damn rock pillars, how they vanished like that and reappeared elsewhere. That hollow tree is a mystery too, but I've seen ships in bottles that have baffled me just as much."

Steve almost blurted out about the floating phenomenon but resisted. It was at that moment he sensed a vaguely familiar stench in the air. A sickening, sweet sort of stench.

Ramsey was the first to actually see it, but Steve smelled it before Ramsey said anything. The officer stopped beside a large oak tree and strained his eyes up the hill. "What the hell is that?" he asked.

Steve followed Ramsey's eyes and spotted the black hole hovering in the air about a hundred feet away, at least six feet off the ground. He gawked without reply.

"What is it?" Ramsey asked again.

"I don't know."

The strange dark hole floated slowly toward them, dilating and contracting as it did when Steve and Precilla saw it. Ramsey pulled his gun from its holster and aimed it at the phenomenon. It drifted toward them like a silent cloud.

From someplace unseen, but seemingly close by, a deafening voice penetrated Steve's head. "Don't fire that gun!" it warned.

Ramsey flashed a glance at Steve, kept his aim.

"Josh?" Steve said in bewilderment.

"Be quiet and still," the voice said. "Let it pass."

Ramsey peered down his gun barrel, kept a steady fix on the hole as it quietly approached. Ramsey inhaled deeply through his nose as though testing an odor.

"Let it pass," the voice repeated softly.

The strange hole streamed slowly past them, Ramsey following it with his gun. It hovered in place momentarily, then began to close in on itself and get smaller. It formed into a mere dot then suddenly vanished from sight. It was gone.

Ramsey remained poised with his gun aimed at nothing. He lingered there a moment, started to lower his arm, but quickly aimed at nothing again. "What's that smell?" he said.

"It accompanies whatever that thing is," Steve said.

"What the hell was that?"

Steve turned in a circle. "Josh?" he said confused. "Josh, was that you?"

Ramsey kept aim but turned his head slowly to each side, his eyes scouring their perimeter. "Was that Josh Clemens' voice?" he asked.

"Yes! I know it was! You heard him, right?"

"I heard someone. Or I felt someone. I think."

"What do you mean?" Steve asked. Steve, himself, sensed the voice had spoken from inside his head, that it wasn't actually an audible tone. He was perplexed, nervous and excited. Shocked.

"I don't know what I mean," Ramsey said. He lowered his gun slightly and carefully walked to where the hole collapsed and disappeared.

"Josh?" Steve hollered.

Ramsey snapped his head around. "Don't do that!" he barked, obviously spooked by Steve's sudden yell.

"Sorry. Josh is here."

"Clemens!" Ramsey yelled. "Clemens, where are you?"

There was no reply. Ramsey lowered his gun to his side and walked slowly toward the brush separating him from the water. He crouched and searched the thickets. Steve searched the trees and the hillside.

"Josh Clemens!" Donald Ramsey hollered loudly. "Josh Clemens, show yourself!"

"Josh!" Steve hollered. "It's okay! The policeman is a friend!"

There was still no reply. Ramsey rose slowly upright and joined Steve. "Are you sure you heard his voice?" he asked.

"Didn't you?" Steve replied.

"I'm not sure what I heard, if anything. Damn it I'm confused! What the hell was that thing? And what stinks?"

"I don't know. Precilla and I saw the same thing before we discovered the Indian in the brush."

"You what?"

"We saw it the day we were threatened by the Indian. It left an odor like the one we smell now."

"What the hell are you talking about? You've seen that floating thing before? Why didn't you tell me about it?"

Steve cocked his head slightly, looked Ramsey in the eyes without reply and let him answer his own question.

"Never mind," Ramsey said. He turned slowly in a circle, holstered his gun and hollered, "Josh Clemens! I'm Donald Ramsey. I have been investigating your disappearance, as requested by your brother, Oren. You're in absolutely no trouble with the law. Steve and I would just like to talk to you. You have no reason to hide or feel threatened."

Steve scoured the trees and hill. There were many places to hide, but it didn't actually seem Josh Clemens was really anywhere around. He had heard his friend's voice, it wasn't imagination, and Donald Ramsey heard him too. But the voice was somehow different. It was almost as though he actually thought it, as though the voice sounded from inside his head. It was a warning voice from within, a signal of some kind; a caution to not fire on the dark hole.

"You've got some explaining," Ramsey said.

"Yes. Now that you've seen that *thing*, I can talk about it."

"From now on, whatever you discover or experience, no matter how ridiculous or unbelievable something might seem, I want to hear about it. I thought we had that understanding when I dropped that building off at your house."

"I didn't know how to tell you about what we both just saw."

"I'm beginning to wonder if we really did see anything," Ramsey said.

"You saw it. I saw it. Precilla saw it. We smell its evidence right now. And you heard Josh Clemens warning you not to fire your gun at it. We experienced the same thing."

"I don't know what I just experienced. Let's search this place for signs of your friend. He's got to be somewhere on this island."

Neither Josh Clemens, nor any signs of him, could be found on the island. The odor left behind by the floating mystery dissipated quickly. Ramsey and Adams spent three hours searching the island but came up with nothing. Besides no Josh, they found no masks in the trees, no Dream Dancers or Amity Pillars. There were no rattles or anything besides the rock painting of the hand and the circle of small stones at the top of the hill where the evil looking Indian had approached Steve and Precilla. They'd done enough searching, Ramsey decided. He became more interested, now, in what else might be revealed in Josh Clemens' manuscript and recommended they return to Steve's house.

*　　　*　　　*　　　*　　　*

Fifteen

Precilla Adams prepared coffee, a pitcher of orange juice and sandwiches, and the threesome went out on the deck to eat and discuss what had happened on the island. She didn't seem too surprised to hear about Steve's and Ramsey's encounter with the floating anomaly. Ramsey had already heard Steve's version of his and Precilla's previous experience, and now he wanted to hear Precilla's rendition of the story. It, of course, was identical to Steve's.

After it was settled and agreed upon that they had all actually seen and experienced the same thing, Precilla informed Ramsey and her husband that she now knew what the mysterious floating thing was. She said it was definitely Kimirente.

Ramsey about spilled his coffee all over his lap as he choked on the word and his last bite of sandwich. He stood quickly to avoid the scalding splash and reached for a napkin. "A what?" he said, coughing.

"Kimirente," Precilla repeated.

"You said you wanted to know everything, no matter how ridiculous or unbelievable it seemed," Steve said.

"What the hell is a Kimirente?" Ramsey asked.

"It's sort of like an apparition," Precilla said. "It's real, but it's like a projected image from someone or something. Josh has several drawings of them and the archeologists have taken pictures of similar images they've found on rocks and clay fragments. I continued reading Josh's manuscript while you two were on the island and I found out what it was we experienced."

Ramsey used the napkin to wipe the coffee off the side of his cup. "Do you want to explain?"

"I'll get my notes," she said. "It's pretty complicated without them."

While Precilla left to gather her notes, Steve briefed Ramsey on the first chapter of Josh's manuscript, explained how the two artists had met face to face with the mysterious Indian with no eyes. He told him the Indian's name, Bright Feather, and how he claimed to live in an area within the wilderness called Loretasia, the Inner Kingdom. He mentioned how Bright Feather encouraged the artists to find, underwater, a fragment from the hand holding the Ulambent. He explained that the fragment from the hand would lead them directly to Loretasia, the Inner Kingdom. Ramsey returned to his seat and listened without interrupting, grabbed another half a sandwich on the way. Precilla returned through the sliding glass door, stood quietly and flipped through the pages of her notebook while Steve completed his story.

When Steve was done, Precilla took a seat on the other side of Ramsey so he would be situated between her and Steve. She said the information she was about to explain wasn't necessarily in the order it came from the manuscript, but it would be easier to clarify things this way; somewhat out of order. She began by telling them a little about the artist, Dakota Chase.

"Dakota Chase calls the area in the wilderness, the highlands. He doesn't explain why, he just calls it that, probably because there are so many high hills out there. When I speak of the area, I'll refer to it from now on as the highlands.

"After he and Cole Madden returned home from their first encounter with Bright Feather, they agreed to meet the following weekend to scuba dive the lake to search for the hand holding the

Ulambent. The Indian told them to find a fragment of the hand, as it would lead them to Loretasia. Since Madden would be gone until the day of the planned dive search, Chase decided to return to the highlands by himself and continue to explore. He was hoping he might again chance upon Bright Feather and get more information out of him."

Precilla settled back, skimmed her notes, then continued. "I'm going to first start with the legend, since everything seems to revolve around that. When Dakota Chase returned to the highlands the following day, accompanied by his dog, Pablo, he did again meet Bright Feather. Bright Feather was actually waiting for him, as if he knew Chase was going to return. The Indian said he wanted to show Dakota a special place in the wilderness and, while he led him to it, he would tell him about the legends of Lore."

She said the roots of The Lore Adventure stemmed from the early stages of the last ice age. She explained that somewhere in the North, as the legend has it, when the glaciers began to move, abrupt shifts in the ice generated tremendous amounts of friction. Unimaginable friction. The immense heat and unbridled energy beneath the ice created a massive explosion. The concentration of that explosion became trapped inside the glacier. As the glaciers crept through the millenniums, gouging and tearing the earth's surface, the volatile massing trapped inside the ice crystallized and formed into a perfect, diamond-hard sphere. The core of that diamond hard sphere continued to swirl and pulsate with its own dynamic energy.

Somewhere along the glacier's journey, the ice mass plowed up from the depths of the earth, a fragment of black, petrified coral. The coral was translucent, shaped like a hand, and clung to the bottom of the ice. The coral hand rode with the ice until it finally settled.

When the glacier's journey ended, and the ice began to melt and recede, the coral hand released itself from the ice and settled back to earth. It settled on the floor of the prevailing glacial lake, Lake Agassiz. As the melting continued and the new lake expanded, the diamond hard sphere that was created by the explosion, also dropped from the diminishing ice and drifted to the bottom of the frigid water. It landed on, and settled into the fingers of the petrified, coral hand. The hand and the sphere now sat together at the bottom of Lake Agassiz.

Precilla stopped for a moment, poured herself a glass of orange juice and refilled Steve's and Ramsey's coffee cups. "There are many off shoots to this legend that I won't go into," she said, "at least not now anyway. It gets complicated, so I've summarized it as best I could."

"I'd like to hear everything," Ramsey said.

"Yes," Precilla replied. "Let me first build the foundation for you, then, if necessary, we can backtrack. The legend is like a giant tree with branches going everywhere. We'll stay on the main trunk and explore the branches later."

"That sounds good," Ramsey said, sipping his coffee. "When do we hear about that mysterious floating hole?"

"Later; that's one of the branches. The legend first." She continued her story, "The crystallized sphere that dropped from the ice to the bottom of the lake I will refer to from now on as the Ulambent. Remember, too, that all the while Bright Feather is revealing this legend to Dakota Chase, he's guiding Chase to some special place in the highlands."

"I thought this Bright Feather character was blind, had no eyes," Ramsey said. "How could he see to guide Chase anywhere?"

"That's another branch off the main trunk," Precilla replied. "We'll get to that later, too."

Ramsey grabbed another half a sandwich off the tray and gestured for her to continue.

Precilla explained that over time, as the Ulambent laid in the coral hand at the bottom of the lake, the energy inside its core began to glow. As the light intensified, a consciousness was born.

Ramsey stopped her. "What do you mean, a consciousness was born?"

"An awareness within the light became inherent. Inborn. Born within."

"This energy of light could think? It was aware of itself? Aware of its own existence?"

"It could think and see," Precilla replied. "The energy became a living consciousness. Over time, according to legend, the energy developed a will of its own. The energy became a life form within the Ulambent."

"And so Josh Clemens' myth begins," Ramsey said. "He made all this up."

"No," Precilla said. "This is the legend as Bright Feather told it to Dakota Chase. Josh simply recorded the legend. You have to realize, as I continue, that all civilizations, including our own, have their own personal and unique myths and legends. This legend I am relating is not out of line."

Ramsey took a bite from his sandwich. "Of course," he said chewing. "I understand that. I won't interrupt again."

"In time," Precilla went on, "the brilliant light released itself from the Ulambent, spewed outward, and spread itself across the surface of the lake. The light reflected its magnificent brightness and resplendent colors off the lake and into the sky. The fury in which the energy fanned its colorful light frightened all the living creatures of the land and they scattered into hiding. The *awareness* within the light saw this; saw the fear it had created, and retracted its radiance into a small, fiery ball. Realizing this dense concentration of energy couldn't remain confined for long, the *awareness* retraced the glacial path and followed it to its origins in the North. It was there, somewhere in the North, near the polar regions, that the *awareness* shed its energies of light into the ice. The *awareness* willed those energies to remain in the ice, where no living things would be frightened by it. Below the ice, the *awareness* then raised a pillar of stones in homage to the energy's splendor. The *awareness* then returned to the land near the Ulambent. From Lake Agassiz and the neighboring lands, the *awareness* could watch the energy it had left in the Northern ice mingle with the energies of space. It watched its beautiful, colorful lights fan magnificently in the Northern sky."

"I'll be damned," Steve said. "A legend for the Northern Lights."

"That part of the legend is very important," Precilla said. "It's one of the hundreds of existing branches, but is very close to the trunk. The many off shoots, or branches from the main legend, are called Lorals. Lorals are Legends of Lore. I'll continue, now, with the main Loral, the Legend of Lore."

Precilla explained that the *awareness* was now an invisible energy, living in the trees and along the lands near the lake with the Ulambent. It was a sensitive energy, experiencing passion for its own existence and a tremendous love, respect and tenderness for all the living things surrounding it. The *awareness* allowed all the living things to feel its presence, as it wanted to be a part of everything. They sensed its existence and accepted it as a part of them, as a friendly and wholesome part of nature.

Humankind eventually appeared in the regions near the Ulambent and the *awareness* was charmed by this new presence. Enraptured by one human in particular, a leader among the people, the *awareness* chose to emerge from invisibility and enter into a new form; a form similar in fashion to this human leader. In a small, spring fed pool, secluded between rocks in the middle of the forest, the *awareness* used its will to reflect the image of the human onto the water's surface. The *awareness* manipulated the image into a personal design, then entered the pool. The *awareness* rose from the pool, dripping wet, cloaked in this new image.

The *awareness* danced and reveled along the rocks in celebration of *his* new form. The animals of the forest gathered in curiosity and watched the ritual. The *awareness* sang aloud a name for himself, sang loudly for all the creatures in the region to hear. The *awareness* named himself Lore. Lore, as he would have it, would mean, "Wise One."

"Wise One," Steve said softly. "Your theory about Lore was correct, then. Earlier in the manuscript, when Chase and Madden met Bright Feather for the first time, they asked him who the Amity Pillars actually belonged to. He told them they belonged to Lore. Your rationale, then, was that Lore was a name for someone and not something. You had figured the name meant *one of knowledge or wisdom*. Wise One."

Ramsey refilled his coffee cup. "You're saying this energy that came from the, what do you call it? the Ulambent? has now transformed into a human form? He calls himself Lore?"

"According to legend, yes," Precilla replied.

"And he now lives among humans?" he asked.

"No," Precilla replied. "There's more. While Lore celebrated his new image, the commotion attracted not only the animals in the region, but the excitement aroused the curiosities of the human inhabitants as well. Lore knew this. He knew they were coming to investigate the disturbance and he knew he would have to hide.

"Lore understood he was the product of a great Influence, inherent from the same origin that created humans and all the living things; but he was not really human, himself. He was different. He knew he couldn't live among the human populations or be a part of humankind. He made a decision. Before the gathering of animals and prior to the arrival of the curious people searching for the commotion, Lore withdrew from his present mass and transfigured himself into a size much smaller." Precilla held her hand up, suggested a size of about an inch between her thumb and forefinger. "With this new size, Lore could now exist in secrecy while retaining the image of man. He could live in secrecy among man."

"So now this Lore character is just an inch or two tall? Existing in the image of a Native American?" Ramsey asked.

"According to legend," Precilla replied.

"That's quite a myth," Ramsey said.

Steve smiled broadly. "It's great," he said. "I love it!"

"While Bright Feather is telling all this to Dakota Chase, where is he leading him to in the forest?" Ramsey asked.

"He's leading him to Loreduchy Swamp. I think it's the swamp with all the masks we discovered while tracking Bright Feather."

"What's special about that place?" Ramsey asked.

"It's a meeting or gathering place for the Loreduchy. Loreduchy are people that become involved with the Lore Adventure."

"The secret society?" Steve asked.

"Possibly," Precilla said.

"What about that floating thing?" Ramsey asked. "What the hell was that?"

"We'll come to that," Precilla said. "I should finish the Loral first."

Precilla continued. She explained that when the people arrived to investigate the disturbance, the animals withdrew and Lore hid himself among the rocks by the pool. Finding nothing, the people retreated to their encampments. Lore, pleased with his new image, wanted to give something to the leader he had patterned himself after. He wanted to give him a gift, more or less, in return for the human image.

Lore removed the beautiful Ulambent from the coral hand at the bottom of the lake and placed it in the water where the leader bathed daily. The Ulambent was diamond hard; a small, smooth and shiny transparent sphere. The sphere was hollow on the inside with uniquely crystallized, interior walls. Because of its crystallized interior, when struck by any kind of light, the Ulambent gave off a dazzling display of vibrant colors.

Steve Adams straightened. "Is that the Ulambent in there? In that building?" he asked excitedly.

"No," Precilla said. "That's just a small crystal ball that represents the Ulambent. The Ulambent was far more than a beautiful sphere; it contained great powers that would later be discovered."

Steve relaxed and Precilla continued with her story. She told them, the following morning, as the leader bathed, he was attracted to shimmering colors sparkling across the rocks underwater. While wading toward the colors, he cut his foot on a stone and bent to pamper the wound. Bowed, holding his foot in his hand, the leader spotted the Ulambent, the source of the brilliant colors. The Ulambent was lying, gleaming, on top of the rocks. He scooped it out of the water, returned to shore and sat on a boulder to inspect it. While holding the Ulambent toward the sky and gazing through its brilliance, it slipped from his fingers and bounced on the boulder by his feet. The leader trapped the Ulambent with his injured foot and instantly his cut was healed. Knowing, now, that the Ulambent was a stone of special powers, the leader wrapped it in cord and wore it around his neck. This pleased Lore.

Lore became captivated by the leader's beautiful mate and their children. He longed for his own mate and to have children of his own. He returned to the pool where he had emerged in the image of man and cast his own reflection into the water. He churned the water and maneuvered the reflection into an image of a beautiful woman. Lore released a part of his energy from himself and poured it into the reflection. The image rose from the pool and joined Lore at his side. He named his new, beautiful mate Aura, in honor of his glorious lights in the North. He then named the spring fed pool, from where they both had emerged, Aurox. Lore and Aura retreated to an island close to the mainland and it was there they made their home and began their family and the civilization of Lore.

"The island," Steve interrupted. "The island with the circle of stones. That has to be Lore's island."

"That would be my guess," Precilla said.

Ramsey snorted. "This is just a concoction," he said, "an elaborate story made up by Clemens. This is what it's all about; this is his plan. He's creating a myth."

"That's very possible," Precilla replied, "but it's difficult to distinguish the line between reality and fantasy. Bright Feather is real, we've all seen him on videotape. Bright Feather is supposedly telling Dakota Chase this legend as he's leading him to Loreduchy Swamp. Josh Clemens simply recorded this legend as Bright Feather told it to Dakota Chase. Myths often stem from embellished truths."

"Well, the truth as I see it," Ramsey said, "is this Bright Feather character is not real at all. He's someone who's been made-up to look old and mysterious, and is simply a part of a plot to try to convince people, you two in particular, that these legends are real. I believe it's all a fabrication by Dakota Chase and Cole Madden, and your friend, Josh Clemens, got on board and is writing stories about it while the artists are creating the visual elements. It's all an elaborate hoax, just as I've said from the start."

"What about the two thousand year old buildings the archeologists uncovered at the dig site?" Steve asked. "How can they be explained?"

"Like Precilla said, myths often stem from embellished truths. I'm not saying all the myths were created recently; some perhaps are from the past. What I'm saying is, I believe Josh Clemens and the two artists are developing a very elaborate hoax around the legends."

"I don't argue that at all," Precilla said. "But there are mysteries involved here that can't be explained. You even admit to that."

"Yes I do, and I'm waiting for your explanation about that floating thing we all witnessed on the island."

"I know," Precilla said, smiling, "but I have to finish the Loral first. I'm condensing it as best I can without omitting the significant elements."

Ramsey nodded and allowed Precilla to continue. She said Lore and Aura used clay from the earth to build their dwelling on the island. They hardened the clay by baking it, as they'd seen the Indians often do. From their new home on the island, they began their family and the civilization of Lore.

Over time, more people arrived into the regions and conflicts arose among the settlements. The leader that Lore had admired from the beginning was killed in one such conflict. Lore was saddened to see this dark side of greed and the lust for power inbred within the nature of man. Lore mourned with the people the loss of their leader; he experienced grief for the first time. The leader's son, whose name was Ur, removed from his father's neck the Ulambent and wore it around his own. Ur became the new leader of the people and Lore was pleased.

As more conflicts arose among the people, one of the *Seekers*, as Lore called Ur's enemies, spotted the Ulambent around Ur's neck and lusted to own it. One night, while Ur slept, the Seeker entered Ur's lodge, struck him with a rock and stole the Ulambent. He left the leader for dead. Lore knew this and went to save the new leader. He secretly entered Ur's dwelling and, using his natural powers, removed the leader from his lodge. He took him to a hollow inside a large hill overlooking his island, and nursed him back to health. For the first time Lore revealed himself to man.

Lore explained to Ur the origin of the powerful Ulambent, and that he would now have to retrieve it from the Seeker who stole it. Lore would hide it for all time. Lore explained that if in the wrong hands, the power of the Ulambent could be used for evil purposes. He told Ur that once the Ulambent was safely hidden, the Seeker's obsession over the Ulambent would drive him to search for it for the rest of his life. He also told Ur that his own life would be in danger until the day the Seeker died. Ur understood this. He allowed Lore to put him to sleep in the hollow hill until that day came; until the day the seeker died.

The Seeker's people left him alone in the wilderness after many years of searching for the Ulambent. Driven by his unsatiable lust to possess the powerful sphere, the Seeker did, indeed, search for it, by himself, until the day he died. On that day, Lore returned to the hollow hill and woke Ur from his deep sleep.

Ur's oldest son, Kaiee, was now fully grown and was the new leader of the people in the region. Ur was proud of his son and did not wish to return to his people and take away the leadership role from Kaiee. Ur's request to Lore was extraordinary. He asked Lore to make him one like Lore and his descendants; to make him small, so he could live like Lore, in secrecy, near his people. Lore granted Ur's wish and made him one like his kind.

One of Lore's daughters became the mate of Ur and they had many children. These children were a mixture of Lore and human. With this new human influence making entry into the civilization of Lore, there entered, also, the nature of greed and power among the inhabitants. This doleful nature incited a desire within one of Ur's descendants to seek the ownership of Lore's hidden, powerful Ulambent of legend. The descendant's name was Noctumba.

"Noctumba!" Steve exclaimed. "He's the one I read about in Josh's notes, remember? The evil one that must be stopped!"

"He's the one," Precilla replied.

"Noctumba?" Ramsey said.

"We've come across the name before," Precilla said, "but we haven't been able to tie the name to anything until now."

"Lore hid the Ulambent after retrieving it from the Seeker that stole it from Ur, didn't he?" Steve asked.

"Yes."

"Did Noctumba find it?"

"Yes. And he used the powers of the Ulambent for his own greedy purposes. Over time, the powers became too great for Noctumba, and he became dangerously out of control. He was overcome with an obsession to control the world."

"How did Noctumba find the Ulambent after Lore hid it?"

"That's really complicated. I had to pool a bunch of Lorals together and condense them all into one short version."

"What's the short version?"

"Lore placed the Ulambent in a shrine he had made out of clay. He chose a secluded part of the forest to place the shrine. All around the shrine he constructed an architectural maze; surrounded the shrine and Ulambent with buildings similar to the one on the dining room table. Upon completion of the architectural maze, the Ulambent disappeared."

"Disappeared?" Ramsey asked. "How?"

"Lore willed the Ulambent invisible. The only way one could gain access to it, or to bring it back, would be to disassemble the maze and shrine. The entire architectural assemblage would have to be disassembled in the reverse order that it was constructed. In the exact reverse order, block by block."

"Noctumba found the maze and shrine and figured out how to do that?" Steve asked.

"He did."

"How?"

"That's where the Regions of Influence come in."

"The Regions of Influence?" Ramsey asked. "You're really beginning to lose me here."

"Bright Feather explained it all to Dakota Chase. The Regions of Influence are the energies that pass through everything, all living things. Those energies are what bind all life into a harmonious One. Lore understood the makeup of the Regions of Influence, realized he was a product of the Influence, and he mastered control of those energies. Lore could channel those energies at will and perform remarkable feats that would seem supernatural to humans. All the powers, the understanding and knowledge of the Influence that were innate within Lore, were also inherited by all Lore's descendants. Noctumba included.

"Within the Influence there also flows something remarkable. The *stream of consciousness*; the consciousness of all living things. When we think silently, the energy of our thoughts leave us and pass into the Regions of Influence. If one has knowledge of, and understands the Influence, one could read the patterns of our thoughts."

"Do you mean to say that while I'm thinking to myself, I'm actually broadcasting my thoughts into the Influence?" Steve asked.

"Something like that."

"And if you understood the makeup of the Regions of Influence, you could read my thoughts?"

"According to Loral, yes."

"Is that how Noctumba found the Ulambent?"

"Yes. Noctumba read the patterns in the Influence. He was very keen to the makeup of the Regions of Influence and he deciphered Lore's design from within the stream of consciousness."

"But didn't Lore hide the Ulambent long before Noctumba arrived?"

"Yes; but for Lore, there is no such thing as time. Time is a convention we humans have introduced to ourselves. We've developed the calendar, sun dial, hour glass and electronic time pieces. People have become slaves to the hour glass; our lives revolve around the clock and everything we do is dictated by time. We plan our entire lives around the calendar and clock. We live a linear life. The Regions of Influence has no calendar or clock; there is no line or particular direction. There are no parameters. Within this great Influence also flows the stream of consciousness. Noctumba entered the stream of consciousness and unraveled Lore's plan."

"Noctumba destroyed Lore's architectural maze? He disassembled it and retrieved the Ulambent?" Steve asked.

"He did. And with the powers of the Ulambent, he deviously sought to rule the Inner Kingdom. The problem was, the powers of the Ulambent were too great for Noctumba and he lost control. He became lost in his fixation; he became dangerous to himself and the entire Inner Kingdom. The Regions of Influence, that delicate thread of energy that keeps the balance between all living things, was at risk of being altered. Altering the Influence would not only affect the Lore civilization, it would affect all living things, including humans, as well."

"So what happened? What did Lore do?"

"You two returned from the island just as I was getting to the part where Dakota Chase and Cole Madden were striking out to go scuba diving in search of the coral hand at the bottom of the lake. I don't know what happened, I stopped reading there."

Donald Ramsey checked his watch, set his empty coffee cup on the tray and leaned back on the bench. "Now that you've established most of the legend for us, tell us about that floating anomaly we all saw on the island. You had a name for it."

"Kimirente," Precilla said.

"Yeah, Kimirente."

"Like I'd said, Bright Feather told all this to Dakota Chase while he was leading him to Loreduchy Swamp. As they entered the valley and approached the swamp, Chase noticed a mask hanging from one of the trees. The mask hung at eye level and as he walked toward it, Bright Feather told him it was a Windtickler Spirit Mask. Inset within the eyes of the mask were two glass crystals. Bright Feather told him if he looked at the swamp through the crystal eyes he would see the makeup of Loretasia, the Inner Kingdom.

"When Chase looked at the swamp through the eyes of the mask, he saw a colorful, kaleidoscopic image of the whole area. Everything was fragmented, surrounded by dazzling colors; everything looking like his recent, colorful paintings. Bright Feather told him he was seeing the Auras of the Influence, the colorful Auras of life.

"As they continued on toward the swamp, Chase spotted the Kimirente hovering above the ground a ways in front of him. Bright Feather told him to be still and quiet, not to attract its attention. He said the image would move on and eventually go away. When Chase asked what it was, Bright Feather said it was an entity from someplace else, a projection from another world."

Donald Ramsey coughed. "A projection from another world?"

"That's what Bright Feather told him. When the Kimirente vanished, Bright Feather said that what he'd seen was actually an entity from someone's mind's eye. He said it was projected by someone from another level of consciousness; someone directing the entity through the region. He told Chase it was an adversary looking for him and that he should be very cautious if he were to encounter it again in the future. He said someone from the Inner Kingdom was trying to prevent Chase and Madden from discovering Loretasia."

"Who?" Steve asked. "Why?"

"Wait a minute," Ramsey said, "you're not actually buying into this are you Adams? You don't really believe this?"

"I just want to hear the whole story."

"I think what we all saw was a projection," Precilla said. "I think it was a Kimirente created by the Indian Steve and I encountered on the island; the Indian that threatened us."

"You're not serious!" Ramsey said. "You don't honestly believe the Indian on the island created that floating thing with his mind; that he projected it with his thoughts!"

Precilla gripped her notebook tightly. "Yes. Yes I do," she said flatly. "Bright Feather told Dakota Chase that within this world there are many unseen worlds, and within those clandestine realms are many things we can't explain or understand. He said all the worlds are adjacent to one another, confluent with the world we know. Bright Feather explained that all the worlds have portals, just off the corners of the eyes, and that the gateways into those domains are open for those who allow their minds to see them."

"Here we go," Ramsey said. "That fine line between reality and fantasy you spoke of earlier—you've just crossed!"

"Do you have a better explanation for what we saw?"

"I have no explanation at all. I was hoping yours was going to be a little more practical; down to earth. I've seen spots before, similar to what we saw. They were created by bright lights, flash bulbs and sun glares, things like that. An explanation along those lines would make a whole lot more sense to me than suggesting it was some kind of a projection created by someone's mind."

"Whatever it was," Steve said, "we all saw it and it was real. It left an odor that we all detected, so it was a physical thing and not just a spot from a light glare. I think we all need to keep open minds here."

Ramsey checked his watch again. "Open minds, yes, but at the same time, realistic. The legends are interesting, I'll give them that, but that's exactly what they are, legends and myths."

"Legends and myths with many unexplained circumstances surrounding them," Precilla said. "Supernatural circumstances."

Ramsey stood. "Unexplained might be the better word; supernatural is a little heavy. I have to get a move on and head out to the dig site now. Milton and Schepp were informed this morning that we're no longer going to keep a man on duty out there. The department can no longer justify the expense of it. They have enough of their own people out there to keep the area secure."

"I'll bet that's not sitting very well with them," Steve said with a chuckle.

"Not at all," Ramsey said. "When I talked to the officer on duty, before picking you up this morning, the archeologists were already unhappy about not being able to relocate that coral hand at the bottom of the lake. He said they really went ballistic when they were told we were no longer providing security for them. I have to go out and clear the air."

"What do you mean they couldn't relocate the hand at the bottom of the lake?" Steve asked.

"Their divers couldn't relocate it. Either it wasn't there or they were diving the wrong area."

"I hardly doubt they were diving the wrong area," Steve said.

Ramsey laughed. "It wouldn't be the first thing that's disappeared, now, would it?"

Steve and Precilla walked Ramsey through the house and outside to his car. He thanked them for the lunch and said he would keep in touch and asked them to do the same, particularly if there were new developments. They waved him off and returned to the house.

"What are your plans for tomorrow?" Precilla asked as they entered the front door.

"I was planning to work on an advertisement. Why?"

"I would like to go back to that large rock we found in the woods while tracking Bright Feather."

"The Rock Tony Williams and his dog led us to? Where Bright Feather disappeared?"

"Yes."

"Why?"

"There's something I would like to see."

"I didn't think you wanted to go back out there after the incident on the island."

"I have to go back there."

"Do you honestly believe that floating thing was a Kimirente?"

"Yes, I do. I know it's bizarre, and Ramsey probably thinks I'm loony, but I honestly believe that's what we saw."

"Well, whatever it was it scared Ramsey, too. He drew his gun on it."

"And you actually heard Josh Clemens' voice?"

"Josh Clemens warned us not to fire the gun. I don't know if I actually heard his voice or thought it, but Ramsey detected it, too. He's as bewildered as you and I."

"Well, I've actually read more of the manuscript than what I led you and Ramsey to believe. I'm about done with it and there's something I'd like to see. I have to see."

"What?"

"Let me finish reading everything tonight and I'll tell you all about it on our way out there tomorrow morning."

"Tell me now."

"I can't just yet. I have to organize things better first, so it's clear for you. So it's clear for both of us, actually."

"What do you know?"

Precilla smiled. "Let me put it all together first."

* * * * *

Sixteen

Steve Adams loved the fragrance of the forest and all the aromas that came with summer. He inhaled deeply as he got out of the Grand-Am and enjoyed the morning's redolence. He'd hardly slept the previous evening, as all he could think about was his experiences on the island. Something had to be very important for Precilla to want to return to the highlands, as Dakota Chase called the wilderness region; something more important than her fears. Precilla obviously knew things he didn't and he just wanted to dive into her brain and consume everything. He was a bit tense with apprehension over what they might encounter in the forest this morning, so he allowed the woodland bouquet to help settle his nerves.

Precilla didn't seem goosey at all. In fact, she appeared quite calm. He could tell there was a lot on her mind because she was preoccupied, but there was no evidence of anxiety. During their drive into the highlands she remained absorbed in her notebook, reading and jotting down thoughts as they came to her. She had spoken little. When she climbed out of the passenger's side of the car she looked ready to go.

"All set?" Steve asked.

Precilla grabbed her notebook, shut the door. "Let's go," she said.

They walked away from the car and followed a narrow path into the woods. The path was convenient, a deer trail that opened a tight passageway through the brush. It was heavily trampled and

filled with hoof prints. The trek into the area with the large
boulder would take about an hour and Precilla would finish Josh
Clemens' story for Steve while in route.

Once inside the tree line, the brush thinned and the deer trail
became less obvious. Steve took a quick compass bearing to make
sure they were headed in the right direction. Several high hills
would lie before them and some of the hiking would be difficult.
Precilla skimmed her notes while Steve took the compass reading
and, in only a moment, they were on their way.

Precilla began her story as they started out. "When I told
Donald Ramsey I believed what we saw on the island was a
Kimirente, he said I had crossed that fine line between reality and
fantasy. He had no idea the measure of that line, if in fact, a line
actually exists. As I proceed, you'll have to determine for yourself,
and come to your own conclusions, what's actually real and
what's fantasy. Most of what I tell you will seem pretty fantastic."

"I'm listening," Steve said. They were approaching their first hill.

"Chase and Madden did meet on the date they had planned to
and went scuba diving in search of the hand at the bottom of the
lake. They borrowed a boat from a resort owner and used Chase's
equipment. It was Madden's first dive.

"They spent the whole morning searching the area where they
believed the hand was supposed to be but they had no luck finding
it. With tanks running low on air, they made one final dive. Madden
spotted an unusual hump rising from the bottom of the lake: An
object, it seemed, covered with dead weeds. The two peeled away the
entanglements and revealed the hand. The unraveling stirred up a
cloud of muck so they surfaced to conserve on air while the murky
cloud settled. They were extremely excited.

"When they returned, the hand was in clear view and they
floated carefully around it, being especially mindful to not stir up
the bottom. Chase noticed a part of one of the fingers was missing

and pointed it out to Madden. He cautiously approached the form to inspect it more closely. It was then he noticed a small fragment lying in the palm of the hand where the sphere was supposed to be. He gently removed the fragment and held it to the broken finger on the hand. The breaks matched up perfectly. Madden signaled to Chase that he was nearly out of air and the two surfaced and returned to the boat.

"Once in the boat, Chase realized the fragment was actually broken on both ends, that there was yet another small piece somewhere at the bottom of the lake. The tanks they were diving with had reserve air and Chase adjusted the valves to gain access. He wanted to make one more dive to try to find the missing piece. Madden stopped him."

Precilla paused to rest and catch her breath. The hill they were ascending was quite steep and over a thousand feet high. Steve was ready for a breather, too.

"Why did Madden stop him?"

"Madden noticed something very peculiar about the fragment. When held to the sky it was translucent, smoky black in color, but remarkably, when he squeezed it tightly, it caused a tingling sensation in his hand."

"What do you mean a tingling sensation?"

"It vibrated. Madden said it reminded him of catching a fly, the way the wings buzzed inside the closed hand. There was no sound, just a tingling sensation. When Chase held the fragment, he felt it, too."

"What was causing that?"

Precilla resumed the climb up the hill. "Besides it being very odd, they didn't know what was causing it. By accident, though, Chase discovered that whenever he faced a certain direction the tingling became more intense, and when he turned in an opposite direction, the sensation lessened. The strongest intensity occurred while facing toward the South arm of Comet Lake; the area of lake with the island."

"Like a signal of some sort?"

"That's how it seemed to them. It was as though the fragment was homing in on something on South Comet Lake."

"What did they do?"

"By this time more boats were on the lake and fishermen were approaching their position. Chase decided not to attract attention with another dive, so the two removed their gear and headed the boat toward the South arm of the lake. Dakota piloted while Cole guided with the fragment. As they got closer to the island, the fragment's vibration became very intense. They were certain, now, it was homing in on something. Something underwater.

"Suddenly the vibrating quit. Madden hollered for Chase to stop the boat and back up some. When he did, the vibration resumed and became so strong, the fragment actually bounced along the palm of Madden's open hand. Chase killed the motor and dropped anchor there. They were both completely perplexed."

"Do you think this actually happened?" Steve interrupted.

They were at the top of the hill and Precilla suggested they sit a moment. "Wait until I'm all done, then form your opinions. It gets better."

Steve and Precilla sat in the grass along the narrow, tree covered ridge overlooking the valleys on each side. The forest floor perked with the vibrancy of the woodland's colorful wild flowers. It was a peaceful spot, with nature's critters chiming in the background.

As they relaxed, Precilla continued with her story. She said Chase suggested they use the reserve air in the tanks to dive that spot. They didn't have a whole lot of time left, maybe fifteen minutes underwater. There was no activity on this part of the lake so their dive would go unnoticed. Both artists were excited and apprehensive over what they might discover.

They weren't disappointed. Dakota Chase first spotted several Amity Pillars rising from the bottom of the lake. Befuddled, they tentatively approached them. A couple of towers rose five or six feet off the floor, while the others were much smaller. As they circled around them, Madden spotted a cluster of small brick buildings a few feet away. They descended slowly toward them.

All the buildings were linked together with bridges and stairways, all minutely detailed with windows and balconies. Resting on one of the balconies was a small black object, similar to the finger fragment Chase was holding in his hand. He carefully picked up the piece from the balcony and held it to the one in his hand. The breaks matched perfectly.

As Dakota touched the matching ends together, they fused! A blue spark accompanied the fusion and in his surprise, he dropped it. The melded fragment toppled from his hands and landed on a window ledge where it teetered. Chase quickly reached for it but the turbulence pushed it into the window and it disappeared.

Disgusted, Chase reached his finger into the window to feel for it; to try to retrieve it. Madden grabbed his arm and pointed to the side of the building. The interior of the building was glowing through the windows. The divers backed away slowly and watched. All the windows of every building began to glow. A streak of light shot from one of the windows and passed beneath them. Brilliantly colored streaks of light began shooting from the other windows and the entire arrangement seemed to melt into a concentrating white light! Bubbles poured out from the windows and floated every which way. The water around the divers churned and moved them in circles. In a frenzy, Dakota Chase pointed upward and they raced for the surface.

As they approached the surface, Chase, looking up, saw his reflection in a swirl of colors. He broke through the reflection and thrashed into the open air. Madden bobbed beside him and the water foamed around them. The boat was gone! Somehow the anchor rope had released itself from the anchor and the boat drifted off. Dakota Chase spit out his regulator and hollered for Madden to swim to the island.

When they reached the island's shoreline, they sat in the shallow water and, in quiet dismay, stared outward toward the lake. The boat had drifted all the way to the opposite shore and the lake had settled into modest ripples.

Precilla Adams stood and stretched her arms and legs. Steve joined her. "That's it?" he asked.

"It's just the beginning."

They walked along the ridge for a moment, then Steve guided them down the other side of the hill. As they descended the grade, Precilla continued.

"Both those poor guys were completely stunned," she said. "Speechless. Chase finally began removing his gear and tossed his flippers onto shore. Madden did the same."

Precilla paused a moment. "Are you ready?" she asked.

"Ready for what?"

She smiled. "Madden saw something on a rock. It looked like a tiny figure, a person, not more than a couple of inches tall. He thought it was one of those GI Joe action figures; the Indian figure. He was dazed. Then the figure moved and Chase saw it. He was stupefied. They just sat in the water and gawked. The figure wore a grassy vine around his waist, walked across the rock and hopped to another. It was like a dream. His skin was golden, his hair long and black, breaking at the shoulders, and his features were Native American. His tiny eyes were black and shiny."

Steve stopped walking. Precilla gave him a moment to digest the story.

"The figure spoke to them and told them not to panic, that they had just shattered their known world and entered another. He said it would take a while to realize it and adjust to it, but eventually they would come around. The figure sat down and waited for them to blink back to reality. As the artists stared dreamily, the little figure introduced himself as Singer, the Singer of Songs. He called himself the storyteller."

"Yes," Steve said, "I remember the name from Josh's notes. Singer. In the notes the character was sitting on a leaf and talking about the stars."

"I remember," Precilla said. "How are you doing?"

"It's pretty fascinating. Quite imaginative."

They continued down the hill. Precilla told Steve that it seemed like an eternity before the artists could speak. When Chase finally did, he just said this wasn't really happening.

The little figure, Singer, chortled and jumped to his feet. He assured them that it was actually happening. He said they had simply passed through their own dimension and expanded their awareness into another realm. He said they had entered the gateway into Loretasia, the Inner Kingdom and that he'd been waiting for them for a long time.

Madden asked Singer if they were dead, if they had actually drowned in the lake and this was some kind of journey into another existence. Singer chuckled and told them they were quite alive, that they had simply augmented their sensibilities and needed some time to adapt themselves to this newly developed awareness. He guaranteed they were both very healthy and alert. It was genuine.

"I'll skip a lot of the early conversation by Singer," Precilla said, "as he was basically talking them out of their bewilderment and reviving them to full consciousness. In time the artists came around some and listened to the little one attentively. When they drifted into disillusionment, Singer clapped his hands and hollered, jolting them out of their numbness. Chase started shivering in the water and noticed the air cooling around them. When he felt the air on his skin he knew it was all real. All of his senses had returned and this little figure talking to him, Singer, the Singer of Songs, he knew was real. Singer was as real as the air chilling him. Madden conceded to it shortly afterward."

Steve stopped her for a moment. "You're talking about two real people here, you know. They're not some fictional characters in a book. Dakota Chase and Cole Madden are real people. Josh Clemens actually wrote this about them? He wrote all this, claiming it to be fact?"

Precilla smiled broadly and winked. "I'm not done yet, I've just begun."

"No wonder Josh Clemens is missing," Steve said. "Those two guys probably bonked him for making such a claim on their behalf."

"Shall I continue?" Precilla asked.

"First tell me what you want to see out here. What are you looking for?"

"The mask with the crystal eyes, for one thing. Do you remember? Dakota Chase spotted the mask when Bright Feather led him down the hill toward Loreduchy Swamp. He had Dakota look through the crystal eyes to see the colors of the swamp. As Chase looked, the Indian told him he was seeing the colors of Loretasia, the colors of the Inner Kingdom. He said they were the colorful Auras of life."

"Yes, I remember. What else are you looking for?"

"We'll get to that later."

They continued their descent. The morning was blossoming into a beautiful day. The early sun splashed across the tree crowns and spread bands of light throughout the forest's corridors. Precilla flipped to a page in her notebook and resumed with her story.

"Singer waved for the artists to follow him onto the island. He leaped from the rock he was standing on and disappeared into the brush. Chase and Madden crawled through the thicket and followed the little one up the hill. As they followed, Chase spotted the rock painting of the hand holding the Ulambent and pointed it out to Madden. At the top of the hill, Singer took a position inside a circle of stones and asked the artists to sit on the ground just inside the circle. As they sat, both noticed other figures skittishly poking their heads out from behind leaves and rocks. It was all so dreamlike. Singer would often clap his hands to keep the two from drifting into disbelief.

"Singer informed them that the circle of stones surrounding them was created by his father, Kintu, a long, long time ago. The circle of stones fringed what Singer called an Amity Point, a place of harmony and calm. A place of peace. He said the world was filled with ever changing Amity Points and people and animals instinctively found their own. They were places outside the world's active energies, places of comfort and peace. Places of safety and solitude. Kintu outlined this Amity Point with stones long ago and later designated it as the meeting place for Chase and Madden.

"The little one told the artists they had been chosen by Lore and lured into the Inner Kingdom to fulfill a very important mission. They were chosen to retrieve the Ulambent from Noctumba. He said it was human greed, through Noctumba, the descendant of Ur, that took the Ulambent away from the Inner Kingdom. It was time now for human goodness, through the deeds of Chase and Madden, to bring it back to its rightful place. Chase and Madden were chosen by Lore to do this because of their rectitude."

"Wait a minute," Steve interrupted. They were at the bottom of the hill and he stopped to think. "Let me guess. Chase and

Madden would have to rebuild the shrine that held the Ulambent and reconstruct the architectural maze that surrounded it?"

"Exactly. And that's just what they did. Block by block they reassembled everything in the proper order."

"How? How could they reconstruct it, exactly as it was, block by block?"

"The same way Noctumba disassembled it to steal the Ulambent. The design was in the Influence, within the stream of consciousness."

"They understood how to see into this stream of consciousness?"

"Singer and others, over time, taught them how."

"What others? Who besides this Singer character?"

"Bright Feather, for one."

"Oh, yes, Bright Feather. Who is Bright Feather? How's he involved."

"He was the person in Dakota Chase's dream."

"What? The one that entered the lake and was struck by lightning?"

"He's the one."

"This is too much," Steve said, looking for a place to sit. He guided Precilla to a large boulder where they both sat. "I could use an Amity Point right now."

*   *   *   *   *

Seventeen

Precilla told Steve that long ago Lore chose Bright Feather to become the first Loreduchy. Loreduchy are the liaisons between humankind and nature, between human civilizations and Loretasia, the Inner Kingdom. Singer told the artists that the first people in the regions, the native Indians, were on a path similar to Lore's. They lived and learned from nature and used nature's wonders and energies to guide them. They understood the powers of nature and the delicacy of her balance. Over the course of human time, however, new people arrived and, through their greed and lust for power, they began aimlessly reaping the earth's energies and destroying the globes natural wonders and powers. The first people understood the mysteries of nature, used the energies without destroying their sources, and replenished them to keep the balance. The new people were oblivious to it.

As the populations increased, the first people were torn from their lives, scattered in disarray and deprived from following their paths. They were forced away from nature, pushed out of the lands, and fettered to the new civilization. The old knew how to use the energies of nature while leaving the sources of those energies in tact. The new consumed and depleted the sources. They destroyed them and used the energies for personal gain and power. The Loreduchy are those that understand all of this and help to lure people back to nature; back to themselves. Humans are a part of nature, but so many are lost and confused. Bright Feather was special to Lore. He lured him to his island to teach him about the Regions of Influence, so he could help guide others back.

Noctumba, however, knew this, as his evil cunning interpreted Lore's plan within the stream of consciousness. Noctumba feared that if Bright Feather were to learn about the Regions of Influence and master how to channel the Regions' tremendous powers, then he could be a threat to his controlling the Inner Kingdom. So Noctumba plotted to do away with Bright Feather.

Steve Adams rose from the rock he was sitting on and rubbed his butt with both hands. "This is definitely not an Amity Point." He moved to a mound of grass and sat. "Noctumba plotted to get rid of Bright Feather? To kill him?"

"So Singer claimed."

"What happened? How did Lore lure him into the Inner Kingdom in the first place?"

"By leaving signs: Amity Pillars, rock paintings and masks. He left a trail for Bright Feather to follow."

"A trail that would lead him to Lore's island."

"Yes."

"Did the circle of stones already exist on the island?"

"Yes. Kintu, Singer's father, had already assembled the stones around the Amity Point and that was where Lore was going to teach Bright Feather the ways."

"But Noctumba stopped him before he reached the island?"

"Exactly. Noctumba set his trap. He built an Amity Pillar at the bottom of the lake and placed the Ulambent on top of it. As Bright Feather descended the hill toward the lake, toward the island, the Ulambent began to glow and attracted his attention."

Steve leaned forward. "So he waded into the water to investigate the source of light and discovered the Amity Pillar and the Ulambent."

"That's it."

"What was the humming noise? The One chant Dakota Chase heard in his dream?"

"A warning. Lore's descendants tried to distract Bright Feather, warn him away, but the power of the Ulambent was too compelling. He submerged and took the Ulambent from its pedestal."

Steve thought. "And just before the lightning struck the Ulambent, the chorus of voices hollered, 'No!'"

"Yes, a final desperate warning. But it was too late. The lightning struck the Ulambent and the flash was so intense, that it blinded Bright Feather and knocked him unconscious. Noctumba retrieved the Ulambent, fled, and left Bright Feather floating in the water to drown."

"But Lore saved him."

"Yes, Lore and Aura revived him and nursed him back. Bright Feather's sight was gone, but Lore taught him how to see without his eyes."

"How?"

"He taught him how to see through his mind's eye, to see through the Regions of Influence. Bright Feather, in time, could see far beyond normal human sight; he could see everything around him at once. He wasn't limited to eyesight, to our stereoscopic vision. He could see everything around him, all directions at once."

Steve leaned back and supported his weight on his hands. "This is incredible! What a legend. Josh Clemens, you're crazy but brilliant." He thought for another moment. "Is the lost city, the assemblage of buildings we videotaped, the site of the reconstruction?"

"No. That's the decoy. Singer told Chase and Madden that some of their activities would surely be discovered, attract attention, that they would have to secretly plan around that. They would have to keep people away from their real intentions and the real location of the shrine and maze. In order to do this, Singer helped Dakota devise a plan.

"Dakota Chase involved his students. He told them all about Lore and the secret civilization. He told them everything; he told it all, except he told it as a fantasy, as an adventure story. The students helped in the creation of the Lost City, the decoy city, while Chase and Madden assembled the real maze in secret. All the while, however, the Lost City and all the masks, Amity Pillars, rock paintings and rattles had their own special purposes besides being decoys. Several major purposes."

"What purposes?"

Precilla laughed softly. "The main reason was to confuse Noctumba, to distract him away from the actual reconstruction site. Another, which was also extremely brilliant, was to lure humans back into the wilderness to search for everything. While in the process of searching, people would rediscover many of the elements of nature. While searching they would discover things they'd forgotten about or never learned; things they never thought about because of their being so caught up in the daily rat races of society. In the process of searching, people would begin to rediscover themselves and rediscover their places in nature. People would get caught up in the Lore Adventure, the adventure created by the artists. They would reacquaint themselves with nature while searching the wilderness for the artists' works."

Steve grinned. "Too ingenious."

"To help attract people into the wilderness," Precilla continued, "Dakota Chase and Cole Madden lured Josh Clemens into their scheme. He began writing stories for newspapers and magazines, and the word got out. It really spread fast. People got involved in the adventure and many began building Amity Pillars themselves. Rock towers started appearing everywhere. It became an active, fun adventure for people. A real adventure with a wholesome plot."

"I'll be damned," Steve said. "This is crazy! According to Josh's manuscript, then, this whole adventure thing was actually an elaborate scheme designed by Lore to get humankind back on track with nature. Even Josh's writings were a part of his plot."

"Precisely. And doesn't that make you wonder about something?"

"What? Wonder about what?"

"What we're doing here. What's our involvement in all this? At the outset, Josh said in his letter to you that *you* were deeply involved. You questioned it yourself, when we left the island the first time, after seeing the Kimirente and encountering the evil Indian; who incidentally, I know who he is. You told me in the car to think about it, to think about our involvement in all this."

"You know who the Indian is? The one that threatened us on the island?"

"Yes. His name is Nefar."

"Who the hell is Nefar?"

"When Noctumba learned that Lore had saved Bright Feather's life and made him Loreduchy, he felt he needed someone himself, a human companion, to become an adversary to Bright Feather. He found Nefar in the wilderness and befriended him, taught him about the Regions of Influence and how to channel those powers at will. They became partners."

Steve rose and approached his wife. "Let's continue this as we walk," he said. They continued their trek toward the area of the granite boulder and Steve began a barrage of questions. "You said a while back that others were involved, assisted the artists with this plan. Who besides Bright Feather was involved?"

"A young Lore maiden named Princess. She was the daughter of one called Lady Magic, a dulcet, or music maker. Lady Magic played the colored waves of light with a stone harp and turned the light waves into music. Her daughter, Princess, caught the eye of Dakota Chase. While inside the stone circle, as Singer was unraveling Lore's plan for the artists, Chase spotted her perched on a tree branch above his head. He was thunderstruck by her beauty. She wore a tendril of miniature daisies and her radiance charmed him. He whispered to himself something like, 'She's a princess,' and their companionship had begun."

"What do you mean, their companionship had begun?"

Precilla beamed. "Dakota Chase named her; he called her Princess. This bonded them. They became friends, bonded for life, and she became his guardian while he was in the highlands. A necessary guardian, as it turned out. She helped protect him from Noctumba and Nefar. Later, Cole Madden became companion to one called Angel. They watched over the artists while they reconstructed the shrine and maze."

"Watched over them. You're saying Chase's and Madden's lives were in danger while they were doing all of this?"

"In grave Peril, yes. Both Noctumba and Nefar were on a quest to stop them from reconstructing the assemblage. Stop them at any cost. They almost succeeded."

"How?"

"Before Chase and Madden left the Amity Point, the circle of stones, and departed from the island, Singer told the artists they had to find an obelisk. While on their next visit to the highlands, Singer had said to them, they were to find an obelisk in the forest; a large granite boulder jutting out of the earth. He said beneath this boulder would be a sign showing them where to locate the reconstruction site. Singer also told them they would find a map that would lead them to Olyqua."

"The boulder! Where we're going!"

"Yes. Singer called it the *obelisk*. Sometime later, when Chase and Madden returned to the highlands, they searched the forest for the obelisk. While searching, they were approached by a friendly, cheerful little denizen that said he was sent to show them the way to it. He guided them. Once there, this friendly little character turned on them and tried to kill them. It was Noctumba."

Steve sorted this in his head as they approached another hill. "How did Noctumba try to kill them?"

"He led them onto the boulder, the obelisk, where they climbed to its pinnacle. Beneath the obelisk, out of sight from their view, were dagger like stakes, protruding through the ground and pointing upward toward them. Noctumba was going to lead them over the edge, onto the stakes.

"Singer and Princess intervened, came to their aid and warned the artists. Princess guided Chase and Madden away from the obelisk and stakes, hurried them to the bottom of the hill toward safety while Singer detained Noctumba. Now check this out. Noctumba pulled from the earth a large boulder and hurled it through the air at the fleeing artists."

"Wait a minute. How big is this Noctumba character? An inch tall? He yanks a boulder out of the earth and throws it at Chase and Madden?"

"Yes."

"How?"

"He somehow manipulates the Regions of Influence and fires the boulder through the air with his will."

"With his will?"

"Yes. Without physically touching it, the boulder pulled itself free from the ground, flew into the air, crashed through the trees and smashed the limbs and branches in its path as it whirled toward the fleeing artists. Singer, using the same method or powers, ripped another boulder from the earth and aimed it at Noctumba's to intercept it. The boulders collided in the air behind the artists. They collided with such a tremendous impact, they literally exploded into fine fragments and granules and the debris razed to the ground."

Steve stopped walking. "Do you remember our first trip out here with Tony Williams and Ramsey? Saber, Williams' dog, followed Bright Feather's trail and led us to the boulder. As we approached it, Williams noticed a sandy, gravely material with rock fragments covering the ground, said it looked like a rock crusher had been in there. Tree branches were snapped and scattered all over the place. Williams said it looked like some object had crashed through the trees and tore everything up."

"I remember very well, yes," Precilla said. "No one had a reasonable explanation for it."

"Pretty fantastic. Josh has an explanation for everything. How, though, does Josh keep Lore hidden from the growing populations of people? I mean, if Lore has been around for thousands of years and his civilization also grew in numbers, how did they remain hidden? Kept in secrecy? Why haven't any of them been spotted by people during all this time?"

"The Lore possess what Josh refers to as *Yul,* or the ways of glamour. They can shift their appearance, or project themselves into any image they choose; chipmunks, birds, anything."

"Like Kimirente," Steve said softly. "In the photographs and on the rocks, those stick figure images with animals, separated by an X, those must be symbolic of their ways of glamour. What did you call it?"

"Yul. Josh called it Yul, or the *glamouring* way."

Steve chuckled, continued walking up the hill. "Do these little people speak English?"

"They speak any tongue. They communicate through, what Josh refers to as, *Soulmit.* They interpret thought impulses and feelings, interpret the thoughts behind the words or language. They can detect deception behind words quite easily."

"Telapathy?"

"I suppose. Josh calls it Soulmitting."

"That's wild. Did Noctumba and Nefar continue with their quest to stop Chase and Madden after the attempt with the pointed stakes and boulder failed?"

"Yes, a couple of times, but the artists had the guardians, Princess and Angel, to protect them. Nefar once confronted Dakota Chase while he was alone in the wilderness. He revealed himself to him. While Chase was building an Amity Pillar, he spotted that mysterious hole in the air not far from where he was working. The hole, or Kimirente, floated close to him, began some kind of metamorphous or change, and unfolded before his eyes. A form slipped out of the hole and unraveled into a frightful looking entity."

"What do you mean, a frightful looking entity?"

"Josh described it as near human, but bat like."

"Bat like?"

"It was black and rubbery looking with a flat snout and fiery red eyes. When the arms unfolded, they were webbed to the body like bat wings. A sharp, pungent odor accompanied the image. Dakota Chase froze in horror. It seemed to Chase as though the ominous eyes had penetrated his innermost being, consumed his thoughts and breath of life. He stood fixed, stone-still, helpless and defenseless."

"What the hell was it?"

"A Kimirente. It was a morbid image created by Nefar to shock and confuse Dakota Chase from his senses. While Chase stood there in icy trauma, the Amity Pillar he had been constructing rose from the ground and tilted toward him. The smaller rocks on top tumbled to the ground, whereas the larger boulders rose higher and angled dangerously over him. The boulders suddenly toppled onto him and pushed him to the ground, nearly crushing him."

"That kind of takes the amity out of the pillar, doesn't it? What happened, how was he not crushed by them?"

"The boulders became suspended in midair, a hair above Chase's body as he lay motionless on the ground. Princess appeared beside him, had somehow caught the boulders, froze them in place, and prevented them from crushing him. The boulders rolled away from Chase without touching him. The entity, Nefar's Kimirente, folded back into itself, slipped back into the hole like a snake slithering into the earth, and disappeared."

Steve quietly absorbed Precilla's story and tried to visualize the event in his mind. He climbed the hill automatically, without awareness of his footing or how steep the grade was ahead of him.

*   *   *   *   *

Eighteen

Steve and Precilla made it to the top of the second hill and paused to rest. Steve scanned the area as he thought about the two artists and his friend, Josh Clemens. These were bold accounts Josh had written. He was writing about real people. Precilla was relating all this without persuasion, simply matter-of-factly, allowing Steve to formulate his own opinions. He asked her, "What do you think? Do you believe any of this stuff?"

"I believe what I've seen for myself. That strange hole in the air we all saw on the island was real, and so was the Indian that threatened us. The hollow tree, the black rock with all the symbols, the Amity Pillars and the small buildings the archeologists uncovered, they're all real, too. There are also many things that can't be explained with logic. How were those huge Amity Pillars removed from the dig site? How did all that crushed gravely material get spread over the ground below the large boulder, or obelisk, as Singer calls it? And the broken tree limbs and branches, what caused that? How did Josh Clemens simply vanish without leaving any signs? What's the coral hand at the bottom of the lake that supposedly led Chase and Madden to the underwater buildings and island? It all sounds like fantasy, there's no question about that, but there are many tangibles backing it up."

"Yes, but you didn't answer my question. I asked you if you believed any of it."

"Before committing myself to believing anything, there's something else I want to look for near the obelisk."

"What?"

"Somewhere in the vicinity of the obelisk, downhill from it, there's supposed to be another small building made of blocks. It's called the place of *Kalon*, whatever Kalon is, and the building itself is referred to as the Makai Shrine."

"Makai? That's familiar. I remember that word, but I don't remember what it means."

"It's a spider. A Kimirente, I think. Among the photographs the archeologists gave us, there are Makai symbols and Josh had made a sketch of one such symbol with the word Makai written under it."

"What's so important about the shrine?"

"The shrine is said to be hideous in appearance, designed as a skull, with stairs leading to an entryway surrounded by gruesome looking fangs. For some reason it was meant to be frightening looking, particularly for the young Lore. It's supposedly a place for some kind of ritual for young Lore, but Josh didn't really elaborate, he only mentioned it. After Chase and Madden discovered the shrine, Bright Feather told them that one day they would, themselves, pass through the shrine and enter a place called the *Chamber of Knowledge*."

"They would pass through the shrine? How big is this shrine supposed to be?"

"The size of the building on our dining room table, I imagine."

"And Chase and Madden were going to pass through the shrine and enter some Chamber of Knowledge?"

"As it turned out, that was figuratively speaking. When Chase knelt to peer into the doorway with the fangs, he saw a large support column in the central room. The support column was a brace for a second level. A balcony. The column was covered with designs, tiny masks and pictographs. Beyond the column, off to one side, he noticed another doorway leading out the back. This second doorway didn't have fangs, but it was very unique. The shape of the opening was exactly the same shape as a large boulder some distance away."

"Do you mean, by line of sight, the front and rear doorways lined up with a rock behind the building?"

"Yes, perfectly, and the rear entry was in the shape of the rock."

"What was so important about the rock?"

"First, the artists were attracted to all the cobwebs around the shrine, especially behind it, where the cobwebs stretched between the shrine and the boulder. The ground sloped dramatically into a deep hollow. The grass was completely covered with web and it formed into a large funnel in the middle. It looked like a white cloud floating above the ground and seemed to be a part of the shrine, as though it was designed to be there. Chase and Madden walked carefully around the web to avoid disturbing it. They were greatly impressed by the entire configuration. They moved away gingerly and made their way to the boulder they'd spotted through the shrine's doorways.

"There was nothing at all unusual or unique about the boulder in appearance, it was simply a large rock. Madden wondered if there might be something beneath the rock, so the two began pushing on it, rocking it back and forth until it finally rolled to the side. They revealed a hole in the earth, a couple of feet in diameter, forming into a tunnel that dropped a good six feet deep. At the bottom of the hole was a slab of stone and the passage widened, exposing a stairway that descended even deeper into the earth."

"Wait a second," Steve interrupted, "there's a cave out here? Chase and Madden discovered a cave?"

"A very complex cave, yes, with different chambers filled with pictographs. In legend, as Josh describes, it's called the

Chamber of Knowledge. Somehow the cave was central to
Kintu's early development, during his early existence as he
matured into adulthood."

"Kintu, that's Singer's father, right?" Steve asked.

"Yes."

"Kintu is part of the title of Josh's other manuscript, isn't it?"

"Yes, it's titled, "KINTU: THE DISCOVERY OF ONE.""

"What's that all about?"

"I haven't had a chance to read any of it yet; I've only skimmed
it. It appears to be a story about Kintu's life, a fable about his
early existence."

Steve removed his compass from his pocket and took a quick
reading. "We have one more hill to climb after we descend this one.
Loreduchy Swamp should be on the other side. Tell me more about
this cave Chase and Madden discovered, what did they find inside?"

Precilla continued with her story as they began their descent.
Dakota Chase, she explained, was the first to enter the tunnel. He
carefully lowered himself to the slab of rock and crouched to
investigate. To his surprise, there was an unlit torch strapped to
the wall along the stairway leading downward. Madden joined
him and the two, after lighting the torch, cautiously descended the
stairs. The short stairway led to an open room.

The granite walls of the room glistened with particles of
reflected light from the burning torch. The entire cavity was filled
with pictographs, including the ceiling. All the paintings and
etchings seemed to be in story board fashion. The stories began
with Lore's creation, the explosion that occurred beneath the
glacier. That pictograph took up most of the ceiling. Both artists
stood in awe of the beauty and the complexity of the chamber.

The artists continued past the first chamber and entered a
narrow passageway leading to another. All along the passageway
were more images, seemingly a continuance of the picture story

they had just left. Then Chase noticed something very odd. He spotted along the walls, pictographs of two human stick figures carrying a torch and investigating pictures that were painted on a cave wall.

Steve Adams came to a halt. "Wait a minute, don't tell me...."

Precilla laughed. "Yes," she said, "the pictographs represented Chase and Madden's discovery of the cave! They represented that exact moment in time!"

"This is too much," Steve said under his breath.

"Too much, indeed," Precilla said. "The artists, in their awkward realization of this, backtracked a ways through the corridor to inspect all the images more closely. They recognized their whole experience etched in the stone wall! The pictographs began with Chase's discovering the first Amity Pillar. From that discovery, the images led the artists all the way to that precise moment in time, to their standing in the passageway looking at themselves. Needless to say, it was more than a little haunting for them."

"Needless to say, this is a little more than outrageous," Steve said.

"Eventually," Precilla continued, "after their dizzying discovery, the artists made their way quietly into the next chamber. The walls, ceiling and floor of that room were covered with Lorals, a few of which Chase recognized from Bright Feather's stories. Most, however, made no sense to him. While they were studying all the imagery, a loud grinding sound echoed throughout the cave and the floor shook, terrifying both of them.

"One of the walls suddenly moved and parted from another. Sand poured from the opening and particles trickled down from the ceiling. The artists dropped to the floor in panic, covered their heads to protect themselves from the falling debris. The crunching noise lasted only a moment and then it was quiet and still again.

"Chase and Madden stood slowly, brushed the fallen sand from themselves and cautiously approached the open crevice between the walls. Chase aimed the torch through the opening and peered inside. It was another cavern. The cavity was painted mostly in blue and covered with green splotches everywhere. They slipped through the narrow gap and entered to investigate.

"Madden determined the blue represented large bodies of water and the green splotches indicated land. Both concluded they were looking at a huge, three-dimensional painted map of the Northern wilderness. The Boundary Waters Canoeing Area, specifically; the area where they suspected the island of Olyqua was located."

Steve motioned for Precilla to follow him down the hill as she went ahead with her story. He was too absorbed and amazed to say anything or interrupt her.

She followed him carefully, as the grade was becoming steeper. "With over a million acres of wilderness making up the BWCA, Chase and Madden had absolutely no idea where to begin looking for Olyqua on this enormous map. Chase, after much study, finally spotted an area that looked somewhat familiar to him. It was an area that he had possibly once canoed. He approached the area with the torch for a better look. That's when something entered the opening to the room.

"A form slipped through the gap between the walls and filled the corner of the chamber. It was a ghastly looking image, covered with a slimy material that reeked with foulness. It was hard to distinguish what it was in the dim light, but it looked like a giant slug with bouncy tentacles and one, oozing red eye that rolled around in the center of the head. It was grisly. Chase and Madden were horror stricken. From the mouth dangled several rubbery whiskers dripping with slime. The form moved slowly, wavered from side to side like a large snake with its head reared high. When the mouth opened, it opened round and wide, exposing greasy, muscular ridges that rippled inward toward its throat. The blubber lips folded back, the mouth opened wider and wider and the form swooped downward toward the artists.

"At just that moment, a tiny figure darted between the two artists. The little figure took a position between them and the hideous form. The torch light suddenly went out! From somewhere in the darkness a voice hollered, "Olyqua!" Accompanying the voice were several violent flashes of light that temporarily blinded the artists.

"Chase and Madden fell to the floor in pain and terror. Chase clutched his eyes, rolled on the granite floor and yelled for Madden. Madden writhed beside him, also experiencing tremendous discomfort from the sudden bursts of light. Dakota reached out with one hand and clasped Madden's shoulder, asked if he could see anything. Both were sightless, detecting only the spotted ghost images resulting from the brilliant flashes of light floating before them.

"In time they composed themselves and it seemed as though their sight was returning. Still, the spots floating before them were very intense. The artists helped each other to their feet and stood a while, blinking and squinting, rubbing their eyes to get rid of the spots. It appeared as though the cave was illuminating and the walls were coming back into view. Chase asked Madden if he was seeing it also. He was.

Dakota Chase scrunched up his eyes and peered at a wall through the spots. He listened for movement in the cave, wondered if he had actually seen that terrible looking slug form or if he had just imagined it. The blue color of the wall and green splotches were once again in focus, though very dim, and the light spots continued to float before his eyes. Madden said he was beginning to see the green shapes along the walls, but the spots before his eyes were obstructing a clear view.

Then Chase all of a sudden realized what was happening. It was all right there before him. He shook Madden's shoulder and told him to follow the spots before his eyes; to look closely at the spots while viewing the wall. He started laughing, asked Cole Madden if he could see it. Madden also laughed.

Seven spots floating before Dakota Chase's eyes lined up perfectly with seven green splotches in the midst of the blue wall. As the ghost image spots dissipated, Chase was left looking at Olyqua! He was looking at an island surrounded by six smaller islands. The seven ghost image spots, resulting from the flashes of light, had lined up perfectly with the seven land masses of Olyqua. He knew it was Olyqua."

"Unbelievable," Steve said. "But what the hell was that slug thing? What was that all about? Was it Nefar?"

"I don't know if it was Nefar or something else. One of the Lorals in Josh's manuscript describes an underground dweller called a *Slaglit*. It was some sort of an underground ruler. It is said to be a repulsive serpent that lives beneath the ground and feeds on the flesh of living things. It supposedly devours the flesh while keeping its victims alive in its innards. The victims watch themselves being slowly digested; they're kept alive long enough to experience being digested. It's quite a morbid myth among Lore, for what purpose, I have no idea."

"That's a bit disgusting," Steve said. They had reached the bottom of the hill. "Just what is Olyqua, do you know exactly?"

"Not really. It's obviously someplace North. Four people are presumably going to meet there and something is supposed to happen. What's going to happen, I don't really know. In Josh's notes, if you recall, it said something like, 'Four will meet at Olyqua and Olyqua shall become One. Olyqua will be victorious and the Inner Kingdom will return to the peaceful Regions.' Maybe it's revealed in Josh's other manuscript."

Steve paused to rest before climbing the last hill that would lead them to Loreduchy swamp. "What did the artists do after discovering the location of Olyqua on the cave wall?"

"They returned to the surface, replaced the boulder over the entryway to the tunnel and went looking for Singer and Bright Feather. They wanted to know what was happening to them. They wanted to know what it was they had just experienced, and why. They wanted to know what that thing was in the cave, that slug like form, and who the little one was that created the flashes of light and hollered, Olyqua!"

*   *   *   *   *

Nineteen

Precilla continued her story as she and Steve rested, "Princess and Angel appeared out of nowhere and guided Chase and Madden back to the Obelisk. The artists were introduced to a new character—an elderly Lore denizen named, From The Rock. Singer was sitting beside the elder beneath the obelisk. From The Rock, as they learned, was some kind of ceremony leader. The obelisk, they were informed, was an area where many Lore ceremonies took place."

"What kind of Lore ceremonies?" Steve asked.

"I'm not sure. The obelisk was apparently a gathering place for celebrations and meetings, but Josh didn't elaborate much. He focused more on Chase's and Madden's activities and experiences, their discoveries. The whole manuscript centered around their discoveries and their building of the shrine and maze that was supposed to bring back the Ulambent."

"Which they did complete, right?"

"Yes. The elder, From The Rock, had Dakota Chase pry a stone loose from beneath the obelisk. The stone was triangular shaped, the size of the palm of his hand. The flat sides of the rock were etched with a map that showed them where to erect the shrine and maze. As Chase and Madden studied the map, Singer told them about a second Ulambent. He told them that another Ulambent existed and that it was just as powerful as the original."

"A second Ulambent? There are two of them?"

"There are two, yes. Singer explained it to them. He told the artists that in the early days, when the Indian leader, Ur, had become one of them, Lore foresaw trouble in the Inner Kingdom. He knew that the human influence among them would bring about greed and power, so he selected one of Ur's first descendants to become a future leader for Ur's clan. This leader would head all of the future descendants of Ur. The leader he selected would become known as Koto, which for Lore would mean, Teacher. Koto would somehow play an important role in the future of the Inner Kingdom.

"Lore introduced Koto to the Regions of Influence and taught him all about the complexities of those energies. Koto valued the delicacy of life and the tender thread that binds all living things together. He understood nature's sensitive balance.

"Lore sent Koto north, to the place of his origin and the place where he had shed the energies of his light into the ice. The new leader discovered beneath the ice Lore's Amity Pillar of homage to the Northern Lights. It was then Koto became influenced by the lights and surrounding energies. The energies penetrated Koto and they became part of him. Then, something remarkable happened. Koto was suddenly repelled from that spot. Without awareness of transport, the new leader found himself standing on an ice cap on the opposite side of the earth; he found himself standing on the barren South pole.

Instinctively, Koto shed the new energies that had penetrated him in the north. He shed his energies into the southern ice. Above him and all around him, the air and the sky began to liven with brilliant, colorful lights. The lights grew intensely and danced like fire above the earth."

"Southern lights," Steve said. "Is there such a thing as southern lights?"

"Oh, yes," Precilla replied. "In the north it is the aurora borealis, the northern lights. In the south it is the aurora australis, or southern lights."

"How do you know that?"

"I looked it up."

"This is too much," Steve said, chuckling. "Then what happened?"

"Koto, in tribute to these Southern Lights, erected an Amity Pillar of his own beneath the ice. Upon completion of the Amity Pillar, Koto realized its significance. He realized the meaning behind all the balanced rocks. The Regions of Influence were clear to him. The rock pillars represented the delicate balance of energies between the poles of the earth, the poles of the galaxies, and the poles of the universe. They represented the delicate balance within the poles of existence, the precious balance within the circle, or globe of life. Koto then returned to Loretasia and Lore explained to him the power of the Ulambent, the power of the crystal cocoon from which he came.

"Lore told Koto that before he hid the Ulambent, willed it invisible within the shrine, he created a second Ulambent. He had made this second Ulambent out of the original. Both Ulambents were equal in power. When he created the second Ulambent, an identical shrine to the one he had built by hand, suddenly materialized out of nowhere. The Ulambents parted from each other and each took a position within its own shrine. Once the Ulambents were inside the shrines, the shrines merged together and became one."

"Hold on a second," Steve interrupted. "Why two Ulambents?"

"The original, of course, belonged to Lore, as it was the Ulambent from which Lore had released himself. The second Ulambent Lore created for Koto. The Ulambents are symbolic of the opposite Poles, or the opposite forces which stabilize existence and create order. The forces within the Ulambents together create One. They create amity, or harmony."

"Did Noctumba know any of this? Did he know that there were actually two Ulambents?"

"No."

"Why not? If he saw within the stream of consciousness how to disassemble the shrine and maze to retrieve the Ulambent, how could he not see there were actually two of them?"

"Lore could conceive the *inward way*."

"The what way?"

"The inward way. Lore can think inwardly without revealing his thoughts into the Regions of Influence. All of his descendants have since discovered the way. It's a way of thinking silently or inwardly without allowing the thought impulses to flow into the stream of consciousness.

"When Noctumba disassembled the shrine, both Ulambents appeared before him and merged back into one. And that was the problem. The merging powers of the Ulambents were too much for Noctumba to control. The forces consumed Noctumba. He became wild with the desire to control the world. He was possessed with greed and power. The powers were far too much and they became his falling. Noctumba began disrupting the harmony of the spheres, the Regions of Influence, without even realizing it. Order became chaos."

"So what happened when the artists finally recreated the shrine and maze?" Steve asked.

"When they added the final block to the shrine, something remarkable happened. The twin shrine, the one that had held the second Ulambent, suddenly appeared before them. It appeared from nowhere."

"They didn't build it?"

"No. It just suddenly appeared, as it did when Lore built the original shrine."

"Were the Ulambents inside? Did they appear with the shrines?"

"Not at that time, but shortly afterward. Noctumba, first, made one final attempt to get rid of Chase and Madden after they completed the maze and shrine."

"How?"

"Chase and Madden left the site quickly to look for Bright Feather, to tell him the construction was complete and that another shrine had mysteriously materialized before them. Noctumba confronted them in the woods before they had gotten far from the site. Noctumba told the artists that they had interfered with his affairs, meddled in something far beyond their understanding and that they were in deep jeopardy. He told them they had to leave the forest at once. He told them they had to relinquish their necklaces to him and leave the forest. They could never return. If they returned, the consequences would be devastating."

"Relinquish what necklaces?" Steve asked.

"The necklaces Bright Feather gave the artists when they first met, remember? When the Indian told the artists to find a fragment from the underwater hand, he gave them necklaces. They were tiny replicas of Amity Pillars, to be worn whenever the artists were in the forest."

"To identify them," Steve said. "Yes, I do remember. I thought it was a little peculiar they were given necklaces for identity. Why did Noctumba want the necklaces? What was so special about them?"

"Apparently they had some kind of special powers."

"What kind of powers?"

"Noctumba leaped to a tree branch above their heads, reached a hand toward the artists, and the tiny stones of the necklace became very hot. Chase ordered Madden not to release his necklace no matter how hot it got. Noctumba fumed, demanded they release them.

"The artists agonized from the heat of the stones burning inside their fists, but neither would release them. Noctumba leaned toward them, told them they were about to perish if they didn't let them go. Chase and Madden stood frozen. Noctumba's eyes suddenly flared red. He gave the artists one last chance. The necklaces burned in their grips.

"Two sudden bursts of light flashed in Noctumba's eyes. Bars of lightning shot toward the artists. Instinctively Chase and Madden held the necklaces before their faces and the bolts of lightning were deflected away from them. A crack of thunder exploded around them and the tree branches behind them split and crashed to the ground. Chase and Madden turned quickly and fled into the direction from which they had come; retreated to the construction site.

"Once they were inside the site, Bright Feather appeared at the tree line. Beside him were Singer, From The Rock, Princess and Angel. Between the twin shrines, in the center of the maze, stood two Lore denizens neither Chase nor Madden recognized.

"Noctumba pursued the artists into the site, but halted between the shrines when he saw the two unfamiliar Lore figures. He froze like a statue. The two unfamiliar Lore denizens confronted Noctumba without a word, but it appeared as though Noctumba was being restrained, held fast by some invisible force. The little one's body began gleaming brilliantly with colors. He glowed like a hot amber in a fire pit. The colors radiated upward from his body and swirled in a circle above his head.

"Suddenly, from inside the swirling circle of colors above Noctumba, the crystal Ulambent appeared. The Ulambent shimmered inside a halo of its own bright light. Noctumba trembled, seemingly fighting with all his might to free himself from his restraint. The Ulambent divided into two Ulambents, parted slowly, each surrounded by their own halos of bright light and swirling colors. The Ulambents floated toward their prospective shrines, entered circular windows designed for them, and disappeared. Noctumba's body suddenly relaxed and he crumpled unconscious to the ground."

"What happened?" Steve asked. "Who were the two Lore characters that confronted Noctumba?"

"It was Lore and Koto that confronted Noctumba."

"What happened next?"

"While Noctumba lay unconscious, the two shrines merged and became one. After they merged, they disappeared."

"Disappeared? Just like that, they disappeared?"

"Just like that."

"Where are the Ulambents now?"

"Someplace where they will never again be found, so legend has it."

"Did the maze, or all the buildings surrounding the shrine, disappear, too?"

"No. They're still in tact and hidden someplace in the forest. It's now a landmark in Lore history or legend."

"Do you know where it is?"

"No. Only Chase and Madden know where it's located."

"What happened to Noctumba?"

"After the shrine disappeared, Noctumba woke. The entire site became filled with Lore denizens welcoming him back. Noctumba had no recollection of what had happened or what he had done."

"None?"

"No. He only realized he'd been missing, but he had no recollection of his evil doings. There was a large celebration over Noctumba's return and Dakota Chase and Cole Madden were honored for their deeds. The artists later met with Lore and Koto and they were told about Olyqua."

"Olyqua," Steve said. "What the hell is Olyqua?"

"I don't know."

*   *   *   *   *

Twenty

Steve gazed at the hill before them, the last hill before Loreduchy Swamp. He gestured they start their climb and he led the way. "What about this Nefar character, did he lose his powers, too, when the Ulambents returned and the shrine disappeared?"

"No. Nefar is still at large, around somewhere, still on a quest of evil."

"Is he here? Is Nefar still in this area?"

"I don't know."

"Listen to us!" Steve said sharply. "We're talking as though all this actually happened!"

"Amazing, isn't it?"

"So that's it? That's Josh's story?"

"Almost."

"What do you mean, almost?"

"Dakota Chase and Cole Madden left for someplace North to help prepare for Olyqua. I imagine Olyqua has something to do with Nefar, though I'm not certain of that. All the signs of the actual Lore civilization in this area will supposedly disappear. How or why, exactly, I don't know. The artists works will remain, however. For a while, at least. The only thing that will remain of the actual Lore civilization is the myth, or legend. All the Amity Pillars, the black rock, the masks and dream dancers—everything created by the Lore civilization—will disappear."

"Why?"

"According to Lore and Koto, their exposures to humans in this region will have served their purposes and they will be moved to someplace else."

"Moved to where? Up north? Moved to where Chase and Madden have gone?"

"That would be my guess. Why, I have no idea."

"But the works the artists made will remain here?"

"Yes, as part of the legend. But over time, many of those will disappear, too. Many will be taken away; stolen from the forest by human greed."

Steve and Precilla made their way to the top of the hill that overlooked Loreduchy Swamp. At the top of the hill they paused before descending into the marsh.

Steve said, "Donald Ramsey mentioned to us that Milton's and Schepp's assistants at the dig site couldn't relocate the coral hand at the bottom of the lake when they went back to further investigate it. Do you suppose it has disappeared?"

"Probably."

"If everything is supposed to disappear, as this legend has it, do you think all the masks will still be in the trees down there?"

"I don't know. I don't know who made all of them. But we'll soon find out, won't we?"

"Come on," Steve said. They began their descent, scouring the tree branches along the way.

Steve and Precilla approached from the northwest. Steve's plan was to stay along the right side of the swamp and make their way south to the Amity Pillars where Bright Feather was caught on videotape; the place where he had left the ceramic rattle. From there they would continue on to the obelisk.

Steve felt excitement beginning to bubble inside him as they approached the swamp. Nefar lingered in the back of his mind but he wasn't feeling the anxieties he'd experienced when they first struck out. Precilla was quiet all the way to the bottom of the hill. Near the edge of the swamp they stopped just long enough to scan the trees in their immediate vicinity; then they began their hike along the swamp's shoreline.

"Did you ever learn anything about the rattle Bright Feather left for us at the base of the Amity Pillar?" Steve asked.

"Nothing," Precilla replied. "There's nothing mentioned about rattles in Josh's manuscript. I know Native Americans use rattles in ceremonies and dances. Medicine men and women, or shamans, use them for their own special reasons, but I have no idea what our rattle represents."

"There must be some significance to it," Steve said. Precilla didn't reply.

As they hiked, Steve became aware of the forest's briskness. The area was alive with birds, squirrels and chipmunks. Frogs leaped and splashed away from their path. Three large blue herons lifted themselves out of the near side of the marsh and took wing to the other side. A doe and two of her fawns bolted up the hill from their drinking spot and watched curiously as the hikers passed by. Lightning quick skinks darted before their footsteps and took refuge in the rocks and beneath scattered patches of mushrooms. Ducks floated quietly away from the shoreline and a large, unidentifiable bird perched complacently on top of a dead tree in the middle of the fen. The swamp and the dense trees rising from within and surrounding it provided a resplendent haven for wildlife. Steve quietly thought about the crow that had led them to the hollow tree and wondered if he and Precilla might see it this morning.

"I wonder how many of these little critters are actually Lore denizens watching us?" Precilla said with a chuckle.

"Look over there," Steve said, pointing a finger. "Just down from that drop off to the right of the swamp." He was pointing at a mask hanging from a low tree branch.

As they approached the mask, Steve noticed that the eyes shimmered and sparkled with color.

"That has to be the mask we're looking for," Precilla said softly. "The one with the crystal eyes; the one Dakota Chase looked through when he was with Bright Feather."

They made their way to the tree, stood beside the branch and examined the mask. The face of the mask was tranquil, a soft amber in color, with an expression of calm. From the chin of the mask hung several ceramic chimes attached to rawhide laces. The wind catcher for the chimes was a red-tail hawk feather. The air was at rest and the chimes dangled in silence.

Steve took the mask carefully into his hand and rotated it slowly to inspect. A soft tinkling rang from the chimes. The eyes were composed of two glass crystals cut with many angles and they glimmered with color as the mask turned. It was a beautiful piece of art.

"Can you see through the eyes?" Precilla asked.

Without speaking, Steve stepped closer and leaned toward the mask as he pulled it to his face. He drew the glass crystals to his eyes and gazed toward the swamp. What he saw was a fragmented, kaleidoscopic view of the trees and water. Everything was surrounded by brilliant colors, the colors of the rainbow. It seemed as though the trees were shimmering in their own radiance, as though they were giving off their own colors—their own halos. It was as though he was seeing the life of the trees, seeing their energies, or the auras of their own energies, surrounding them.

As he turned his head slowly, the colorful fragmented view of the swamp swirled before him, dazzling in splendid light, sparkling with unimaginable beauty. It seemed as though he was gazing into a thousand fiery swamps, each a different and individual world, filled with its own elegant luster. He stared in quiet fascination.

"What do you see?" Precilla asked excitedly.

"It's amazing," Steve replied. "It's fantastic." He pulled himself away and held the mask for Precilla to see.

She stepped forward and leaned into the mask. "Oh, my!" she exclaimed. She took the mask into her own hands and held it to her face. The chimes tingled with soft melody.

"Oh, Steve, this is incredible!"

While Precilla viewed the swamp, Steve scoured the trees surrounding them, looking for more masks and dream dancers. Finding none, he searched the direction ahead and spotted the Amity Pillars where Bright Feather had left the ceramic rattle. He scanned the hill descending toward the pillars, remembering the painted rock at the top, the rock with the painted crow.

"The Amity Pillars are just ahead," he said, turning to Precilla.

She was facing him, looking at him through the mask. "You're beautiful," she said.

He laughed. "I know."

"No, really. Your color is beautiful. You look so warm."

"We'd better keep going," Steve said.

"Look at me through this first; see what colors surround me." Precilla turned the mask around and handed it to Steve.

He took the mask into his hand and pulled it to his face. As he looked at his wife, she glistened in a warm halo of seemingly pure amber. She was beautiful and her smile charmed him.

"What do you see?" Precilla asked.

"A beautiful, young woman. A beautiful woman shining in her golden light."

Steve released the mask gently and let it swing away with its music. It almost seemed as though the beautiful halo remained around his wife. Her blue eyes danced with excitement.

"This is unbelievable," Precilla said softly.

"Come on," Steve said, "the Amity Pillars are just ahead."

They walked toward the pillars, both looking for more masks. "They're all gone," Precilla said. "All the masks that were here before are gone."

"As the legend said they'd be," Steve replied.

"There's a couple over there," Precilla said, pointing ahead. "But I see only two. The trees used to be filled with them."

As they approached the Amity Pillars, Steve thought about Chase and Madden and their discovery of the underwater buildings. He thought about the divers as they shot to the surface of the water after the buildings emitted the turbulent bubbles and frightning streaks of light. Precilla had said that Chase, as he neared the surface, saw his own reflection surrounded by dazzling colors. He had broken through his reflection of colors as he splashed into the open air. Later, he remembered, after the artists met Singer by the island's shoreline, Singer had told them that they'd just left their known world and entered another. The little one told them that they had augmented their sensibilities and entered another level of consciousness or awareness. They had entered another realm. He said they had entered the world of Loretasia, the Inner Kingdom.

They stopped beside the Amity Pillars to see if anything had changed. Steve asked Precilla, "Do you suppose the colors in legend are somehow related to the entry into Loretasia or the Inner Kingdom?"

"How do you mean?"

Steve reminded her about the artist's experiences as they surfaced from the underwater buildings, how they broke through their own reflections of colors as they thrashed into the open air. He reminded her of what Singer had told them about leaving their accustomed world and entering another realm.

"It could very well be," Precilla said. "The colors definitely have something to do with the whole legend, but it's not clear yet as to what they represent. I'm sure the mask back there was telling us something, but I don't know what it is. It's obviously there for a reason. I'm certain that soon it, too, is going to disappear as the other masks have disappeared. I'm sure it has served its purpose, whatever its purpose was supposed to have been."

"Well, these are still here," Steve said, gesturing toward the Amity Pillars.

"Chase and Madden must have built these. Their works are supposed to remain in tact. At least until they're either destroyed or stolen by explorers."

"Where do you suppose the real site for the shrine and maze is located?"

Precilla studied the trees. "I don't know."

"Well, there's nothing more here," Steve said. "Let's continue to the obelisk."

A ways beyond the pillars, Steve and Precilla angled from the swamp and followed the direction they had taken previously with Donald Ramsey and Tony Williams. Neither saw but a few masks while they walked. It was a little disappointing, as they had looked pretty spectacular hanging from the limbs when they first discovered them.

As the obelisk came into view in the distance, Steve scanned the trees along the hillside and spotted the unusual pathway through the crowns. Even now, dead branches dangled from the course. Some were split into threads, as though something violent had traumatized them. All along the ground were dried branches and limbs, piles of dead twigs scattered everywhere. Steve approached a tree in which its trunk's bark had been torn away.

As he examined the skin where the bark was removed, he noticed fine sandy granules imbedded deeply into the surface. Closer examination revealed stone fragments protruding from parts of the tree as far up as his eye could see.

"Look at this," he said to Precilla. "The forces that created this damage and blasted this gravely material into this tree must have been extraordinary."

"All the trees are imbedded with sand and rock chips," Precilla replied. "Look at this one here, there's a chunk of stone the size of my hand sticking out of the trunk!"

Steve walked to where Precilla was standing and latched hold of the rock fragment she was referring to. He tried to wiggle it free but it wouldn't budge. "This is insane," he said. "I can't imagine the force it would take to do something like this."

They continued slowly in the direction of the obelisk, examining the trees along the way. All of them, it seemed, were affected by whatever it was that created the disturbance and blazed the pathway through the crowns. The trees were healing well, however, with new branches and leaves forming. All these signs revealing something catastrophic had happened here would soon be gone. They would disappear like everything else.

Steve and Precilla paused a few yards below the obelisk and studied its colossal mass protruding from the earth. It created its own enigma as it stood alone and towered over the hill.

"This is the place where Lore ceremonies supposedly take place," Precilla said, "and the place where Chase and Madden were shown where to build the shrine and maze."

Steve approached the outcropping and crouched beneath it. He dragged his hand over the ground and pulled dried leaves out of a hole the size of his fist next to the base.

"What are you looking for?" Precilla asked, joining him.

"This, I guess," Steve replied, cleaning out the hole. "The elderly character, From The Rock, had Dakota Chase pry a triangular rock from the ground. It was the one with the directions to the construction site."

"This, too, is the place where the artists met Noctumba," Precilla said, backing out from beneath the boulder. "This is where Noctumba was going to lead the artists onto the pointed stakes."

Steve joined his wife and they walked up the hill and around to the backside of the obelisk. Together they climbed the rising mass to its peak and stood looking out over the hill.

"Pretty amazing, isn't it?" Steve said.

"Do you think the original Amity Pillars are still at the site where Tony Williams rediscovered them?" Precilla asked.

"I don't know. I imagine they're gone too, like everything else. Let's take a walk over there, it's just over the hill to the South."

"Let's go the other way first," Precilla said, "to the hollow tree. I'd like to see if anything there has changed."

As they backed down off the obelisk, Steve asked, "Where's the building in the shape of a skull located? The building that led Chase and Madden to the cave?"

"Somewhere below us, presumably not too far from here. That may be difficult to find, if in fact, it's actually there."

"Do you think there really is a cave? A chamber of knowledge?"

"I don't know. So many things exist that are mentioned in Josh's notes and manuscript. It's difficult to know what to think or believe. Those two artists and Josh Clemens have gone to great lengths to bring this legend to life."

Steve and Precilla made their way to the hill leading to the hollow tree. In the back of Steve's mind he was hoping to see the black crow sitting on the tree branch. This whole experience was like a dream to him and he tried to retrace its course, beginning with the discovery of the Amity Pillars during the police search for Josh Clemens. How could Josh have simply disappeared like that? Vanish into thin air? And later, too, the Amity Pillars, how could they have been removed from the site and placed elsewhere without leaving any signs of disturbance? He was becoming too confused thinking about it, so he dropped it as they descended the hill toward the tree.

The first thing Steve noticed as they approached the tree was that the small Amity Pillars that had previously stood below it were now gone. As they got nearer, he noticed, too, that the small bricks that once surrounded the hole at the base of the tree, were also gone. He removed his keys with the penlight and knelt at the trunk to peer inside.

The once matted pathway leading into the hole was already grown over with grass and there were no signs of animals using the hollow as a refuge. He turned on the light, aimed it into the opening and looked inside.

"All the feathers are gone," Steve said. "The stairway that circled the inside of the hollow is also gone. There's nothing here. There's no evidence that anything was ever here."

Precilla knelt, took Steve's light and looked for herself. "It's astounding how everything has returned to its natural state so quickly. You'd think there would be some kind of sign remaining that would suggest those things were here."

Steve rose and scanned the area. "Let's head over to the site with the Amity Pillars," he said.

Precilla stood and handed him his keys and light. "Would you care to lay a little wager on the pillars being there?" she asked.

"I only bet on sure things."

"Oh, I think it's a sure bet."

Steve took his keys and they started up the hill. As they climbed, Steve snickered.

"What?" Precilla asked.

"I was just thinking of when we discovered the mask near the rock with the crow painting."

"What was so funny about that?"

"You were. We must have looked like a couple of nitwits while we were taking it down from the tree branch. I think I still have a welt on the top of my head from where you bashed me with that thing."

"You were wobbling so much while I was on your shoulders, I thought you were going to drop me down the hill."

"What are those masks all about, anyway? What's the purpose behind them?"

"I read in Josh's notes they represent the spirit or the vitality within individuals. They represent the spirit or the crux of life. The balanced rocks of the Amity Pillars represent the delicate balance between all living things and the Windtickler Spirit masks represent the basic nature, or the fervor of the individual. The wind is life's journey and life's influence on other things. The chimes are the songs behind the influence—the songs of life. Windtickler, I guess, represents the spirit in the wind, the passion within the walk or the journey of life."

"Is Windtickler one of the Lore denizens?"

"I really don't know. Josh has so many notes, many of them Lorals, or short anecdotes dealing with the legend. I've barely scratched the surface. An entire book of Lorals could be written from his notes."

"Give me another example of a Loral," Steve said. They were nearing the top of the hill.

"I've already told you about the Northern and Southern Lights."

"I know. Do you remember any others?"

"There are so many, all of them are interesting. One comes to mind, though, that I thought was really neat. It's called the Lady Fly of the Clover."

"What's that about?" Steve asked. He pointed South as they reached the top of the hill and angled in the direction of the Amity Pillars.

"On a very dark night, a Lady Fly was flying over a lake, lost and confused while looking for its mate. By accident, the Lady Fly landed on the water, and with drenched wings, was unable to lift itself from the lake. Eventually it sank from fatigue and drifted downward to the bottom. The Lady Fly settled on a round, crystal ball, the Ulambent, and the Ulambent began to glow. As the Lady Fly clung to the Ulambent, its energy was restored, and with the restoration, the light from the Ulambent penetrated the abdomen of the Lady Fly.

"With revitalized energy, the Lady Fly swam to the surface. Its tail began glowing brightly as it lifted itself into the open air. As it flew higher into the sky, its glowing tail grew even brighter and began to flicker. The flickering light assisted the Lady Fly in seeing its way to safety in the meadows away from the water. While settled and resting in the clover, the lighted, flickering tail of the Lady Fly attracted its mate and they were once again united. From that time on, all the offspring of the Lady Fly were born with glowing, flickering tails. They have since dazzled and beautified the nighttime summer sky with their sparkling lights."

"The fire fly," Steve said with a smile. "Amazing. That's a Loral, huh?"

"There's a ton of them."

Steve and Precilla reached the crest of the hill above the Amity Pillar site. From there they noticed the pillars were gone. Before descending into the site, Steve scanned the whole area around them, looking for any signs of Lore.

"Are you surprised?" Precilla asked.

"No. I'm amazed."

"There's something very profound at work here," Precilla said.

"A lot more at work than the capabilities of the two artists and Josh Clemens, that's for sure."

"Do you want to go down and have a look?"

"I just want to see what the ground looks like where the pillars stood," Steve replied. They descended into the site.

As Steve had suspected, the ground was undefiled where the pillars once stood, and there was no matting or disturbance in the grass showing work of removal.

"How can any of this be?" Precilla asked quietly.

"Do you think that skull shrine actually exists?" Steve asked. "Or if it does exist, do you think it's still here, in this forest?"

"I don't know. Everything we've witnessed is gone, as though none of it was ever here. As told in the legend, everything except the artists works will disappear from this region."

"Should we even look for it?"

*   *   *   *   *

Twenty-one

A crow cawed from someplace off to their left, from the east, in the direction of the swamp below them. Steve stiffened and looked into Precilla's widened eyes. His whole body chilled. Without speaking, Steve took Precilla's hand and they descended the slope away from the Amity Pillar site. They descended carefully in the direction they'd heard the crow.

The ground leveled off some before them, then seemed to drop abruptly into a narrow hollow. They approached the drop off and examined the ground below. Steve immediately spotted a white, soft cloud, seemingly floating above the grass. The cloud sloped from all directions toward its center where it formed into a perfect funnel. It was the most massive and intricate spider web he'd ever seen.

On the near side of the web stood a building in the shape of a skull. From where they stood, it seemed as though the backside of the building was attached to the cloud of silk; as though the building was the key attachment point for the webbing. As they studied the area, a crow cawed and launched from a tree branch above them. The sudden disruption startled them both and they reared back in surprise.

"Damn it, I'm going to have a heart attack!" Steve blurted out. Precilla clung to his hand with all her might. The crow winged out of sight, leaving the two gawking at the trees.

"What now?" Precilla asked. Steve could feel her trembling.

Steve stepped closer to the drop off. "Let's have a look."

Precilla continued to hold tightly to his hand. "Do you think there really is a cave down there?"

"Look, over there, on the opposite side of the hollow. There are a lot of rocks. Some of them are pretty large. We'll see if the entryways to the building line up with one of them."

Steve gently pulled Precilla close to him, then sat on the edge of the drop off and dangled his legs over the side. He released her hand, carefully eased himself over the edge and slid to the bottom. He turned, held up his hands and gestured for Precilla to join him. "Come on," he said, "I'll catch you."

Precilla sat down and scooted herself over the edge. She let out a short yelp as she came to rest in Steve's arms. Small rocks and clumps of dirt tumbled after her and landed by their feet.

"Are you okay?" Steve asked.

"I'm fine. Look at that building," she said softly, peering around his shoulder.

Steve turned and looked. The building was fashioned in the shape of a monstrous skull, with terrifying fangs in a mouth opened wide and yielding to its entrance. A stairway, partially covered with vines, led to the gruesome opening. The vines crept upward along the face of the structure, clinging tightly and thickening near the top and around the backside. "It's just like you described," he said, "maybe a little more taunting in real life."

Precilla stepped around him and walked tentatively toward the shrine. "It's awesome," she said with a voice of dismay. "This thing looks really old."

Steve joined her and knelt on the ground in front of it. "That cobweb is the most magnificent thing I've ever seen."

"I hate spiders," Precilla said.

"If that funnel in the center of the web is any indication of the spider's size, then it's a Rottweiler with eight legs."

Steve spun quickly, barked like a dog and grappled at Precilla's feet.

Precilla screamed and leaped back. "Steve!" she yelled.

He laughed and turned again to the shrine.

"Don't do that!" she whined.

"This thing is amazing," he said. "Look at this detail. The whole thing is made of tiny blocks, formed and fitted perfectly together." He lowered himself to peer into the opening.

A large column, covered with designs and symbols, rose in the center of the main chamber. A circular staircase curved upward along the interior walls. As Precilla had described in her story, the column was a support for a second story balcony. The windows of the upper level were shaped as scorning eyes and emitted eerie bands of light into both levels of the complex. Suspended from the ceiling of the central chamber were tiny masks with chimes.

"This is incredible," Steve said. Precilla knelt beside him and looked for herself.

As Precilla studied the interior, Steve sat up and looked across the hollow toward the large rocks. "Do you see a rear entry?" he asked.

"There's light seeping through the backside of the main room but it looks like a vine or something is blocking the view."

Steve leaned over the shrine and examined the vines that had wrapped themselves around the building. On the backside he spotted a short stairway leading away from an obscured doorway masked with small leaves. Gingerly he parted the leaves with his fingers. "Take a look now," he said, "do you see anything?"

"Oh, yes," Precilla said. "I can see right through the building to the other side."

"Do you see a rock?"

"Perfectly. It fits right inside the shape of the doorway you just opened."

Steve looked at the rocks. "Which one is it?"

"That tall one. It's kind of pyramid shaped."

Steve spotted the boulder. It stood a good four feet off the ground. "That thing is huge," he said.

"It fits right inside the doorway, just as I had read." Precilla replied. She pulled herself away from the building and sat up. "Have a look."

"Trade places with me and hold these leaves away from the opening."

Steve and Precilla traded places and Steve looked through the doorway. Remarkably, the rear entryway was in the exact shape of the boulder Precilla had mentioned. He rose again and studied the area around the boulder. A small hill rose behind it, then seemed to slope downward again in the direction of the swamp. "Let's go over and have a look."

"Are you going to try to move it?" Precilla asked.

"In the story you told, Chase and Madden were able to roll it to its side. You and I might be able to do the same."

"Those were two men that pushed it over; I don't have the strength to do that."

"We'll see," Steve said, standing. "Come on." He offered Precilla his hand.

Precilla took his hand and stood beside him. They walked carefully around the shrine, mindful of the intricate cobweb while staying clear of the grass immediately fringing it. "What did you say this place was called?" Steve asked.

"It's called the place of Kalon and the building is referred to as the Makai Shrine. I have no idea what Kalon means, but I'm certain Makai is a spider; or it means spider."

"Just look at that silk," Steve said as they circled the area. He looked at the tree branches hanging low over the cloudy form. Dozens of dragonflies and other insects dangled in neat vertical rows. They were entwined in sticky thread that led from the massive web to the branches above. They looked like trophies all lined up in an orderly fashion.

"Yuck," Precilla said. "That's gross."

When they reached the other side, Steve walked immediately to the boulder and examined it. Near its base, facing the shrine, he spotted a mark. "Look here," he said, kneeling and pointing to it. "There's something scratched into the rock." He cleaned the surface with his finger and revealed a small etching of a spider.

"What is it?" Precilla asked.

"An image of a spider carved into the rock. I don't see any other markings."

"Do you think you will be able to move it? It's awfully big."

Steve rose and leaned into the boulder and braced his feet firmly to the ground. He pushed with all his strength but the boulder didn't budge. "It's as tight as a wisdom tooth," he said.

"You and I will never be able to move that thing," Precilla said.

"Give me a hand; let's try from the other side and see if we can at least rock it a little."

Steve and Precilla moved around the boulder and both readied themselves to push on it. Steve gave the "Go" and they pressed their weight and strength against it. The boulder moved slightly but not enough to raise the base.

"Let's look for a tree branch or something to use as a lever," Steve said, standing upright.

"It's too big for us," Precilla said.

Steve left the boulder and started up the small hill behind it. "It moved a little when we both pushed on it, so if we can find a limb or something to use as a lever, we might be able to get it rocking enough to roll it to its side."

"There's a dead limb under that tree over there," Precilla said. "Is that what you're looking for?"

Steve turned. "Where?"

Precilla pointed. "On the ground near the base of that big tree."

Steve followed his wife's aim. Below a large oak tree laid one of its limbs, bigger around than his arm and at least seven feet long. The limb's smaller branches had broken off, making it suitable for a lever, provided it wasn't rotten or spongy. "I'll check it out if you want to find a couple of rocks to use for a fulcrum."

Precilla scavenged for rocks while Steve examined the limb. It was perfect. The bark around the limb was peeling loose, but the wood, itself, was hard with little flexibility. He cleaned it off and returned to the boulder.

"Will these do?" Precilla asked, puffing and struggling with a large rock in her arms. She dropped it near Steve's feet where it clacked against others she had found.

"Those will do fine," he said. He knelt and rolled one close to the base of the boulder. "I don't know what I'm going to believe if we find a passage to a cave under here."

"What do you want me to do?" Precilla asked.

Steve rose and wedged the large end of the limb tightly between the boulder and the fulcrum. "Kneel against the boulder and push upward while I push down on the limb."

Precilla took her position. "I'm ready," she said.

Steve clasped the limb tightly and leaned over it. "Push!" he commanded, bearing down with his weight. The boulder tilted away slightly and the stench of mildew escaped from its base.

"Hold it there!" he grunted, struggling with the limb. "Grab one of the smaller rocks and stick it under the base."

Precilla fumbled with a rock and pried it under the boulder. She removed her hands quickly.

Steve eased off on the lever and the boulder settled onto the rock Precilla had placed beneath it. He moved the fulcrum closer and reset the limb. "If I can raise the base higher, take that larger rock and slip it underneath."

Precilla readied herself with the rock and Steve pushed down on the limb. The boulder leaned further back and Precilla quickly rolled the larger rock into place.

"There," Steve sighed, relaxing and pulling the limb away. The base of the boulder was raised high enough to where he would be able to see beneath it.

Precilla leaned close to the ground and examined the exposed area. "Steve," she said, "it looks like there's a deep hole underneath it."

Steve crouched, removed his keys and penlight. "This can't be," he said with disbelief.

"It smells wet with mildew," Precilla said.

Steve laid down close to the opening and reached his arm beneath the boulder. "There is a hole under here."

"What are you going to do?"

"Have a quick look."

"You're not going to put your head under there!"

"A quick look," he said.

"No way! It's not safe!"

Steve scooted closer and stretched his head under the boulder. He heard Precilla's disapproval behind him. "Don't be ridiculous, Steve, if that rock gives way you'll be crushed!"

Steve turned on the light and peered into the hole. It dropped five or six feet to a slab of stone where he could faintly see several steps leading deeper. "I don't believe this!" he exclaimed. "There are steps down there, just like you'd said."

"What's that smell?" Precilla asked.

"Mildew. It's pretty dank in there."

"No," Precilla said, "what smells out here?"

Steve pulled himself away from the boulder and sat up. He breathed in through his nose. He recognized the odor.

"It's the same odor we experienced by the ring of stones on the island," Precilla said.

"It is the same." Steve rose to his feet and scanned the area.

"There!" Precilla whispered sharply, pointing toward the hill they'd descended to reach this place.

Steve saw a human form dart between trees and disappear. It moved too fast to recognize, but it definitely dashed upright on two legs.

"Someone's up there," he whispered. "Come on, let's get behind the oak tree."

They slipped low profile away from the boulder and backed cautiously toward the tree. Steve kept his eyes fixed on the hill where he'd seen the figure.

"Who is it?" Precilla asked.

"I don't know." Steve guided her quietly behind the tree where they both knelt and scoured the hill.

"Be very still," a voice said softly from someplace behind them. Steve and Precilla spun their heads around.

The old Indian, Bright Feather, stood several feet away. "Don't disturb the air," he said.

Steve froze speechless. His heart bashed against his chest. Precilla dug her nails into his arm.

"He's just looking; he doesn't know you're here," Bright Feather said quietly. "Control your fears."

Steve gawked in fascination. It was as though he was fixed in a vacuum and all time had suddenly come to a halt. Precilla remained transfixed in her own stone posture.

"He's leaving," Bright Feather said. "He's descending the other side of the hill."

"He?" Steve responded automatically.

"You've found the cave," Bright Feather said.

Precilla remained speechless. Steve's eyes stuck to the old man. "We've found the cave, yes," he said.

"I'm Bright Feather."

"Yes, we know." This wasn't happening!

"What do you plan to do now that you've found the cave?"

Steve tried to turn his head to look at the boulder but he couldn't peel his eyes away from the Indian. "Do?" he replied dreamily. "What are we going to do?"

"Are you going to enter that place?"

"I was going to take a look, yes." This was so dream like. So uncanny.

"I'm Precilla," Precilla finally spoke. She sounded dazed.

"Yes. Josh Clemens has spoken highly of both of you. He spoke the truth."

"I don't understand what's going on here," Steve said.

"Josh Clemens is waiting for you up north," Bright Feather said.

"Up north? Olyqua?"

"Near the place of Olyqua, yes."

"He's all right? Josh is all right?"

"Josh Clemens is well, yes. He's waiting for you."

"Waiting? Why doesn't he come here?"

"He has reason to be there, in the north; he no longer has reason to be here. Your reason for being here is complete, also."

"Our reason for being here?" Steve said. "What reason? Why are we here?"

"Josh Clemens will explain everything to you soon."

Steve was beginning to regain his senses. "Who was that on the side hill?"

"That doesn't matter, he's gone now. What matters, now, is that the two of you go north to meet with Josh Clemens."

"But the cave," Steve said, finally able to glance back over his shoulder at the boulder. "I'd like to see the cave, the Chamber of Knowledge."

"Are you ready for that?" Bright Feather asked. The large boulder suddenly toppled over by itself and landed on its side with a loud thump. "Are you ready to face what's inside?"

Steve snapped his head back at Bright Feather. "What? What's inside?"

"How did that boulder fall over like that?" Precilla asked.

"You already know what's down there," said Bright Feather.

"The Slaglit!" Precilla blurted out. "There's something evil down there, isn't there?"

Bright Feather turned to walk away. "You may enter that place if you feel you must," he said. "Or you can accept what you know is there and find your way north to Josh Clemens."

Steve and Precilla stood. "Why not both?" Steve asked. Enough of this enigma, he thought. "Why can't I first see the Chamber of Knowledge, then find Josh Clemens?"

"You can't do both," Bight Feather said.

"I can't? Why can't I do both?"

"I don't know how to answer that."

"Come on! This is all nuts!" Steve said, frustrated. "What the hell's going on?"

"Whatever decision you make will be the right one," Bright Feather said. He started walking away.

"What's Kalon?" Precilla asked.

Bright Feather paused for a moment and smiled toward them. "Before Makai was Kalon," he said. "Josh Clemen's choice in you was very good."

"That's it?" Steve said. "Why don't you tell us more? Stay here and visit with us longer."

"That's not necessary, and I'm needed elsewhere," he replied. "You've already made the right decision as to what you're going to do."

"How do you know we've made our decision?"

Bright Feather continued to walk away.

"How do we find Josh Clemens?" Steve asked.

"Go in the right direction, he'll find you."

Steve turned back toward the cave. The boulder that had toppled away from its entrance was again standing upright over the hole! "What the…"

"Steve, look there," Precilla said. "Look at what's hanging from the tree branch."

Steve followed Precilla's eyes and spotted two necklaces hanging from the leaves. The necklaces were tiny replicas of Amity Pillars, suspended from rawhide laces. These were the same types of necklaces that were mentioned in the story; the same types of necklaces the Indian had given to Dakota Chase and Cole Madden when they first met by the rock towers with the lightening bolts.

Bright Feather was gone. Steve and Precilla approached the necklaces and removed them from the leaves. Precilla closed her eyes and shook her head in obvious wonder.

"It's time for us to leave, too," Steve said. "I think we're about to find out what all of this is about. It's coming to a head." He looked in the direction where Bright Feather had disappeared.

"Did you really decide not to enter the cave?" Precilla asked, staring now at the boulder that had mysteriously reset itself above the tunnel.

"Yes. Right when I was given the choice between entering the cave or meeting Josh Clemens up north. For some reason, I felt if I entered the cave, everything would end right here and now. We would never know what's really going on."

"Let's go home," Precilla said.

*   *   *   *   *

PART FOUR

The Light In The Wilderness

Twenty-two
The Light In The Wilderness

Steve Adams had a horrible thought. He turned to his wife who was sitting in the passenger's seat, quietly thumbing the tiny necklace of stones hanging from her neck. She had spoken little during their drive to the archeologist's dig site. "Do you know what my instincts tell me?" he asked.

"What?" She appeared to be in deep thought.

"If we had entered that cave, that's where we'd be right now, and possibly for all time."

"What do you mean?" The remark had obviously grabbed her attention.

"The figure we saw on the hill above the cave entrance, that was Nefar. If we had entered the cave, he was going to seal us inside."

"Why?"

"I don't know why." Steve guided the car along the two track road leading through the forest. "When Bright Feather gave us our choice of either entering the cave or meeting Josh Clemens up North, the thought of entering the cave left me cold. Something inside me warned me against it."

"Bright Feather never told us who that was on the hill," Precilla said.

"No. Thinking back on it, he didn't have to."

"Do you really believe entering the cave would have led to our death?"

Steve pondered for a moment. "Yes. Yes I do."

"Do you know what else is strange?" Precilla asked.

"Besides everything, what else?"

"While talking to Bright Feather, I never once noticed his eyes. I can't even remember his eyes."

Steve suddenly realized he hadn't noticed them either. "He was suddenly there, then gone, just like that. I think I was too stunned to realize anything when he appeared. It was like a dream."

"Who toppled the rock away from the cave entrance, then replaced it?" Precilla asked.

"Bright Feather."

Precilla gaped at Steve. "Bright Feather?"

"Don't ask me how he did it, but I know it was him. At the very moment I made my choice about not entering the cave, he replaced the boulder. Something else tells me there is no longer a cave there. The shrine and everything that has to do with that chamber of knowledge is gone. If we went inside, we'd be gone too." He felt a sudden chill.

It was quiet for a moment. Precilla held up her necklace, asked Steve, "Have you noticed this about the stones on these necklaces?"

"What about them?"

"The stones come apart. They're like powerful, tiny magnets." Precilla pulled the stones apart then put them back together.

"They are magnets," Steve said surprised. He touched the stones of his own necklace hanging from his neck. "What are these for, anyway?"

"I don't know. In Josh's story, they somehow protected Dakota Chase and Cole Madden from Noctumba."

"Noctumba," Steve repeated. He chuckled, said, "Now if one of those little guys suddenly appears before me, I'll know for sure I've completely lost it, gone wacky."

"What's our part in all this, Steve? Bright Feather said our reason for being here is complete. He said that about Josh Clemens, too; that Josh's reason for being in this forest was complete. What did he mean?"

"I don't have a clue. All I'm thinking about now is what Josh said in his very first letter to me. Do you remember? He said that I was deeply involved in all of this."

"I think he meant it to be plural when he said that; I think that statement was meant for both of us."

"I think you're right."

"Why are we going to the dig site?"

"I have to get a bearing on Olyqua off the black rock. I have to find out where it is so we can find Josh."

"Bright Feather said he would find us."

"Yes, but he also said to go in the right direction. We can't just aim North from any point; I'm sure we have to be on a specific course. I can get a bearing off the black rock, then map it out."

"Do you think Milton and Schepp ever relocated the hand at the bottom of the lake?"

Steve smiled. The thought of Milton and Schepp going ballistic over the disappearance of the hand tickled him. "I don't know, but we'll soon find out."

Steve aimed the Grand-Am around the last corner before reaching the point where he had normally parked his car when visiting the site. To his surprise, four police cars were parked right in the middle of the grass road.

"What's going on here?" Precilla asked.

"I don't know." Steve came to a stop, looked at several officers he didn't recognize. Then, Tony Williams appeared from behind one of the cars and approached with his dog.

Steve and Precilla got out of their car and waited for him.

"Hi Steve, Precilla. Did Ramsey get a hold of you yet?"

"No," Steve replied, "has he been trying to?"

"Oh, yeah, all morning."

"Why? What's up?"

Tony laughed. "Your two friends, Milton and Schepp, are a little beside themselves." He laughed harder. "I mean, they are absolutely livid!"

"Why? What's happened?"

Tony Williams shook his head. "Everything at the dig site is gone. The black rock, buildings, photographs, everything!"

"What?"

"Everything has disappeared, just like those rock towers we first discovered." Williams stopped beside Steve's car and petted Saber.

"When? How?"

"When was this morning sometime, how I don't know. Milton and Schepp left early this morning with their divers to look for that hand form at the bottom of the lake. Everything was intact and normal when they left. After an unsuccessful attempt to find the hand, they returned, and everything was gone. Poof!"

"Is there any evidence of removal?" Steve asked, shocked. "Any signs of people or equipment that could have removed it?"

"Nothing. Everything has vanished, the same way those rock towers disappeared." Tony laughed again. "Ol' Ramsey has definitely got a mystery on his hands."

"Where are Milton and Schepp now?" Precilla asked.

"We don't know. They stormed out of here in their Jeep, practically screaming all the way. They're threatening law suits on everyone: Ramsey, the Sheriff's Department, the county—everyone."

"Where's Ramsey?" Steve asked.

"Looking for you. I tried to reach him quickly on the radio when I saw your car coming but I couldn't get a hold of him. I'll call dispatch and leave word that you're out here."

"No," Steve said, "tell him we're headed for home. We've had kind of a complicated day ourselves."

"If this stuff has been placed elsewhere like those rock pillars," Tony said, "do you have any suggestions as to where we should start looking for it?"

Steve smiled and shook his head. "Don't even bother looking. I've got a feeling everything's gone for good." Tony Williams didn't seem at all surprised by that statement.

Steve and Precilla climbed back into the car. "How was your vacation?" Steve asked.

Tony smiled broadly. "Fantastic. I could use another one right now, believe me. There's a place just ahead on the right where you can turn around."

"Thanks, Tony. Good luck."

"Yeah. I'll leave word with Ramsey you're headed home."

Steve drove ahead to the turn around. Precilla asked, "How are you going to find Olyqua now?"

"I don't know."

*   *   *   *   *

Twenty-three

Precilla was the first to notice the peculiar odor when she got out of the car in their driveway. She looked at Steve. "Is something burning?" she asked.

Steve stood still for a moment and sniffed. "It smells like stale smoke, but it's kind of sweet smelling."

"It has a chocolate smell," Precilla said.

"Chocolate...," Steve said slowly. "Milton!" he yelped, looking toward the house. He shut the car door and hurried to the front entrance.

"What's the matter?" Precilla said, quickly following.

Steve entered the front door and walked immediately to the dining room. The small brick building that had sat on the dining room table was gone. "Damn it!" he cursed.

He quickly made his way to the editing suite in the basement. When he got to the bottom of the stairs he noticed everything was gone! All of Josh's notes, manuscripts, the box they came in—everything was gone.

"Damn them!" Steve growled, moving to the editing machine. "They've taken everything. They've even stolen the video we made!"

"Do you think it was Milton and Schepp?"

"Who else? They were definitely here. I could recognize Milton's tobacco smoke in the middle of a forest fire."

"What are you going to do?"

"Call Ramsey and have those two picked up for breaking and entering. Burglary! How dare they enter our house like that!"

"I think someone's here," Precilla said, listening. "I just heard a car door shut."

"Our little thieves, I hope."

Precilla led the way up the stairs and into the living room to the front door. Donald Ramsey was just about to ring the bell. Precilla opened the door and invited him in.

"Wow," Ramsey said, looking at Steve, "what's with the stone face?"

"Those two puppets, Mutt and Jeff, stole everything from our house! The building you brought over, Josh's notes and manuscripts, the tape we made…they've taken everything."

"When?" Ramsey asked. He stepped inside and closed the door behind him.

"Today. I don't know when, exactly, but it had to have been sometime recently; I could smell Milton's tobacco smoke lingering outside when Precilla and I got home. We just got home a few minutes ago."

"I just passed their Jeep on the way over here," Ramsey said.

"What? Let's go get them!" Steve barked, going for the door.

"Hold on a second, settle down. They couldn't have rifled through here and taken everything that fast."

"What do you mean? They've had all morning."

"No. No they haven't. I've been following them all over, ever since they tore out of the dig site. They've been to the court house, the police station, a lawyer's office and, just a while ago, they checked into a motel. I've been on their tail all day."

"But you just said you passed them while you were on your way here."

"Yes. I was at their motel trying to settle them down when I got the call from dispatch telling you you were on your way home.

They were emphatic they come to see you. I had to fill my car with gas, told them I'd be right behind them. I only pumped five dollars worth because I wanted to be here when they arrived. I couldn't have been more than five minutes behind them at the most."

"Five minutes?"

"If even that. There's no possible way they could have entered this house and taken everything out in that short amount of time. Your suspicions are wrong."

"I can't be wrong."

"Oh, you're wrong all right. You said you smelled Milton's tobacco smoke when you got home, right? Well, he was puffing like blazes and blowing a smoke trail a mile long when I passed them. I imagine when they got here and discovered you hadn't arrived yet, they just hightailed it back to their motel. They're a bit confused right now. There's no way they had time to take anything out of here."

Another vehicle entered the Adam's driveway. Donald Ramsey peered through the door window. "Ah," he said, "your burglary suspects have just returned."

Steve stepped around Ramsey and opened the door. Milton hopped from the Jeep and his pipe sailed out of his mouth and hit the driveway with an explosion of sparks. "Damn it!" he cried. "What a day I'm having!"

Steve lost it. He erupted into laughter, turned and left for the kitchen. He heard Ramsey cackling behind him. "I'm going to put on some coffee," Steve snorted.

"Come on in," Precilla said in a wavy voice. "Steve's making coffee."

"I don't want coffee," Milton said. "I want my photographs."

"Yes, well, come in anyway," Precilla replied.

Milton, Schepp, Ramsey and Precilla entered the dining room and stood by the table while Steve fumbled with the coffee pot. He was still laughing with his back turned to them.

"Is something funny, Adams?" Milton growled.

"Geez, I don't think so." He set the pot down and doubled over.

"What's so blasted funny?" Milton demanded.

"Oh," Steve sighed, regaining his composure. "I'm sorry." He turned to them. "With everything that has happened today, I imagine I'm just relieving tension." He was struggling with all his might to hold back his hysterics. He didn't dare look at either Milton or Schepp.

"Yeah, well, I see no humor in anything that has happened today," Milton said. "We have come to get the photographs we leant you."

"Yes. I think they're with the small building that was sitting on the dining room table," Steve said, turning again to the coffee pot.

There was a moment of silence. "And where's that?" Milton finally asked.

Steve poured water into the well of the pot, then joined them by the table. "Have a seat," he offered all of them.

"We don't want a seat. We don't want to stay," Milton said. "I just want to pick up our photographs and return to the motel."

"We have a little problem with that," Steve replied. "Come on, have a seat."

"What kind of a problem?" Milton asked. His eyes darted back and forth to everyone.

"I don't have your photographs. They're gone."

"What do you mean they're gone? You just said they were with the small building."

"That's where I think they are."

"Then where's the building?"

"That's gone too. Everything is gone."

"What do you mean, everything is gone?"

"Everything in our house that had to do with this Lore Adventure business is gone. It has disappeared. For a while I thought you and Schepp had taken it, until Ramsey straightened me out on that notion."

Milton pulled a chair out from beneath the table and sat. He put his elbows on the table and his head in his hands. Schepp, Ramsey and Precilla also sat. The only sound in the house was the gurgling from the coffee pot.

"I'm sorry," Steve finally said, joining them. "Everything in the forest is gone, too. Not only from your dig site, but everything else. Precilla and I went to check on the Amity Pillars today and discovered them missing. Everything that was in the hollow tree is gone. Most of the masks that hung in and around the swamp are also gone. The only things that remain are the artworks the artists had made."

"How?" Milton asked, raising his head. His eyes looked swollen and red.

Steve now felt compassion for him. "I have no idea how."

"I'll pour coffee," Precilla said, solemnly.

"Do you have anything stronger than coffee?" Milton asked.

"Add Kahlua to all of them," Steve said.

Precilla looked at Ramsey to confirm his. "What the hell," he said.

The five sat and visited around the dining room table for at least an hour, then retired to the deck. Precilla made sandwiches, more coffee, piled store bought cookies onto a tray, then joined them. The afternoon passed quickly. Neither Steve nor Precilla mentioned anything about the skull shrine or the cave. They only told them that they had searched the forest and discovered everything missing. Precilla didn't even mention, that in Josh's manuscript, he proclaimed that all this was going to happen.

Donald Ramsey's expressions during most of the conversations told Steve that he knew he and Precilla were holding back information. Those expressions became vocal after Milton and Schepp retired to their motel. When the archeologists left, they were still very confused but their anger toward everyone had diminished. Ramsey wasn't about to leave until he heard it all.

Steve and Precilla told him everything that had happened. Ramsey listened attentively, without mockery. The befuddled officer admitted there were too many strange occurrences that had happened since Josh Clemens' disappearance, including Josh's disappearance. He said there was no reason to doubt Steve and Precilla's stories. He was very curious about the cave and decided to go there in the morning with Tony Williams to check it out. Steve said he was certain there would no longer be signs of any cave or skull shrine remaining in the forest. He finally told Ramsey that Josh's manuscript claimed everything in the forest was going to disappear. Ramsey made no comment. Steve waited for Donald Ramsey to ask him if he believed any parts of the Lore legend, but the policeman never asked. Ramsey said he had enough for one day. He excused himself from the deck. As he left, Steve and Precilla walked him outside to his car.

"Precilla and I have one major problem yet to solve," Steve said, as Ramsey opened his car door.

"What's that?"

"How do we find Olyqua? How do we find where we're supposed to meet Josh Clemens? The black rock with the direction to Olyqua is gone."

"It's up North, isn't it?"

"North is a pretty big area," Steve said.

"I suppose," Ramsey replied. He tapped the door with his fingers and thought quietly to himself. He looked at Steve and asked, "Didn't you say that Clemens declared everything the Lore civilization created would disappear from the forest?"

"Yes. And it has."

"And didn't you also say that everything the artists made would remain?"

"Yes. Why do you ask?"

"Didn't Precilla mention in her story that Dakota Chase made a transfer rubbing of the black rock? He made a rubbing of all the etchings that were on the rock."

"That's right!" Steve remembered.

Donald Ramsey pulled a notepad from his shirt pocket and wrote something down. He tore the page out and handed it to Steve. "Her name is Misty Lymaars, a friend of Dakota Chase. She lives with him, or at least stays at his residence. She's a printmaker of some sort, a very nice gal, really attractive. I don't think they're sweethearts, just good friends. You might want to run over there tomorrow and talk to her. She may know where that rubbing is. The address is on the paper."

Steve took the paper and scanned the address. "Thank you," he said.

"If you get your hands on that rubbing, give me a call. I have something you can use that might help you find your destination."

"I'll do that," Steve said, smiling.

"Later, then," Ramsey said, climbing into his car.

*   *   *   *   *

Twenty-four

Misty Lymaars greeted Steve and Precilla jovially. She opened the door wide as though she was expecting a whole house full of company. Steve and Precilla had tried to call her by phone before they stopped by but there was no answer. They took a chance, anyway, and popped in unexpectedly.

"Hi," she greeted warmly. She was genuinely cheerful.

"Misty Lymaars?" Steve asked.

"Yes, I'm Misty. Are you friends of Dakota's?"

"No, not really, we've never met. My name is Steve Adams and this is my wife, Precilla."

"Oh, Steve and Precilla, yes, I'm glad to meet you. Please, come in, Dakota said you two would be by sometime early this summer to pick up a map."

"He did?"

"Yes, before he went up North for the summer. That was a month or so ago."

"A month ago?"

"At least a month. Come on in; I know right where it is. That is what you're after, isn't it?"

"Yes, but, how did he know we would be coming for a map?" Steve asked. He and Precilla entered the house.

"I don't know anything about that," she replied, ushering them into a large room with hardwood floors. The ceiling was at least ten feet high and the extended walls were filled with artworks signed by Dakota Chase. The side of the room facing the street was all glass.

"All Dakota said before he left was two people would be stopping by sometime to pick up a map. Then he wrote your names on a piece of paper and attached it to the cardboard tube he keeps it in. I see your names all the time when I'm dusting around one of his sculptures."

Steve and Precilla stared at each other. Misty studied them for a moment. "Is something the matter?" she asked.

"No," Steve responded quickly. "No, there's nothing wrong. I'm just glad the map is here."

"It's a pretty big map; I'll run and get it for you. You can sit if you'd like," Misty said, pointing to a couple of wicker styled chairs. "Make yourselves comfortable."

"Are all of these Dakota's works?" Steve asked, scanning the paintings on the walls. Most of them were traditional landscapes. The dates showed the paintings to be several years old.

"Yes, but they're older works. Dakota's not real fond of them. I'm taking them all down and replacing them with his newer things."

"These are quite nice," Precilla said.

"Yes, but they're not really Dakota. He calls these prostitution works because they sell readily and make quick money for him. The real art collectors aren't into this stuff, but they're taking a very serious look at his latest things. He's gotten really spunky with his colors lately and, quite honestly, they're excellent."

"Are there any examples of his latest works here?" Precilla asked.

"Oh, yes, would you like to see them?"

"Could we?"

"Of course. Just up the three steps to the next level and around the corner, there are several hanging on the wall. His studio is pretty much off limits, so I'm afraid I can't take you down there."

"We wouldn't expect that," Precilla said.

"Go ahead up, I'll fetch your map. Would you like some coffee or a soda? I have Coke, 7-Up, Pepsi...."

"No, thank you," Steve said, "we don't want to be a bother."

Misty laughed. "I'm having a Pepsi. What would you like?"

"Pepsi sounds good," Precilla said.

"Coke, then, if you have it," Steve said. "Thank you."

"Go ahead up," Misty said. She turned and exited through a doorway.

Steve and Precilla walked to the steps leading to the other level. A large brick archway opened to the adjacent area. As they climbed the steps, Precilla asked, "How did Dakota Chase know we were coming? A month ago?"

"Eerie, isn't it?" Steve replied. "Maybe she made a mistake. Maybe Ramsey called her last night to let her know we might be stopping by and she's confusing us with someone else."

"That's a possibility," Precilla said. They walked through the room and turned the corner.

"Wow!" Steve said, stopping short. "Look at these paintings!"

Along the wall, around the corner they had just turned, hung five large paintings. The paintings shimmered with color. They were abstract works suggesting landscapes with trees and water. All the imagery looked fragmented, as though the paintings were views through a kaleidoscope.

"It's just the way the swamp appeared while we were looking through the crystal eyes of that mask we found yesterday," Precilla said.

"I can't believe these colors," Steve said. "They're exactly as Cole Madden had described; the paintings look like they've been dipped in a rainbow."

"These are incredible, Steve. Look at that one on the right, it's of the Amity Pillars. Some of these places look very familiar."

Steve stepped back a ways for a better view. "There's the obelisk," he said, recognizing the giant boulder. "Everything is glowing with colors. These are fantastic! They just hold you."

"Do you like them?" Misty asked. She appeared holding a small tray with the sodas and a long cardboard tube tucked beneath her arm.

"I've never seen anything like these," Precilla said. "They're marvelous."

Misty lowered the tray onto a small table near the wall and handed Steve and Precilla their drinks. She laid the cardboard tube on the floor by the table, then joined them. "Dakota is rarely satisfied with anything he does, but he really likes these." She took a sip of her Pepsi and added, "They're so full of energy and life."

"How long has he been painting like this?" Precilla asked.

"A long time, actually, but they've just recently appeared on his larger canvases. He has smaller paintings and studies that have been stashed away for a couple of years, maybe longer. It's hard to say. His studio is cluttered with wooden crates filled with drawings and paintings. He about knocked me off my feet when he showed me the first of these larger works."

"Does he exhibit his works anywhere?" Precilla asked.

"Yes, but he doesn't like the museum or gallery scene very much. He says they're too stuffy. He loves working outdoors in the wild."

"How long has he been working on the Lore Adventure project?" Steve asked.

"That's hard to say," Misty replied. "Dakota has always loved the wilderness and, for the past few years, he has been spending a lot of time in forests around the country. He and Cole Madden do a lot together but, to be honest, neither talk about it very much. At least, they don't speak openly about it. I know it's very important to them, though. They've done a ton of work."

"Do you have a studio here, too?" Precilla asked. "Donald Ramsey said you were a printmaker."

"Who?" Misty asked.

"Donald Ramsey. He's with the Sheriff's Department."

"Oh, yes, now I remember the name. He came by once looking for Dakota and asked all sorts of questions. He scared me to death. I thought something was wrong, that there was an accident or something. Then he explained they were just looking for Josh Clemens. I wished him luck. When those guys venture off, nobody is ever going to find them. But, anyway, to answer your question, yes, I do have a printmaking studio here. I do lithography."

"Have you had a chance to look at the map over there?" Steve asked.

"Yes, I've seen it. Dakota transferred the images from a large rock that he and Madden had found in the woods. It's pretty impressive. Last month he gave it to me and asked me to keep it ready for you two, that you'd for certain be by sometime to pick it up. Your names are written on the paper that's taped to the side of the tube."

Steve walked over and picked the tube up from the floor. One end of the tube was open with an inch or so of the rolled map sticking out. He wanted to pull it out and unroll it right there on the floor but avoided the temptation. He sipped on his Coke and studied his and Precilla's names written on the piece of paper attached to it.

"You seem surprised by something," Misty said, watching Steve. "Are you sure nothing's the matter?"

Steve smiled. "Nothing is the matter, really. We're just grateful for this."

"Have you heard from Dakota since they went up North?" Precilla asked.

"No. I don't expect to until July or August. I don't know exactly what it is they're doing up there, but I know they're really back in the bush someplace, withdrawn into some far off remote area. They love that stuff, getting as far away from the rat race as possible."

"Yes," Steve said, "that would be nice. I wouldn't mind spending a little time away, myself."

A phone rang in some other part of the house and Misty excused herself to answer it. Steve and Precilla returned to Dakota Chase's artworks hanging on the wall. "So," Steve said softly, "what's going on? How the hell did Dakota Chase know we were coming?"

"She doesn't seem to know any more than we do," Precilla replied. "She seems like a really nice person."

Steve held the tube out vertically in front of him. "I want to get home and take a look at this thing."

"So do I."

Misty returned. "I'm sorry, that was a business call and I have to run. You're certainly welcome to come back anytime. I'm glad I was here when you arrived; if this phone call came twenty minutes ago, you'd have missed me."

"Thank you again for this," Steve said, waving the tube, "and the sodas."

"You're welcome. It was very nice meeting both of you. Dakota has wonderful friends and associates."

"I'd like to see your work sometime," Precilla said.

"Come back again and I'd be happy to show you some things."

Steve and Precilla took one last glance at Dakota's paintings as they left the room. Misty Lymaars escorted them to the door and thanked them again for coming by.

*　　　*　　　*　　　*　　　*

Twenty-five

Donald Ramsey was an expert with maps. He had Dakota Chase's transfer rubbing all laid out in the cavity of the dig site where the black rock had been. In no time, he had directions drawn onto a Minnesota map for Steve and Precilla to follow. He removed a small nylon case from his belt and fumbled with some kind of instrument that was inside it. Steve and Precilla watched quietly from the edge of the crater, while Tony Williams sat beneath a tree nearby, petting Saber.

The dig site was quiet this afternoon and looked very stark with everything gone. Milton and Schepp, along with their assistants, were off somewhere in the forest searching for the things that had disappeared. Steve figured any kind of a search would be in vain, but he wasn't about to shatter their dreams by telling them that. He was glad he didn't see them today, as he felt sorry for them and wouldn't know what to say to them.

When Ramsey called Steve early in the morning, to find out if Steve had found Dakota Chase's transfer rubbing, the officer told him that he and Tony Williams were leaving to investigate the cave Adams had mentioned. He told Steve they would meet him and Precilla at the dig site at around three in the afternoon. When they met, Steve right away asked if they had found the cave. Ramsey said they would talk about it later, after he plotted a map for them. The map was now plotted and Donald Ramsey hoisted himself out of the crater and sat on the rim of the trench.

"Do you know what this is?" Ramsey asked, holding the instrument he had been working with toward Steve.

"No, what is it?"

"It's called a GPS, which stands for Global Positioning System. Have you heard of it?"

"I've heard of it, yes, but I'm not real familiar with it."

"It's a pretty remarkable little toy. It's a computerized gadget that's linked to satellites orbiting the earth. The satellites feed it information pertaining to exact locations on the ground—where you are now, where you're going, and where you've been. You can create routes to any locations in the world, store the locations and routes into memory and return to them at any time. For the buck, it's the best navigation tool around. It's yours to use when you and Precilla head up North. North, North-East, actually."

Steve took the device and looked at it. "It looks complicated," he said.

"It looks complicated, but it's very simple to use. I would teach you how to use it right now but you'd forget. It's best to play with it and learn its capabilities by using it and experimenting with it. It doesn't take long to learn."

Steve sat down beside Ramsey. "What are these numbers here?" he asked. He was looking at a tiny monitor type screen showing numbers.

"That's where we are right now, our precise location on the globe. I've already stored those coordinates into memory. I've also projected a course for you with an exact bearing on Olyqua; or in the direction of Olyqua, at least. That's stored into memory, also, so you don't have to worry about losing it. As you practice with that thing and learn how to operate it, you'll discover that it will tell you when you deviate even the slightest bit off course. It will tell you how far off you are and how to get back on track. When you park your car in the woods, take a reading of your location and store your position into memory. The GPS will guide you right back to it when you want to return."

"You're letting me borrow this?"

"Yes. Lock in on anything you find up there and store the locations into memory. That way, if you ever have to go back, this thing will take you to the exact locations."

"I appreciate this," Steve said.

Precilla sat down beside Steve. Tony Williams and Saber joined them. Precilla examined the GPS.

"How did it go this morning?" Steve asked. "Did you and Tony find the cave?"

"We found a sink hole," Ramsey replied.

"A what?"

"A sink hole. We found the ledge above the hollow you had told me about, but there was no building or shrine in the shape of a skull. Tony's dog actually led us there, followed your scent all through the woods. On the opposite side of the hollow, where you said you'd discovered the rock that covered the cave's entrance, we found a sink hole, where the ground had caved in. It had happened very recently."

"What do you mean the ground caved in?"

"Sink holes aren't uncommon around here. Where you said you'd seen the cave, the ground was collapsed inward."

Steve and Precilla looked at each other confused. Ramsey added, "We did find your pyramid shaped rock, however, and the engraving of the spider was still there."

"It was?"

"The rock was laying on its side, partially sunk into the ground. If there was a cave there, it no longer exists."

"What if we had been inside?" Precilla said in a shallow voice.

"Then you would no longer exist either," Ramsey said flatly. "It's probably good you chose not to go inside."

"This is unbelievable," Steve said.

"When are you planning to go up North?" Ramsey asked.

"This coming weekend," Steve replied. "I have to finish some work before we go."

"Use some common sense while you're up there. Don't go venturing off into dangerous places. There are a lot of bogs in that area and many of them are dangerous. Often, what looks like might be firm ground is actually shallow peat floating over a deep marsh. You don't want to fall through that stuff; you could disappear forever."

"I appreciate your concern," Steve said sincerely.

"I'm very concerned," Ramsey replied. "We don't know what's really going on here. The events that have happened in this forest are unexplainable, and I'm at a complete loss for explanations over some of the things I have experienced personally."

"What are Milton and Schepp going to do now?" Steve asked. "Are they going to stick around and continue with their search?"

"For a while, I'm sure. They'll keep looking until they burn out or find something. They've pulled up stakes here and are presently living out of the motel. They're a couple of lost souls, I can tell you that."

"We're all a little lost right now," Precilla said.

"Josh Clemens," Steve chortled as he said the name. "He sure had it right on the note he left with his box. He wrote that something very unusual was going to happen."

"What did he write exactly?" Tony Williams asked.

"He wrote, 'Before long, something very unusual is going to happen that will baffle many people. Don't get caught up in other people's doubts and suspicions; accept it as a real phenomenon that can be explained.'"

"I'll be looking forward to your return from the North so you can explain it all for us," Williams said.

Steve Adams laughed and stood. "I'd be more than happy to explain all this if I could."

The others also stood and Ramsey handed Steve the vinyl case for the GPS. "Don't lose that thing," he said, "they're not cheap."

"Doesn't it come with a tracking device?"

Everyone laughed as they picked up and left the dig site.

*   *   *   *   *

Twenty-Six

Steve and Precilla headed east to Lake Superior, then north along the north shore drive until they reached the Superior National Forest. It was a beautiful, scenic route that they had driven several times in the past while on camping trips. Steve was familiar with some of the areas within the national forest, as he'd trout fished many of the rivers and streams that flow into the lake. Much of the terrain in the area was very rugged and he knew he and Precilla had their work cut out for them. He also knew there would be no hiking trails or roads for them to follow during their search for Josh Clemens. Their journey on foot over the irregular terrain would often times be dangerous.

The road leading to the national forest was an upward climb into the mountains that overlooked Lake Superior. Precilla wasn't at all surprised by her ears popping as she watched the reading of the altitude change on the GPS mounted on the dashboard of the Grand-Am. Over the past few days, Steve had experimented and became quite proficient in the use of the instrument Donald Ramsey had given them. At present, the GPS showed they were fifteen miles away from their plotted route that would lead them north to Josh Clemens. At least, that's where they hoped their route would lead them.

The Superior National Forest was a vast woodland comprised of rocky, mountainous terrain, low wetlands, and innumerable lakes, rivers and streams. The lush forest canopy was a resplendent hideaway for wild life. It was a rough and often jagged country filled with visual wonders. It was a country that commanded respect from its visitors.

The six hour journey by car led the searchers to a rustic, national forest service campground where they planned to base camp for two days while familiarizing themselves with the area. The secluded campground was nestled in the woods along the edge of a scenic river. It was a quiet spot that had room for only a few campers. All the other sites were vacant. Each campsite was tucked away in the trees and out of view from the others. This was as secluded as Precilla wanted to be at the outset, until they at least had a plan as to how they'd begin their search for Clemens.

After getting the tent set up and the campsite organized, they laid out a map of the national forest on the ground and marked all the gravel roads and logging trails that were in the vicinity of their plotted course leading north. There weren't a lot of them, but any trails along or near the route that led through the sometimes jungle thick terrain would be appreciated. Steve knew how easy it was to get turned around and disoriented in the bush and he was aware there would be countless obstacles in their path. They would have plenty of detours, surely. He became more and more grateful for the GPS Ramsey had given them. It would constantly show them how far off course they were and how to get back on track.

Once all settled, Steve and Precilla hopped in the car and began looking for some of the gravel roads and logging trails they had marked on the map. The back seat was filled with coolers and food, as they couldn't leave it in the campsite for the bear to get into and ransack. The area they were camping in was notorious for that. The bear and wolves weren't of real concern to Steve during the search, but he did think about the moose in the area. He didn't want to spook up an agitated bull in some removed tract where they couldn't get out of its way should it be threatened by an intrusion on its territory.

It was early summer and the swamps, rivers and streams were still at high water level from the spring thaw. That could be a problem, Steve knew, in the lower marshy areas, where wading would be the only way to reach a destination. Some of the rivers passing through their route ran through deep, rocky gorges that would be hazardous and near impossible to negotiate. Struggling across the slippery rocks and boulders of the fast moving rivers and streams also caused concern for Steve, as Precilla wasn't a very strong swimmer. Reconnoitering like this was important and would save time and eliminate a lot of problems in the long run.

The gravel road they were now traveling on ran east and west. It followed the ridge of a steep hill that overlooked deep, pine filled valleys on each side. Steve stopped the car along the edge of the road and got out to look. Precilla climbed out of the passenger's side with binoculars. The view was panoramic. The forest stretched for miles on all sides of the ridge, stretched as far as the eye could see.

"Look at this," Precilla said, "there's nothing but forest. You can see nothing but wilderness." She held the binoculars to see through.

"Look directly to your right, toward north," Steve said. "We are right in line with the route Donald Ramsey plotted for us. What you see probably looks a lot like the areas we're going to have to walk through."

Precilla turned and looked into the valley and the mountain ridge beyond. "Do we have to hike through all of that?"

"I hope not this area." Steve reached through the car window and removed the GPS from the dashboard. "We're quite a ways south from the boundary waters area. We have a lot of hills and valleys like this between us and there. I feel certain Josh Clemens isn't this far south. We're going to ridge hop for now."

"What does that mean, ridge hop?"

Steve saved their present position into the GPS memory, naming it 'S1,' then walked around the car to join his wife. He pointed north across the valley on the right side of the car. "look straight across to the top of the hill on the other side of the valley. That's where we're going next. From that ridge we will look beyond to the next one."

"We're walking there?"

"No. Or at least I hope we don't have to walk between here and there. The map shows a low maintenance road that runs close to that ridge over there, so we're going to go and find it. Hopefully from that point right there," Steve pointed again, "we'll be able to see even further along the line of our route."

"I don't know anything about directions, so I don't know what you're talking about."

Steve laughed. "Draw a straight line with your eyes from here to that other mountain. Imagine that line is a string that stretches from here to there and keeps right on going beyond the other side of that mountain. We have to follow the string, but we can't see the rest of it from here because it disappears behind the mountain. We have to get over to that other mountain to see where the string goes. Josh Clemens is somewhere on that string, somewhere beyond that mountain."

"I think I get it. Let's make a sandwich."

Steve shook his head. "Everything's in the back seat. You make. I'll drive. I don't want to waste our daylight."

As Steve drove, Precilla made sandwiches and they ate along the way. Low maintenance for the road they were looking for was an understatement. It was barely passable. Steve had to stop and park a half mile early because of the deep ruts and washouts. Precilla wasn't overly thrilled about taking the Grand-Am in as far as he did. They hiked the remaining distance, then climbed to the top of the hill so they could look back across the valley to the area where they'd just come from.

Steve held the GPS before him and pushed a button that said, "Go to." His previous position, 'S1' came up and he pushed 'Enter'.

"Look at the X on the GPS monitor," he said. "That's where we just came from." He pointed through the trees to the other mountain ridge they'd previously been. "That's where we stopped the car and got out to look over here. In fact, you can barely see the gravel road from here. The GPS says it's two miles away." He turned around to look in the opposite direction but the forest was too thick to see through.

"So now what?"

"Now we try to find another road to the north of here that crosses our path leading to Josh Clemens."

"I hope it's not like the so called road you just drove over."

"There are not too many roads north of us from here on out. The only one that travels deeply into the forest this far North is the Gunflint Trail. I think that's the one we'll have to take."

"Gunflint Trail? Is it like the rutted out path you just drove across?"

"No, not at all. Much of it is paved and leads to a place called Trail's End. I've actually been up there a couple of times. It's beautiful, very remote."

"What do you call this?"

Steve led Precilla back to the car and they continued to drive for a couple of hours, then returned to their camp. While there was yet a considerable amount of daylight remaining, Steve and Precilla visited the river near their campsite to try their luck at trout fishing. It was a peaceful area. The river cascaded gently around large boulders and slipped moderately beneath the overhanging forest. Steve loved the constant trickling sound of the river's flow. It was like the heartbeat and soul of everything around them.

After catching three nice brook trout and untangling Precilla several times from webs of fishing line, they made their way back down stream to their camp. That's when Precilla spotted the Amity Pillar along the river's edge beneath a large pine tree. It was tucked away in the shadows of the bank beside a calm eddy.

"Look over there, Steve," she said, pointing.

They waded into the eddy and approached the pillar. Just above the small rock tower hung a mask a few inches below one of the tree's branches.

"A mask," Steve said. "I would guess we're in the right area."

It was obvious the Amity Pillar had been built a long time ago because of its moss cover and the cobwebs clinging to it. The mask was also covered with fungus and appeared as though it had been hung at the same time.

"Coincidence?" Precilla asked.

"Let's get back to camp. I'll clean the fish quickly, then we'll have a look around the other campsites along the river to see if there are more of these."

"And if there are, what would that mean?"

"I'm more concerned if there aren't more. If there aren't more, then it would make this a whole lot less coincidental."

"I feel like a pawn in someone's chess game. We're being moved in directions at someone else's will."

"I feel that way, too, actually."

"Do you think Donald Ramsey has any part in this?"

"Ramsey?" Steve responded with a laugh.

"Why laugh? He directed us to Misty Lymaars to get the transfer rubbing, and he plotted out our whole course with it at the dig site. Maybe he's a silent actor in all this. Ramsey is the one who called you at the outset, when Oren Clemens reported Josh missing. He's the one who got you into the forest to help with the initial search for Josh."

Steve chuckled again. "Ramsey called me because Oren had told him Josh and I were close friends. Ramsey asked if I knew of Josh's whereabouts, and if I would care to join in the search for him. I hardly doubt Ramsey has a part in any of this."

"Well, I'm not ruling it out," Precilla said.

"Let's hurry and check out the other campsites. I'll fry the fish and fix supper afterward by the campfire."

Daylight was fading. After having scoured the river's edge near the other campsites and finding no signs of Amity Pillars or masks, Steve and Precilla returned to their own area and prepared their evening meal and ate by their small campfire. Beneath the light of a butane lantern, Steve examined his map of the Superior National Forest and marked the areas he planned on visiting in the morning. He decided he would break camp early, pack everything up and head north to the Gunflint Trail. There was no need staying in this spot for two days like they had originally planned.

The Gunflint Trail was nearly a sixty mile jaunt into the wilderness from its point of entry at Grand Marais. Grand Marais was a beautiful village, with a lot of history, located on the north shore drive of Lake Superior. The Gunflint ended at a place called Trails End, which was nestled between two lakes along the southern border of the Boundary Waters Canoeing Area. After examining the trail and maps closely, Steve didn't figure he'd be driving all the way to Trails End.

One lake, in close vicinity to Ramsey's outlined map, attracted Steve's attention. It was located in Canada, straight north from where the Gunflint Trail ran east and west near the U.S. and Canadian border. It was called Northern Light Lake. Precilla raised her eyebrows to the name of it and looked closely at the map.

"What's the name of that island?" she asked, pointing to the northern part of the lake.

"Paradise Island."

"Do you think that could be Olyqua?"

"No. Olyqua has six small islands surrounding it."

"What about those islands near the bottom of the lake?"

"There are several islands surrounding the larger one, but I don't know if that's Olyqua. I just don't know. I'm going by gut instinct."

"That's a long ways up there, Steve, with no roads or trails to follow. There are several lakes to cross. How are we going to do that?"

"Let's get some sleep and figure this out in the morning. I'm beat."

The magnificent thing about this whole wilderness area, an area called the Arrowhead region, was its peacefulness. It was far removed from the hustle and bustle of traffic, noise and air pollution, phones, and people. The only sound in the night, as they retired to their tent, was the trickling water as the river flowed confidently into the darkness. It was a restful lullaby.

The early twilight mornings were what Steve enjoyed most. He rose before dawn, and while being serenaded by the birds of the forest, he prepared fresh coffee and fried bacon over the open fire. The aromas and textures of the morning's resonance attracted Precilla from the tent and she joined Steve by the fire where she was handed a cup of freshly squeezed orange juice. Both sat quietly by the softly crackling flames and listened to the natural sounds around them.

"This is the way it all once was," Precilla said airily. "I can see, hear, smell, and feel the past all around us."

"It will be even more primitive where we're going today," Steve replied.

"Do you think we will have to walk the whole distance to the lake on the map we looked at last night?"

"No. If worse comes to worse, we can head up to Grand Portage and cross into Canada at Pigeon Bay. We'd be able to drive close to Northern Light Lake through Canada, but it's mostly gravel and a very long route. I hope it doesn't come to that. For some reason I feel we're going to see Josh Clemens today, somewhere north of Gunflint. I don't know where exactly, but I just feel he's there, waiting for us."

★   ★   ★   ★   ★

Twenty-Seven

It had looked like as good a place as any to pull off the main road. Steve aimed the Grand-Am up the remnants of an old two track pathway that led north, away from the Gunflint Trail. He had driven in as far as he dared, then locked the position of their car into the GPS. They struck out on foot. With tent and sleeping bags, backpacks filled with provisions for two days, Steve and Precilla ventured off. They had walked and struggled through the scrub for three hours before they took their first break in a remote clearing that made them both feel quite insignificant in the midst of the vast wilderness surrounding them. The ground was firm here, cluttered with rocks and knee high grass. Both were drenched from the waste down from pushing through marshy areas leading to this place.

Precilla sat on a large rock and rubbed the mosquito bites on her arms and neck. "Do you have any idea where we're going?" she asked.

Steve removed his backpack and sat beside her. "None," he said.

"This is hard walking," Precilla said. "What made you decide to come this way?"

"I wanted to avoid some lakes. We have no way to cross them. I figured it was as good a route as any."

"I hate the thought of going back through those swamps," Precilla said. "All the while we were wading through them I was remembering Ramsey's warnings about not sinking out of sight."

"I was more worried about that over there," Steve said, pointing to the tree line.

Grazing along the edge of the tree line before them, in an area of open water and rushes that stretched into the shadows of the woods, stood a huge bull moose. Its head came up from the water dripping like an open faucet and long weeds and debris dangled from its enormous rack. It stood poised like a statue for a moment, then lowered its chewing mouth again to the water and all but the rack and part of its back disappeared.

"That thing is enormous!" Precilla said.

"Yes, well, be still. They're as blind as a bat and as dumb as a slug, but they can hear and smell very well. I don't want to get him upset and come charging after us." Steve looked for the nearest trees they could climb just in case.

"What are we going to do? He's between us and the direction we're heading, isn't he?"

"He's in that vicinity but the water is too deep for us to cross there, anyway. We'll have to detour around. Further to the left is a hill and dry ground. We'll go that way when it's safe to continue."

"What a picture," Precilla said softly. The moose raised its head high and the sunlight glistening off the water running from its face made it look majestic.

They sat quietly and watched the moose move slowly eastward along the edge the trees. It moved through the water gracefully, half swimming and half trotting. It was a spectacular sight.

"I didn't realize they could move that easily," Steve said. "I thought they were clumsy critters. This is a sight few will ever behold."

"It was worth the hike," Precilla whispered.

Steve drank water from his canteen as he watched the moose glide quietly around a bend and disappear. Wood ducks and herons took its place in the marsh by the trees. The dry ground they were on stretched like a half-moon toward the tree covered hill he had decided to approach. As he studied the hill from where they were sitting he saw a vertical form in the shadows at the base of the rise. He held his binoculars to his eyes and saw it was an Amity Pillar in the midst of scattered rocks and boulders.

"What are you looking at?" Precilla asked.

"An Amity Pillar below the trees over there. Someone has obviously marked our trail for us."

"Is it safe to continue?"

"I think so," Steve said, rising. He grabbed his back pack and slung it over his shoulders. "If and when we see Josh, I don't know if I'll hug him or wring his neck."

"Whatever you do, I'll do the other."

Steve and Precilla made their way cautiously through the clearing toward the Amity Pillar and rise. At the base of the hill the ground was soggy and covered with enormous hoof prints. They approached the pillar and scanned the tree branches for masks.

"It looks like a rain forest in there," Precilla said.

Moss and vines dangled from the trees and the ground was covered with a thick mat of tightly woven grass. The chambers between the pines were dim and dank and very quiet. "It looks rather ominous, doesn't it?" Steve said.

Precilla examined the Amity Pillar. "Do you think Josh built this?"

"That would be my guess, but this is all so strange. How would Josh or anyone else know we'd be coming this way? We're quite a ways off from our plotted route."

"Let's climb the hill and see what's on the other side," Precilla said.

Steve led the way into the trees and they made their way up the rise. Their feet sunk several inches into the spongy ground as they climbed upward. Both noticed the temperature change cooler in the dim light. The air was moist and still but free of mosquitoes. It was quiescent. Even their sinking footsteps were silent. Neither spoke as they made their way to the top of the hill.

At the top they stood on the ridge and looked outward over the slope leading down the other side. The pines thinned below them, yielding to a grove of shorter, green leaf trees that stretched far across the valley to another hill. The canopy of the copse was crowded. It looked like one continuous mesh of heavy foliage. The leafy umbrella was roost for hundreds of birds that were singing and cackling to the afternoon sun.

"From moderate rain forest to tight jungle," Precilla said.

"I hope it's not as dense below the crowns. If it is, we'll never get through it." They descended the hill.

At the base of the hill they stood before a grove of young trees just three times their height. The slender trunks rose but a couple of feet apart from each other and the branches interlaced and sprawled into a drapery of round green leaves the size of silver dollars. A gentle breeze stirred the leaves and they fluttered and rattled throughout the valley.

"Listen to that," Precilla said softly.

"Quaking Aspen," Steve said. "I've never seen a stand like this before."

"Just listen," Precilla repeated. "What does that sound like?"

"Fluttering leaves."

"What else?"

Steve stood quietly and listened for a moment. "A river?"

"What else?"

"I don't know. A rattle?"

Precilla looked at him and smiled. "Our rattle. Listen closely. It sounds just like the rattle with the sculptured leaf Bright Feather left on the ground beside the Amity Pillar. The sound is unmistakable!"

Steve's eyes widened with his realization. "That's it," he whispered in dismay. "That's it exactly."

"These trees are telling us this is the right way," Precilla said enthusiastically. "The rattle with the sculptured leaf is a clue to this place. I know it is; I feel it!"

"As crazy as you sound right now, I believe you're right." Steve felt a chill on his neck and forearms.

"Look in there," Precilla said, "there are passages throughout the grove. They look like tunnels just wide enough to walk through."

Steve entered their position into the GPS, then removed his compass from his pocket. "I'm sure the GPS won't work in there because of the thick cover. The compass will help us continue North."

Steve entered first, holding his compass before him and Precilla followed quietly behind. The pathway was tight and lowly lit, obviously natural, as the grass wasn't beaten or trampled down by animals. As other corridors intersected, Steve kept with the ones leading in the most northerly direction. Though they couldn't feel the occasional breeze inside the thicket, the leaves overhead flitted and rattled throughout the valley. Steve couldn't keep his mind off the rattle Bright Feather had left for them to find.

"You're right about that rattle," Steve said, aiming through the path. "It couldn't be more obvious. How would they know we'd end up here? What's our purpose in all this?"

"I'm sure we're going to find out shortly," Precilla replied.

Steve thumbed the small rock necklace hanging from his neck. "Are you wearing the necklace Bright Feather left us?"

"Yes."

"You don't actually believe that stuff about the artists, do you? About the necklaces protecting them from that Noctumba character?"

"You're not a gambler, Steve. You always say you only bet on sure things. Why are you wearing your necklace?"

"Look," Steve said, stopping at an intersection leading east. In the middle of the path leading away from their northern route, stood a rock with a pictograph of a leaf painted on its face. "What does that mean?"

Precilla moved close behind him and peered around his shoulder to look at the rock. "Do you think it's a trail mark?"

"That path is heading in the wrong direction."

"How do you know that?"

"I'm assuming we should continue north, on the path we're on now."

"I think we should go that way, the direction the rock is showing us."

Steve pondered for a moment. "We can always come back to this spot if we're wrong. We'll try it." He aimed east along the corridor with the rock.

The path zigzagged toward the east for a short ways, then shifted abruptly north again. As more passages intersected, Steve continued to rely on his compass to determine which ones to take. They hiked for two hours in the maze, seeming as though they were meandering throughout the entire valley. Finally the trees began to open up and thin out a little. The ground was gradually sloping upward.

"I think we've reached the other side of the valley," Steve said.

"Do you have any idea where we are?"

Steve removed the GPS from its case and moved into an open area in the trees. He turned the unit on and recalled the position where they had parked their car. "We're a little over four miles from the car," he said, "We're over four miles northeast from where we parked."

"We've walked more than four miles," Precilla said.

"Yes we have; considerably more. This just shows a straight line between us and the car."

"So, now what?"

"Let's get out of this maze and head up the hill. We'll find a place to set up the tent, grab a sandwich, then we'll have a look around."

"A look around what? More woods? Olyqua is on a lake; shouldn't we be looking for the lake?"

"Josh Clemens is supposed to find us, remember?"

"In a million acres of this?" Precilla said, gesturing toward the trees. "He's going to find us in this?"

"Come on; let's find a place to drop our gear."

Steve aimed up the gradual slope away from the maze. The aspens thinned and mixed with pines and the ground became rocky and hard as they climbed upward. Several hundred feet of ground led to a small clearing before an abrupt outcropping of granite. Scattered rocks and boulders dotted the clearing in front of the sharp rise. Between the rocks and boulders laid a patch of earth that was covered with a soft bed of pine needles. Steve dropped his gear on the soft spot and sat down on a boulder.

"This is a good place to pitch the tent," he said.

"Our little Amity Point," Precilla said with a chuckle.

Steve opened his backpack and removed a couple of sandwiches Precilla had prepared before they left. He handed one to his wife. "Are you hungry?" he asked.

"A little."

He grabbed his canteen of water, stood, and climbed to the top of the granite outcropping to sit and eat. Precilla followed and sat beside him. They perched with their legs dangling over the edge of the crag and ate quietly while looking out over the tree maze they had just left. Beyond the maze they could see the hill they had descended to get to the dense grove.

"This is so peaceful here," Precilla said quietly. "Look out there; it's all wilderness. There's not a sign of civilization. The only sounds are coming from the birds and animals."

"Along with the sound of our mysterious rattle coming from the trees below us," Steve replied. "I still can't believe it."

"What's the nearest lake from here?"

"I'll have to check the map. We're really a long ways off the beaten path."

"What's next?" Precilla asked.

Steve looked at the rocks and boulders below them and smiled. "I'm going to build an Amity Pillar."

"What?"

"Right down there," he said biting his sandwich and pointing. "Everybody else is building them, I might as well, too. It's a perfect spot for one."

"You're crazy."

"I think we're both teetering a bit over the edge," Steve said, finishing his sandwich. He washed it down with water, set the canteen beside Precilla, then dropped to the ground below the outcropping. "Come on, let's mark our spot."

"No, you go right ahead and do your thing. I'm just going to sit and rest for a while."

Steve walked to a large rock and rolled it close to a boulder protruding from the ground. He knelt and hoisted the rock onto the boulder and moved it around until it sat steady on its own. He stood back and looked at it for a moment, then scanned the area for another one to place on top.

"You look ridiculous," Precilla said, laughing.

Steve snickered, found another rock and struggled with it until it rested securely on top of the others. The balanced rocks stood about five feet high.

"You're going to need a ladder pretty soon," Precilla said, amused.

Steve found a narrow, triangular shaped rock and set it on top of the others. He then placed a smaller rock on top of that one. Nearby, another boulder lay on the ground and he struggled to roll it close to the base of the pillar he had been working on. Precilla continued to watch quietly from above.

"Can you give me a hand with that one?" Steve asked, pointing to a long flat rock a few feet away.

"What are you going to do with that?"

"Make a bridge between the base of that first pillar to this boulder. Then I'm going to build on top of it; make a second pillar."

Precilla exhaled with a sigh, climbed down from the outcropping and joined Steve. "Shouldn't we be setting up the tent?"

"We have a lot of daylight ahead; plenty of time."

"Then we should be looking for Josh while we have all this daylight."

"There's an old saying: If you stay put long enough, people will find you."

"Or your bones," Precilla replied. "Are you planning on staying right here?"

"For a while. Give me a hand with this." Steve grabbed hold of one end of the flat rock and Precilla took the other.

"How long is a while?" Precilla grunted as they hoisted the stone off the ground.

They staggered with it to the Amity Pillar and carefully bridged the two large boulders.

"We'll finish the Amity Pillars, then go to the top of the hill and have a look around."

"I can't believe I'm doing this," Precilla said.

Steve spotted a round rock that looked flat on two sides. Precilla helped him with it and they set it on top of the bridge.

"That looks kind of neat," Precilla said, wiping perspiration from her forehead. "It really does."

Steve stepped back a few feet to look at it. "It does, doesn't it? Two pillars bridged together to make one."

"Look at that crooked rock there, behind you Steve, could we move that one?"

Part of the rock Precilla was looking at was imbedded into the ground and twisted upward at least two-feet. Steve pushed and pulled against it until it finally pried loose from the earth and toppled to its side.

"This one's pretty heavy," he said.

"Let's roll it over to the others." Precilla helped tumble the rock to the bridge, then together they labored to erect it on top of the last rock they had placed. It took several minutes to manipulate into perfect balance.

Precilla found an almost perfect granite sphere and carefully balanced it on top of the crooked rock. "Look at that," she said. "That's awesome."

"Not as colossal as the originals, but just as unique."

"You know, you're both a part of the makeup of that delicate balance," Josh Clemens' voice came from the ledge above them. "It's a nice representation of the two of you."

Steve wheeled in shock. Precilla froze beside the Amity Pillar.

"Josh?" Steve sputtered.

Josh Clemens was sitting on the outcropping with his legs hanging over the edge. His wide, round face was beaming with a broad smile. His lively brown eyes danced merrily between Steve and Precilla. "It took you long enough to get here," he said.

"How long...?" Steve stammered, unable to finish his question.

"How long have I been here?" Josh asked. "A while. I've been watching you work. You almost have it perfect."

"What do you mean?" Precilla asked.

Josh picked up a small piece of paper rolled into a tube and tossed it down to Steve. "Have a look."

Steve caught the paper. Still dazed he unrolled the paper and gawked in disbelief. He was looking at a drawing of an Amity Pillar. The drawing was done with such skill, it looked like a black and white photograph. The picture stunned him, not because of its beauty, but because it was a drawing of the Amity Pillar he and Precilla had just completed!

Precilla looked. "Oh, my...," she said, stepping back. She turned to the Amity Pillar they had just built. "That's it, Steve. That's our pillar!"

"How can this be?" Steve asked.

"Dakota Chase drew it for you a few days ago," Josh Clemens said. "But if you notice, you're missing one small rock on the very top of that first structure you built. Other than that, it's an uncanny likeness, isn't it?"

Steve Adams lowered the paper to his side and looked up at Josh. "What's going on, Josh? What's happening?"

Josh Clemens smiled warmly. "You've been chosen, Steve. You and Precilla have been chosen for something very important. Something very special."

"Chosen for what?" Precilla asked dreamily.

"To help prepare for Olyqua."

"What's Olyqua?" Steve asked.

"Now that I can't answer because I'm not real certain myself. Chase and Madden don't even know yet."

"Where are they?" Precilla asked.

"On the island."

"Is that where we're going?" Steve asked.

"Not just yet. You and Precilla are returning home to finish your devoir."

"Our what?"

"Your task. Your responsibility."

"And just what is our responsibility?" Steve asked.

"Before Olyqua can be completed, we have to attract the right people. Four people are needed for the completion."

"Who?" Steve asked. "What four people?"

"If I knew that," Josh said grinning, "I'd go get them myself."

"If you don't know who they are, how are we supposed to know?" Steve asked.

"You don't know. Dakota Chase and Cole Madden don't know. It's your job to help bring them together."

Steve Adams laughed in his confusion. "Do you mind telling us just what the hell's going on Josh and quit talking in riddles."

"All I can tell you, Steve, is that four people are needed for the completion of Olyqua. I don't know what Olyqua is, though I do know where it will be. You and Precilla were chosen to help bring the four people together."

"How?"

"They'll be lured by your story."

"What story?"

"Yours and Precilla's. The story of your discoveries and the Lore legends."

"Just who do we tell this story to?" Steve asked.

"To everyone, of course."

"To everyone?" Steve laughed. "And just how do you propose we do that?"

"I've already started things for you, and Precilla has practically completed everything with her notes. They just have to be organized now. Organized into a book."

"A book?" Precilla gasped. "Write a book? Steve and I don't write, we wouldn't know where to begin."

Josh Clemens leaned forward. "Someone will help you."

"Who?" Steve asked.

"You're a little confused right now, but you'll figure it out. We have a common acquaintance, a friend, that's a pretty good storyteller. He'll put it together for you and get it published."

"Then what?" Precilla asked.

"Then, of all those that read it, four people will be enticed and merge together on the island. Olyqua will be complete." Josh Clemens stood.

"This is all a fantasy, Josh," Steve said, feeling unsettled.

"A wonderful, living fantasy," Josh replied. "When you return home, concentrate on the Kintu legend I left with you. Kintu will guide you through all the mysteries of the Inner Kingdom. The chosen four will have to realize those mysteries before they merge."

"Everything is gone," Precilla said. "There is no Kintu story or anything else. Someone has taken everything from our home."

"It's all there where you left it. Everything is back in place at your house."

"You look like you're getting ready to leave us," Steve said. "You can't leave now! You have to tell us everything! Tell us where you've been, what you've been doing and why. Tell us how all that stuff in the woods, the black rock, Amity Pillars, appeared and then suddenly disappeared. How did you disappear? Don't just leave us hanging here!"

"Believe me," Josh said, "before you get back to your car, you'll learn all about that. Just remember, when you return home, find your storyteller, then concentrate on Kintu."

"Where are you off to?" Precilla asked.

"I have to join Chase and Madden."

"We'd like to come along," Steve said.

Josh shook his head. "Not now. Tell Oren I'm fine."

Precilla stepped close to the outcropping. "Is Donald Ramsey involved with any of this?" she asked.

Josh smiled at her. "Yes. He doesn't know it yet but, yes, he's involved. He'll play an important part in Olyqua."

"So that's it?" Steve asked. "We've traveled all the way up here, hoofed through all that mesh to find you, and you're leaving after five minutes?"

"That's all that's needed. Find your storyteller, concentrate on Kintu, and Olyqua will become complete. And, by the way, the old wive's tale about the pot of gold at the end of the rainbow? Well, there's a whole lot more than a pot of gold, believe me. You'll see."

"What do you mean?" Precilla asked.

"When you see the light in the wilderness, step into it, you'll see." Josh Clemens smiled. "Alayu, my friends."

"Alayu?" Steve repeated.

"That's a Lore salutation," Josh said, turning. He started walking away up the hill and disappeared from sight. "It's a greeting or an I'll see you later thing," his voice traveled back to them.

"Alayu?" Steve said again.

"You've got it."

Precilla looked at Steve. "Are we dreaming?"

"Josh!" Steve hollered. There was no reply.

"Blast him!" Steve barked.

"What now?" Precilla asked.

"Let's get out of here. Let's go home."

Precilla reached for her backpack, but instead picked up a small oval stone lying on the ground beside it. She bounced it in her hand for a moment, then climbed onto a boulder next to Amity Pillars. She reached high and placed the oval rock on the very top of the first pillar Steve had built. Steve unrolled the drawing he'd been clutching in his hand and looked at it. "That's the final rock," he said softly. "That's the rock in the drawing, the one that was missing."

Steve and Precilla quietly gathered their gear and descended the hill away from the clearing. Neither looked back. They paused for a moment before entering the maze of passages leading through the aspen.

"Let's go," Steve said, leading. He was feeling confused and empty. Disappointed. Angry.

A while into the grove, Precilla finally broke the silence. "What do you suppose Josh meant about stepping into the light in the wilderness?" she asked.

"I don't understand anything Josh mentioned," Steve replied, disgusted.

"Do you know who the storyteller is? Who it is that's supposed to help us write this book?"

"I don't have a clue. Do you?"

"Yes."

"Who?"

Precilla smiled. "Who do you know that's full of it up to his ears and can come up with a story about anything?"

"I don't know. Who?"

Precilla laughed. "Think of someone very close. Close to you and Josh."

Steve stopped for a moment and thought. "Oh, yes!" he blurted abruptly. "He'd have a field day with this story!"

"Steve, look over there," Precilla said. "Look at that band of light coming through the trees. Just off to the left of that passage."

Steve turned and spotted the band of light Precilla was referring to. It was sunlight pouring through a hole in the tree crowns and lighting the ground brilliantly. He moved slowly toward it and stopped just shy of the lighted ground.

Precilla whispered, "Josh said to step into the light when we see the light in the wilderness. Is this it? Is this the light in the wilderness he was talking about?"

Steve gazed around the lighted area. The band pouring through the trees was hazy. "We see this all the time when we're walking through a forest."

The rock necklaces hanging from their necks raised slightly off their chests. Both ogled at them without a word. Steve moved into the light and turned to face Precilla. She stared at him.

"Is anything happening?" she asked.

He shrugged his shoulders. His necklace now dangled normally. Precilla joined his side and they turned in a circle to observe the whole area. It was extremely quiet, except for a soft fluttering directly above their heads. They tilted back to look toward the familiar sound.

Several leaves vibrated in the sunlight, quivering and flapping as though being pushed by a gentle breeze. One of the leaves bent downward revealing something clinging to it. Steve squinted into the light. As his eyes adjusted he saw a tiny figure hugging the stem of the leaf. He felt Precilla's hand fold around his. The figure stretched over the green leaf and looked Steve in the eyes.

"Alayu, Steve and Precilla. I'm Singer, the Singer of Songs. Welcome to the Inner Kingdom, the land of Loretasia. We've been waiting for you."

All around the lighted area, leaves parted, revealing other tiny figures as they poked their faces through the foliage to look at them. Snickering broke the stillness in the air as the little figures became charmed by this new presence.

Singer reached his tiny hand toward Steve and Steve automatically reached toward the greeting. Their fingertips touched and a colorful rainbow poured over the entire area. All the trees, leaves and grasses turned colorful, radiating within their own halos of colorful light.

From the corner of his eye he saw Precilla gleaming beside him. He felt her hand tightening firmer around his own.

"Oh, Steve," she breathed. "Oh, my...."

The Beginning

Something's out there...something in the woods

*   *   *   *   *

Jim Fletcher grew up in the forest covered mountains of Connecticut. There he recognized the wonders and mysteries of nature. Fletcher, a teacher and an artist, has exhibited his artworks around the country. He and his wife, Dee, reside in Minnesota. They enjoy their family, the lakes and the outdoors.

Glossary

Alayu (Ah-lay-you): Respectful Lore greeting, salutation. Used in greetings and departures. There is no such thing as "Good-bye."

Amity Pillar: A tower or pillar made of balanced rocks. The balanced rock pillar is a token to the energy (Regions of Influence) that binds all living things into a harmonious "One." It is symbolic of the delicate, harmonious balance between all living things.

Amity Point: A point of comfort, peace. Ever changing points on the face of the Earth that are conducive to serenity and repose. Points of stillness and calm. Humans and animals instinctively seek out points of peacefulness and tranquillity.

Angel: Female Lore denizen of legend (Loral). The Lore denizen was given the name Angel by artist, Cole Madden. According to Loral (Lore legend), naming one of the Lore inhabitants binds the *name giver* and the one *named* together in eternal friendship. Angel became companion and protector to Cole Madden.

Aura (Owe-raw): Lore's mate. The name Aura pays homage to Lore's colorful, Northern Lights.

Aurox (Owe-rocks): The Pool of Origin. The spring fed pool in the middle of the forest where Lore and Aura emerged in human form. Lore named the pool Aurox in honor of his mate.

Bright Feather: The first Loreduchy. As Loral (Lore legend) tells, Bright Feather is the first person chosen by Lore to become a liaison between the Lore civilization and humankind, between the "seen" world (Earth's outer kingdom) and the "unseen" worlds of the Inner Kingdom, the worlds of Loretasia.

BWCA: Boundary Waters Canoe Area. The wilderness area (over one million acres) located in the Northern third of Minnesota's Superior National Forest. The BWCA borders Canada's Quetico Provincial Park wilderness area.

Chamber of Knowledge: Cave of Lore legend. The chamber walls are decorated with pictographs describing Lorals (Legends of Lore). Loral (Lore legend) has it that the images decipher fables from the past, stories of the present, and insights into the future.

Cole Madden: artist, friend of Dakota Chase. Legend tells how Cole Madden, along with Dakota Chase, discover Loretasia, the Inner Kingdom and the civilization of Lore. Cole Madden is one of the modern day Loreduchy.

Dakota Chase: artist, friend of Cole Madden. Legend tells how Dakota Chase, along with Cole Madden, discover Loretasia, the Inner Kingdom and the civilization of Lore. Dakota Chase is one of the modern day Loreduchy.

Donald Ramsey: Police investigator in charge of the search for Josh Clemens.

Dream Dancer: Life size human figure made of kiln fired clay. Decorated with polished stones, paint, feathers and other objects. All joints and limbs of the Dream Dancer are fashioned to move independently; elements of the figure are chimes that ring in the wind. Several Dream Dancers hang in trees in the wilderness area Dakota Chase calls the highlands. The Dream Dancer is similar in fashion to the Windtickler Spirit Mask.

From The Rock: Lore denizen, one of the elders. A leader of Lore ceremony who resides at the *obelisk* of legend. Lorals (Lore legends) tell of his great powers and his insights into the Regions of Influence.

Glamouring Ways: The charming ways of Lore. The Lore denizen's methods of alluring and fascinating; their means of tricking humans into seeing illusions or things not there. The Lore manner of deception and their ability to change their personal images or appearances.

Highlands: The name Dakota Chase gave the hilly wilderness regions where he and Cole Madden discovered Loretasia, the Inner Kingdom.

Inner Kingdom: Loretasia, the realm of Lore and the Lore civilization. The Inner Kingdom is the unseen region (comprised of different worlds—and levels of higher consciousness) within Earth's Outer Kingdom (the *seen* worlds of Earth). The Inner Kingdom is a part of the makeup of the Regions of Influence. Lorals (Lore legends) explain that portals into the Inner Kingdom lie just beyond the peripherals of the eyes. These gateways move around the borders of sight and are sometimes glimpsed upon as being light flickers or fleeting shadows. The only way through these portals and into the Inner Kingdom, Loretasia, is by way of the mind and the imagination. Lorals explain that children can see and enter the domains with ease.

Inward way: Thinking inwardly without revealing thoughts into the Stream of Consciousness; thinking silently, inwardly.

Josh Clemens: Freelance writer and friend of Steve Adams. Writer of unpublished drafts of two Lorals (Lore legends): LORE: THE LEGEND and KINTU: THE DISCOVERY OF ONE. Josh Clemens disappeared from the highlands and left clues for Steve and Precilla Adams to find Loretasia.

Kaiee (Ki-eee): Early American Woodland Indian, leader of his clan, son of Ur, a former leader of the clan.

Kalon (Kuh-lon): A place of Lore ceremony and ritual for young Lore and the location of the Makai Shrine. The place of Kalon was named after the Lore denizen, Kalon.

Kimirente (Kim-er-en-tay): A projected image from someone's mind. The phantom is produced by means of the glamouring ways. The practice of Kimirente is used for deceiving and fascination the unsuspecting. The Kimirente may become a tangible, physical entity, depending on the power of the one creating it.

Kintu (Kin-too): Lore denizen, father of Singer, the Singer of Songs. In Loral (Lore legend), Kintu is the guardian of the Chamber of Knowledge.

Koto: Leader of Ur's descendants, Lore's correlate.

Lady Magic: Lore denizen, a dulcet—music maker. Mother of Princess. Lady Magic plays a stone harp—the strings of the harp are colored light waves. Lady Magic tickles the light waves and turns the spectrum's frequencies into beautiful melodies.

Lake Agassiz: A large lake that once covered a great part of Minnesota. The lake resulted from the receding glacier at the close of the last ice age.

Loral: Lore legend. Lorals are stories about Lore, the inhabitants of Loretasia, the Inner Kingdom. Lorals weave between the Inner Kingdom (Loretasia—the unseen worlds) and the Outer Kingdom (the *seen* worlds of Earth).

Lore: Founder of the Lore civilization; the name for the inhabitants of Loretasia, the Inner Kingdom. Lorals (Lore legends) tell how Lore released himself from a crystal sphere at the bottom of Lake Agassiz. Lore was born of powerful energies (energies of the Regions of Influence), resulting from tremendous friction caused by moving glaciers during the last ice age. Lore and his descendants have existed in secrecy for thousands of years—have inhabited wilderness areas, inhered to nature.

Lorechitecture: Lore dwellings. Edifices constructed from clay.

Loreduchy: Loreduchy are people that participate in the Lore Adventure; those that seek to learn about the mysteries and wonders of nature. Loreduchy are the liaisons between humankind and nature—between the human realms and the realms of the Inner Kingdom. Somewhere along the line, people coined Loreduchy as "Dukes of the Lore."

Loreduchy Swamp: A meeting location or gathering place for Loreduchy. Loreduchy swamp is somewhere in the wilderness regions Dakota Chase calls the highlands. The trees around Loreduchy swamp are garnished with Windtickler Spirit Masks.

Lost City: A miniature village hidden in the forest. Individual structures are constructed from tiny blocks of clay; each is kiln fired. The buildings were made by students. The Lost City in Loral (Lore legend) is a decoy city; while this miniature hamlet was being constructed and placed in the forest to draw public attention, another was being fabricated in secret by Dakota Chase and Cole Madden.

Makai (Mack-eye): Spider. Pictographs depict Makai as a large spider, linked to the Makai Shrine, somehow part of rituals for young Lore denizens.

Makai Shrine: A small building in the wilderness at a place called Kalon. The shrine is designed as an appalling skull. In Loral (Lore legend) the skull is designed to frighten young Lore; it consists of haunting eyes and fearsome fangs; used in rituals for young Lore. The shrine is the focal point for the vast web of Makai.

Milton (Dr. Milton): Archeologist investigating Lore relics, colleague of Dr. Schepp.

Misty Lymaars: Artist, printmaker, friend of Dakota Chase.

Nefar: A person of evil intent, desiring to control the world, ally with the Lore denizen, Noctumba. Nefar was befriended by Noctumba to help alter the Regions of Influence in order to gain control over the Inner and Outer Kingdoms.

Noctumba (Nock-toomba): Powerful Lore denizen possessed with greed and a passion to rule and control the world. Noctumba stole Lore's powerful Ulambent of Loral (Lore legend) and consumed the Ulambent's energies. The energies of the Ulambent overpowered Noctumba and he lost control of himself and went mad.

Obelisk: A large granite boulder jutting out of the earth in the middle of the forest. A place of Lore ceremony and home of the elderly Lore denizen, From The Rock—ceremony leader.

Olyqua (O-lee-kwa): A significant place in Loral (Lore legend) where a momentous event is suppose to take place; an island in the Northern wilderness, surrounded by six smaller islands. Each island is represented with a different color. A meeting place for four, future Loreduchy.

Princess: Female Lore denizen of legend (Loral). The Lore denizen was given the name Princess by artist, Dakota Chase. According to Loral (Lore legend), naming one of the Lore inhabitants binds the *name giver* and the one *named* together in eternal friendship. Princess became companion and protector to Dakota Chase.

Precilla Adams: Wife of Steve Adams, friend of Josh Clemens, helping to investigate the disappearance of Josh Clemens.

Regions of Influence: Energies between the poles of existence, the poles of life. It is the energy that passes through every living thing; the energy that binds all living things together into a harmonious One. It is the energy between the poles of the earth, the poles of the galaxy, the poles of the universe, the poles of existence. It is the Harmony of the spheres.

Schepp (Dr. Schepp): Archeologist investigating Lore relics, colleague of Dr. Milton.

Seekers: Those filled with greed; seekers of wealth, power and control.

Singer: Lore denizen—the Storyteller, Singer of Songs, son of Kintu. Singer has knowledge of all the Lorals (Lore legends).

Soulmit: A Lore way of communicating; feeling and thought impulses disseminated into the Stream of Consciousness—part of the makeup of the Regions of Influence.

Steve Adams: Husband of Precilla Adams and friend of Josh Clemens; helping to investigate the disappearance of Josh Clemens.

Stream of Consciousness: Part of the Regions of Influence, the flowing stream of energy embodying the wavelengths of individual's thoughts and feelings. The wavelengths are interpreted through Soulmit.

Tendril: Clothing worn by Lore denizens; made of woven vines, grasses, leaves and flowers.

Tony Williams: Police officer with the canine unit, friend of Donald Ramsey, helping to investigate Josh Clemens' disappearance.

Ulambent: Diamond hard sphere of Loral (Lore legend); Lore's derivation. The Ulambent is hollow, glass smooth on the outside with crystallized interior walls, uniquely cut to separate light into its visible spectrum. The Ulambent glistens with color. Loral (Lore legend) tells of the Ulambent's origin, created by an explosion caused by the friction of a moving glacier during the last ice age. The Ulambent is said to contain tremendous energy and power.

Ur: Early American Woodland Indian, clan leader, son of the early woodland leader Lore patterned himself after. Lorals (Lore legends) tell how Ur was transformed into a Lore denizen.

Windtickler: The spirit of the wind; the passion within the walk or journey of life.

Windtickler Spirit Mask: Token of the spirit or vitality within individuals, symbolic of the spirit or crux of life, the basic nature or fervor of the individual. The wind is life's journey and influence on other things; the chimes are the songs behind the influence or the songs of life.

Yul: The practice of *glamouring* (the glamouring ways); the act of charming or alluring. The act of deception.